SOUL
MURDER

Also by Andrew Nugent

Second Burial for a Black Prince
The Four Courts Murder

SOUL
MURDER
ANDREW
NUGENT

Minotaur Books
New York

A THOMAS DUNNE BOOK FOR MINOTAUR BOOKS. An imprint of St. Martin's Publishing Group.

www.thomasdunnebooks.com
www.minotaurbooks.com

Library of Congress Cataloging-in-Publication Data

Nugent, Andrew.
    Soul murder / Andrew Nugent. — 1st U.S. ed.
        p. cm.
    ISBN-13: 978-0-312-53656-5
    ISBN-10: 0-312-53656-9
    1. Boarding schools—Fiction. 2. Murder—Investigation—Fiction. 3. Police—Ireland—Fiction.
I. Title.
PR6114.U36S68 2009
823'.92—dc22

                                                                2009017707

First published in Great Britain by
Headline Publishing Group

First U.S. Edition: August 2009

10 9 8 7 6 5 4 3 2 1

The dying boy Markel said:

'Every one of us is responsible for everyone else in every way. And I most of all.'

Mother could not help smiling at that. She wept and smiled at the same time. 'How are you,' she said, 'most of all responsible for everyone? There are murderers and robbers in the world, and what terrible sin have you committed that you should accuse yourself before everyone else?'

'Mother,' he said, 'you must realise that everyone is really responsible for everyone and everything. I don't know how to explain it to you, but I feel it so strongly that it hurts.'

F. Dostoyevsky, *The Brothers Karamazov*

Preface

The advice given to budding authors is: *write about what you know*. I know about boys' boarding schools, having been in one for eight full years as a youth, and having worked in another for half of my adult life. Both schools had castles on campus – castles, I suppose, being deemed fairly boy-proof. I have used both castles, very approximately, to create a vague aura of gothic horror for my story.

St Isidore's School does not exist, nor is it a code name for any school that does exist. The entire cast and setting of my novel are wholly fictional. What is not fictional but I believe true, is that life is a slow-release miracle. Accordingly, there will always be people in my novels – and especially young people – who, faced with the challenges and even the tragedies of life, grow, develop and deepen.

There is another more sombre truth; in the case of some people, for the miracle to happen, it can also mean to be broken open. This will not be a triumphal progress but – as a Christian – I would understand it as *a way-of-the-cross*. This can happen to the best, the most innocent, and especially the most vulnerable people. To such as these this book is dedicated with profound respect.

I should like to acknowledge the patience of Martin Fletcher and the support and encouragement that I have received from him, Thomas Dunne, Ruth Cavin, Breda Purdue, Jo Stansall, Ciara Considine, Ross Hulbert, Toni Plummer and Nancy Webber. A very special word of thanks to my agent, Mary Pachnos.

This book has not been easy to write. I am grateful to colleagues and confrères who have understood what I was trying to do and why it was important for me to do it.

Chapter One

'Midnight barbecues are the pits. I mean, in the jungle or some place roasting they might be okay. In Ireland, they're the *pits*.'

Wasn't that typical of Gilhooly. Always bitching!

'Get lost, will you, Gilhooly,' Jim Higgins exclaimed.

'Piss off,' the little French boy added. He was practising his idioms. But Gilhooly persisted, as if thirsting for martyrdom.

'Well it's true, isn't it? We're all frozen to death. These sausages are only half cooked. That other mess tastes like puke. Plus we'll all be wrecked in the morning.'

'That's what I hate about you, Gilhooly,' Higgins retorted disgustedly, 'you never agree with anything we plan, but you always insist on tagging along and belly-aching every inch of the way. Why didn't you just stay in bed, snoring and farting, like you always do?'

Seven third-year boys – average age fifteen – were struggling to have a midnight barbecue in late October. In Ireland, this is simply not possible; and St Isidore's boarding school, as Gilhooly implied, is in Ireland. Everything else that Gilhooly said was also true: that is why the others found him so annoying. They were frozen, the food was awful, and they would very likely be sick and shattered in the morning.

So why did they do it? Why did they hold these miserable midnight barbecues that nobody in his right mind could possibly enjoy at all? Addiction? Or for a dare? Routine sado-masochism perhaps – or one of these crazy things that people do for charity?

None of these motivations played any part at all. These boys were on manoeuvres for the single and most compelling reason in the code and lexicon of boys' boarding schools everywhere and wherever – tradition.

The midnight barbecue was one of the most hallowed traditions at St Isidore's. It was an essential rite of passage, one of the evil deeds absolutely necessary for salvation. The midnight barbecue was like stealing fire from the gods. Even such punishments as having your liver fed to eagles or rolling boulders up mountains for all eternity – which is what happened to Sisyphus, or one of those Greek dudes – did not deter the stout hearts of St Isidore's. After all, a man's got to do what a man's got to do, and these men did it with gusto – even several times.

Successive headmasters had laboured mightily to stamp out this deplorable and dangerous custom. Still boys persisted in disappearing into the forest by night, in spite of all the terrors and discomforts of that time and place. Truth to tell, even in the best of circumstances, they cannot have enjoyed the experience very much. But there are more things to life than crass enjoyment. The young scholars of St Isidore's, like adolescents everywhere and at all times, were putting down markers, pushing out boundaries and generally giving notice to their elders that they had arrived on the planet and would not be going away any time soon. Folksy wisdom has always acknowledged that boys will be boys. There are depths and demands in that seemingly innocuous proposition. That is why the boys of St Isidore's were doing the barbecue thing. And that, too, is why the headmaster was trying to stop them.

'It won't look good at the inquest,' the current headmaster, Dr Derwas Fisher, had said on more than one occasion, shaking his head gloomily. He seemed convinced that there would inevitably be an inquest eventually. At midnight in the forest, accidents are just queueing up to happen, and the track record had not been reassuring. One boy had fallen down a deep ravine in the dark and broken his wrist. Another had been attacked by a badger that had crunched his big toe between powerful teeth. Still another had nearly been shot by poachers hunting for deer. And one legendary hero from the dim and distant past had had to be rushed to hospital to have his stomach pumped out, having drunk some lethal distillation, half learned in chemistry class.

So the school authorities had grown rigorously vigilant about these nocturnal adventures. They could not very well lock the boys into their dormitories by night. There had been too many horrific cases in various parts of the world where this had been done, and dozens of children had perished in flames because they could not get out of a blazing inferno. Instead, at St Isidore's, in the summer term and again in early autumn, there was a policy of frequent random checks in all dormitories at any and every hour of the night. This tactic had proved that it had teeth and several arrests had followed, usually whole dormitories at a time. Summary justice was meted out in the shape of mandatory suspension for a week.

In the days when school authorities smacked children, which was really a form of body language – provided one was careful to speak that language correctly – being caught on a midnight barbecue was regarded as a fair cop, and even as part of the excitement of living dangerously. But political correctness had put paid to anything as uncivilized as corporal punishment and replaced it with excruciating and mean-minded scoldings, followed by mandatory suspension.

Suspension was a pernicious and inequitable punishment, simply because it meant totally different things in different households.

In one, 'Oh, darling, how lovely to see you. I'll cook your favourite supper.'

In another, 'You little brat, disgracing us before all the parents.'

In a third, 'Brilliant! We'll go waterskiing!'

And in a fourth, 'You will not put a foot outside that door for the entire week, and *no* television. You can catch up on your school work, which you have obviously been totally neglecting.'

This last remark really hurt. That boy was not the brightest blade in the pack, God knows, but he had been working really hard, just trying to keep up.

Another boy, whose parents were divorced and both remarried, was heard to complain sourly to his dormitory companions as they went into exile: 'It's all right for you buggers. I have *four* of them, and the only thing they can all agree on is that *I* am a total asshole.'

He got lucky, and his grandparents took him. He had a happy week. Grandparents and grandchildren have one deep conviction in common: the parents are pretty dumb.

Meanwhile the boys of St Isidore's had no alternative but to change the rules of the game and even to move the goalposts. Instead of holding midnight barbecues in summer or in autumn, they would hold them in early spring or even in the depths of winter. This meant risking either hypothermia or setting half the forest ablaze, and themselves with it, as they spewed petrol or paraffin on what could too easily have been their own funeral pyres.

There had even been a barbecue in the snow where one sanguine youth – too good for this wicked world – had appeared in pyjamas and football boots. In twenty minutes he had turned blue with the cold and could hardly speak. Gilhooly, who had been reading with avid interest about sailors shipwrecked in Arctic waters, suggested gleefully one way to induce a sharp rise in body temperature. The innocent iceman, shocked to the depths of his sensitive soul, had found enough voice to croak 'Like shit, Gilhooly, you queer' before stumbling off to his bed, which he should never have left in the first place.

Gilhooly could be odious. When the headmaster from time to time scolded his companions for being horrible to 'Eddie', the answer was always the same. 'You don't have to live with him, sir!' On the other hand, Gilhooly had his uses. For one thing, he seemed to know a lot about sex. For instance, on the basis of his superior knowledge in this department, he had been able to tell his classmates authoritatively when would be the best night for a barbecue.

'Have you seen that chart thing that Tyson has pasted up on his wall?'

Mr Tyson was the housemaster, and some of them had indeed noticed the chart and wondered what it was.

'Well, that proves that *this* would be a brilliant night for a barbecue.'

'Why?' they all said.

'Aha!' Gilhooly explained. 'Because this is a temperature chart.'

'So?'

'So, this is a chart of Tyson's temperature. It shows exactly when it is safe for him to have sex without having a whole load of unwanted babies as well.'

There was an undeniably pregnant silence. Then Martin Wilson said: 'I thought it was the lady who, sort of, that you had to have the temperature of.'

'You perfect ignoramus,' Gilhooly snapped. 'What has the woman got to do with it?'

Martin did not rightly know, so he remained silent. Gilhooly resumed magisterially, 'Anyhow, I can tell from this chart that tonight is the night.'

'Why?' they all said again.

'Because the temperature is precisely spot on, and the coast will be clear. Tyson, as soon as he thinks we are asleep, will be spending the night – elsewhere.'

The boys looked at each other, bewildered. Karl Hogan said: 'I don't believe you, Gilhooly. Tyson is very old, you know, nearly fifty or something. I mean, you're over the top, like, from that point of view, I mean, years before you get to be fifty.'

'Nonsense,' Gilhooly snorted. 'Half the guys in the Bible had kids when they were five hundred or something. They were begetting like crazy.'

'Yeah,' Martin interjected, 'but they had to work overtime, to get the world population up and running, like. It's different nowadays.'

Gilhooly smiled acidly. 'Really? How different? Do your parents still do it, Martin?'

There was a shocked silence. There are things that even boys do *not* talk about. Martin blushed scarlet.

'Shut your face, Gilhooly, will you? Just shut your face!'

Whatever wild theory Gilhooly might have had about Mr Tyson's 'temperature chart' – which was, in fact, nothing more exciting than a record of local daily rainfall, made at the request of the national meteorological service – his effrontery was such that the other boys tended to believe what he said. When, therefore, that night, Mr Tyson had indeed left his room about twenty minutes after lights-out, and had even turned off his own light, which he would not have done if he had intended to return there any time soon, they had waited for another half an hour.

Then Higgins, who by common consent was the natural leader of the band, gave the signal.

'Go for it!'

So they went for it.

Chapter Two

From its foundation, thirty-five years previously, St Isidore's School had been housed in a mock-Gothic Victorian folly built in the early eighteen thirties by a noble knight who had made his money out of South African diamonds. Set in the lush Golden Vale of North Kerry, Ireland, it was almost a success. Rather less than a castle, but definitely more than a mansion, purists might and did say that whichever architect had dreamed it up was having nightmares. It was all turrets, flying buttresses, gargoyles, spiral staircases and secret passages, a perfect compendium of the unlikely, the unnecessary and the impractical.

St Isidore's had even had a moat and a drawbridge. That was in the last century, or rather in the one before that. The moat had gone two thirds of the way round the castle, mostly in front of it. It had attracted rats, which is probably why it had also attracted Lady Mabel Randler's pet sausage dog – Lady Mabel was the great-grandmother of the last baronet to inhabit the castle. The hound had plunged merrily into the moat convinced, like so many people, that it could walk on water. Its silly little legs were quite inadequate for moat-bank-climbing, so, inevitably, it finished the day belly up.

Lady Mabel discovered the tragedy herself. She had to spend six weeks in Switzerland to recover from the bereavement. Applying the common law doctrine of the deodand, which states that *Whatever moved to do the deed / Is deodand – and forfeited*, she decreed vindictively that the moat should be drained of every drop of water and never filled again this side of the end of the world. This was a bit hard on the moat which could not really be said to have *moved* at all.

The drawbridge survived until the castle became a school, and it did not seem reasonable any longer to be lowering a drawbridge every time a miserable schoolboy with holes in his drooping socks approached the premises.

Still, the pile served well enough as a boys' school, if only because, with walls three to six foot thick, it was more or less boy-proof. Avid readers of Harry Potter, who were sent to St Isidore's, thought they were in heaven. On the other hand, such is the influence of environment that Old Isidorians – which is what the alumni were called – retained in later life something gently whimsical, tinged with the macabre, and more than vaguely off-the-wall.

Mr Tyson was responsible for fifty boys in the middle school. These were housed in dormitories for five, six, or seven, with a few lucky youngsters having single rooms which were raffled at the beginning of every term. The Middle House, as it was called, occupied space on the second floor of the castle. Mr Tyson's own rooms and one dormitory for seven, inhabited by Higgins and his crew, were housed in a round tower up a further flight of stairs. No doubt on the basis that possession is nine tenths of the law, this was called Tyson's tower. An architectural mushroom, it resembled nothing so much as the control tower of an airport, in the days when safety depended on who was looking out of the window.

When Higgins gave the word, everybody stole out of bed and wrapped up as warmly as impatience would allow. Each boy hurriedly made a shape with his duvet and pillows which he fondly imagined would fool an experienced housemaster into believing that there was a recumbent body in his bed. Then they crept down three flights of stone steps and into the night. It was nearly half past eleven.

Once outside, the boys collected their food from a clump of rhododendrons where they had hidden it earlier in the day. This time, fortunately, it had not been gnawed by rats or dogs. That did happen from time to time, but if the damage was not deemed *too* bad – for which it would have to be *very* bad – standard practice was to brush the affected area robustly with a grubby hand or on a trouser leg, and to hope for the best. The boys, of course, were perfectly aware that much higher standards of hygiene applied in home economics class. They even knew the solid principles on which those higher standards were based. But none of all that stuff applied when the lads were having fun.

A midnight barbecue was one of those privileged occasions when the laws of nature are deemed to be suspended in favour of young people, or so they seem to think. When the young are having high jinks, *surely*, nobody ever gets frightful diseases, babies are never conceived, and teenagers can drive like there's no tomorrow without its becoming a self-fulfilling prophecy. The discrepancy between wishful thinking and sombre reality in all these matters is a series of tragic statistics.

Higgins meanwhile, operationally at least, was taking no risks. He led his cohort out of the gable end of the castle, which was constructed as a massive Norman keep and had only one small window high up in its blank expanse. This was the safest way to cross, unseen, the eighty yards of open terrain between the school and the forest. Once under cover of the trees, the adventurers could move less furtively. But they still had to travel most of a mile before they could have their barbecue safely. Anything less would be courting disaster because sounds, smells of cooking, smoke, and even the flicker of a fire, can be detected across phenomenal distances in the still of the night.

In the days of the noble baronets, the castle had had attached to it a fine tillage farm of several hundred acres. Sir Neville Randler's ancestors had diligently cultivated this holding. His father, however, had been far too lazy to exert himself unduly, or even duly. So he had sold the tillage farm. It was Sir Neville who had eventually given up the unequal struggle and sold the castle to the trustees of St Isidore's School. He was still living in the neighbourhood.

There remained for St Isidore's to inherit nearly eight hundred acres of deer park and forestry, containing two small lakes and a bigger one connected by a network of brooks and streams, and a spectacular gorge gouged out, it was said, by a glacier. The gorge was a mile and a half long, deep, and overgrown with the wildest and weirdest of vegetation. Some of the boys ardently believed that a prehistoric tribe of poison dwarfs, together with extinct reptiles with five hundred teeth apiece, were hiding somewhere in these impenetrable thickets and living off each other – which, admittedly, would have been a neat ecosystem all of its own. The boys were torn between the hope and the fear of finding either or both of these colonies.

If Harry Potter could have been quite at home in the castle, Jungle Jim would have been in his element down in the woods.

The posse was headed this evening for a familiar site, much patronized by clandestine barbecuers. At the end of a long incline which eventually rose higher than the top of the castle, this site was safe, according to schoolboy wisdom, because sound, smoke and smells all rise still further into the air.

So they could not be detected, the boys argued, unless the headmaster invested in a satellite or at least in a helicopter.

At the summit of this modest hill, there was a bowl-shaped depression, tailor-made for wrap-around chumminess at barbecues. This might have been caused by a random-shot meteorite colliding with St Isidore's several million years ago at trillions of miles per hour. On the other hand, it might have been specially designed by a provident intelligence foreseeing that the scholars of St Isidore's would be needing a congenial barbecue site some aeons into the future. The difficulty about this second theory was that it seemed to range the provident intelligence on the side of the lawbreakers.

This particular barbecue was long on random shots but sadly short on intelligent design. It was, as a boy called Jack O'Toole described it with spontaneous alliteration, 'an *effing* fiasco from flag fall to finish'. There had been failures of communication on a massive scale, which meant that pratically no one brought what he was expected to bring. It was like the GUM supermarket in Moscow before the fall of Communism: all chamber pots but no lavatory paper. Demand and supply were not singing out of the same hymn sheet. Sausages, but nothing to fry/grill them in/on, unpopped popcorn, tins without openers, and a bottle of wine, 'borrowed' from Martin's father's cellar, or garage actually, but no corkscrew. Most serious of all, nobody had thought of dry firewood, with the result that they never got a convincing blaze going, whether to cook meat or to warm people.

They stuck it out for an hour and a half. Anything less would not even register on the Richter scale of barbecues. But enough was enough. Everything that Gilhooly had said about this barbecue was too true, which, as already noted, did not make the others love him any the more. A perspicacious if indiscreet teacher had once said to the whole class, 'Gilly is the kind of guy who will die happy if his last words can be, "There, I told you so!"'

It was about half past one in the morning. With any luck, they would be in bed by two o'clock, then up again at half past seven, which was much too little sleep for growing boys. They would stagger through the next day on automatic pilot, sore of throat, sour of stomach, dull of wit, and constipated – or more likely the opposite. If they had class tests that day, they would fail miserably, and if they had rugby training, it would be like dying for the faith under torture.

At least, getting down the hill which led to the

school was easier than climbing it with so much ill-assorted and ultimately useless equipment. They went in single file, almost in silence. They could all remember tales of hilarious barbecues from which the revellers had returned as high as kites. Indeed, one of the times that a group had actually been caught, it was not because of anything clever the headmaster or a housemaster had done, but simply because they came back into the castle at three o'clock in the morning sounding like the sack of Rome.

The forest was dense as Higgins and his followers approached the school. Used as they were to the sudden appearance of the castle, it never failed to take their breath away. One saw none of it, and then all of it, as if it had materialized in a split second before their astonished eyes. Built of grey-red sand-stone, by day – and even by night – it could look warm and benevolent, a safe and protective strong-hold. But this night it seemed massive and sinister, a Count Dracula's castle. A cold cheerless moon sluiced light on the battlements, like icy rain on a row of tombstones. The little French boy said suddenly, 'I am afraid.'

Martin, who was close to him, took his arm and whispered conspiratorially, 'So am I, Bertrand, but let's not let on.'

They went in through the cellars that housed the central heating plant. All was quiet at this hour of the night except one maverick pump, wheezing away eerily like a vampire who has overslept in his coffin. The pitch black darkness of this subterranean dungeon was pierced randomly by menacing points of red light: bloodshot eyes, each threatening some cruelty that the mindless apparatus to which it was attached itched to inflict on the unwary. The boys scuttled through quickly, arms and hands close to their bodies, for fear that even a little finger could unleash a dozen demons.

They got to the second floor, where Middle House territory begins. The final gauntlet was there before them. Seven pairs of eyes lifted apprehensively in the direction of the spiral stairs leading to Tyson's tower. Even when a rocket has been all the way to Mars and back, there remains the tricky manoeuvre of re-entry. It must spoil all the fun of even the most thrilling cosmic odyssey if one is to crash and burn in the last two minutes.

Jim Higgins had just put one hand on the fire door at the bottom of the spiral stairs when he snatched it away again like a scalded cat.

'Scatter! Tyson!' he hissed, and dived for cover himself.

Jim had heard the unmistakable sound of a foot-fall on stone. There was somebody coming down those steps from the tower, and perhaps only two or three twists of the corkscrew away from catching them all red handed. This person could only be Tyson – simply because there was nobody else left up there, since they themselves were the only other residents. Tyson had obviously discovered their villainy and was eagerly awaiting their return. Indeed, charmingly, he was coming halfway to meet them.

Seconds passed. Nemesis, the Greek goddess of vengeance and punishment, giving a last twist to the screw, metaphorically sealing their coffins, abruptly appeared through the fire door. The boys flattened themselves against the wall and suspended breathing. They realized that it was almost certainly too late. Tyson must have seen them, and the game was up.

But, to their amazement, the housemaster turned and walked away quickly in the opposite direction from where the naughty boys were spreadeagled against the wall. Six mouths fell open in blank aston-ishment. The seventh mouth had so much orthodontic hardware within it that opening and closing had to be conscious decisions.

'I don't believe it!' Martin whispered excitedly.

'He never saw us. Perhaps he doesn't even know that we're out.'

'But where is he going – at this hour of the night?' Gilhooly asked.

Karl Hogan said, 'I don't think that was Tyson at all. It was too small.'

'Well who was it then,' Jack O'Toole asked, 'and what was he doing up there, in our empty dormitory?'

'Perhaps it was Lady Macbeth,' Martin Wilson suggested.

Lady Macbeth was the literary name for the class sleepwalker, an inoffensive youth whose real name was Harry Lewins. Harry never did himself or anybody else any harm on his nocturnal rambles. The boys had strict instructions to leave him alone when he was sleepwalking, which they did willingly, being a bit in awe of Harry's unusual affliction – if indeed it was an affliction, and not some higher state of consciousness or mystical experience. They, and even he, were never sure how aware he was of what was going on around him during his walkabouts, though he insisted that he had no recollection of where he had been or what he had done the following morning.

Jim Higgins cut short on the speculation. 'Maybe

so, and maybe not. If it *wasn't* Tyson though, then he's still up there, and we're not home and dry yet. So, you guys, move it!'

They crept up the last flight of stairs as noiselessly as a pride of kittens. Mr Tyson's door was closed and there was no telltale strip of light from under it. Elated, they scurried past and into their own dormitory.

'No lights!' Higgins reminded them in a hoarse whisper. Quickly, they undressed in the dark and undid the dummy figures they had made with pillows and duvets. Then they tumbled gratefully into bed.

There was a short silence. Then the little French boy said: 'Ah! My bed is all wet!'

'How, all wet?' Martin asked.

Gilhooly chimed in, his voice absurdly high pitched and squeaky, '*Oh, là là!* 'ave we been doing *oui oui* in our leetle bed?'

A flashlight flickered briefly. Suddenly, the French boy panicked.

'Higgins, turn on the light, please! I'm all blood. Oh please, I am bleeding very badly. I am going to die!'

His tone was so urgent that Higgins did not hesitate. He jumped out of bed and flicked on the light. The French boy's bed was indeed drenched in blood.

Higgins ran towards him, without knowing what he would do when he got there. Then he stopped in his tracks, mouth open, his face ashen white. With a visible effort, he forced himself to continue. He caught the little boy's hands and started to pull him out of the bed.

'Bertrand, you are all right, do you hear? You are all right, okay? But come with me now, come with me! No, don't look back, Bertrand! Don't turn round!'

He dragged the little boy towards the door, calling urgently to the others, 'Everybody OUT! Please! Don't ask. Just do it, immediately. OUT! DO IT!'

Some of them saw it, some of them did not. Between the little French boy's bed and the window, Tyson was lying on his back on the floor in a pool of his own blood. His throat had been cut from ear to ear, and it looked as if his head was half off. He was certainly dead. It was not a pretty sight. Jim Higgins was to wake up screaming for months afterwards.

Chapter Three

'Molly, isn't that what you call *déjà vu*?'

'Isn't that what you call what?'

'You know, *déjà vu*, like when you've been here before.'

The speakers were Superintendent Denis Lennon and Sergeant Molly Power of the Garda Síochána, the Irish police force, who were driving down from Dublin to Kerry to investigate a shocking murder in a boys' boarding school. All murders are shocking, it goes without saying, but any death in a school – let alone murder – seems particularly shocking.

Lennon went on: 'Well, I have actually been here

before. It must be forty years ago, before the castle was a school. The owner was a young chap, Sir Neville Randler, quite an eccentric and a spend-thrift, people used to say. He had to sell his castle eventually.'

'So what were you doing there?'

'That was a laugh. Some obscure royal was due to call, the duke of somewhere or other. The bad bold baronet demanded a security presence. So P. J. Connolly and myself were sent all the way from Templemore – we hadn't even completed our training at the time. They called it work experience. The Gardaí were way ahead of anyone when it came to saving money. We were despatched on a big black motorbike that was used to break in outriders in cop school. We had to do – what? eighty or a hundred miles on that yoke, and the same to return. P. J. was driving and I was on the pillion seat, clinging on for dear life.

'Naturally, P. J. contracted a terrible thirst and we kept stopping for "just one pint". The result was that by the time we arrived, the duke, or whatever he was, had come and gone, and P. J. could hardly get off his motorbike. To tell the truth, I wasn't much better myself.'

'You must have been boiled in oil for that one,'

Molly exclaimed, quite shocked at the thought that Lennon, the paragon of police probity as far as she was concerned, had ever been so irresponsible.

'Not a bit of it.' He laughed. 'The duke and the baronet had been doing exactly the same thing themselves. The bart was on his ear. We told him that we had arrived bright and early but that our instructions were to be unobtrusive – indeed invisible – while at the same time being ready to pounce at a moment's notice if the IRA tried anything. So P. J. and myself, we said, had forged a ring of steel round the castle – an invisible ring of steel, of course – and felt that we could let it go at that. The baronet was pure delighted. He showed us round the whole castle, fed us, and lubricated us again liberally. I don't know how we ever got back to Templemore that night.'

'I'm shocked!'

'Yes, I suppose you probably are. But those were more innocent days. Besides, I'm not sure that what we have got now in this country is better. In fact, I'm sure that it is worse.'

Lennon fell silent for a time, presumably reflecting on the good old days. After an interval Molly asked, 'What became of the bold bad baronet?'

'He must be in his seventies now. I think he still

lives in the neighbourhood. The locals used to call his place Hatter's Castle when the old boy still had it. I believe that the trustees of the new school had a hard time losing that name. It was not at all what they wanted for their posh academy.'

They made good time from Dublin and were driving up the long tree-lined avenue to St Isidore's by eleven o'clock on a bright October morning. Three days had elapsed since the murder. In the interval the local police had been in charge of operations. Their task had been to preserve the scene until the State Pathologist arrived and, in her wake, what Lennon described as 'the powder-puff brigade'. These were the almighty technicals for whom seeing is not necessarily believing and who can, in any case, see round corners with the periscopic vision of their diverse technologies.

Tyson's body had been removed within a few hours, and within a day the police had been able to hand over the clothes and personal effects of the seven boys who had occupied the dormitory where the body had been found. Dr Fisher, the headmaster, explained, 'Of course, you could not expect these boys ever to sleep in that dormitory again. Indeed, it will probably never be used as a dormitory at all in the future. Boarding schools have powerful mythologies, you see. That room will almost certainly be haunted – or be said to be haunted – in perpetuity. For ever.'

Lennon noticed with wry amusement that the headmaster had added the last two words for the benefit of the police people, who might be presumed to have difficulties with expressions like 'in perpetuity'. One of his strengths as a detective was that people often thought Lennon was slightly dim and, consequently, harmless. In appropriate cases, he positively encouraged that opinion of himself.

Silver haired, sixtyish, domesticated, still married to his first wife, Mary, with two daughters and one son and an increasing flock of grandchildren, on whom he doted, Lennon was not cut in the contemporary mould of police detectives. He was neither hard-boiled nor world-weary – although he did increasingly express a degree of perplexity about 'what the world was coming to'. Lennon did not chain-smoke, drink heavily, habitually sleep in his clothes, or eat only junk food – Mary would never have allowed such things – and he was pretty good at his job.

The headmaster's study was a particularly splendid Gothic horror of a room. Perfectly circular, it was the interior of one of two cylindrical towers to the left and right of the great entrance to the castle. Situated on the ground floor, it would rise two storeys to become the base of Tyson's tower two floors above. At the centre point of the study there was a massive pentagonal pillar with an open fireplace on one of its five faces and tall mirrors set into each of the others: a cunning architectural feature to reflect and increase the sparse light admitted by five narrow windows on the room's circumference. The ceiling of the study was, literally and architecturally, its crowning glory: an intricate and geometrically sublime culmination of a network of ascending pillars, deep ribbing and pointed arches, the whole papered in a heavy damask material mottled with gold stars on an ice-blue background.

'You could imagine the thumbscrews,' Lennon commented afterwards. 'A real Star Chamber. That room must make even the lustiest lads quake in their boots.'

The headmaster seemed indeed rather gaunt and Gothic himself. Perhaps in his late forties, he stooped already at the shoulders, like a depressed vulture with worms. He was tall, thin and hollow cheeked, with limp and colourless hair – Molly called him afterwards Count Dracula. Lennon, in somewhat more complimentary vein, countered with Sherlock Holmes.

'Look at those hawk's eyes,' he said. 'They don't miss anything. I would feel extremely uncomfortable if I was a schoolboy trying to spin him some tall story.'

Dr Fisher had been headhunted by the trustees of the school more for administrative astuteness than for his educational philosophy. 'Horses for courses,' the chairperson of the trustees had exclaimed. Fisher made the place pay, while Tyson and others like him got on with the educating.

Molly asked the headmaster if anything would be done to the seven boys who had ventured out for their barbecue on the night when Tyson had been murdered.

'I mean, as a punishment. After all, these midnight barbecues are surely against the rules, aren't they?'

The headmaster permitted himself the kind of smile he probably reserved for slow learners.

'They most certainly are, Sergeant. The normal punishment for such behaviour is suspension for sometimes even a week. In this case, the circumstances are highly unusual. After all, these boys have had a most hideous shock, which is punishment enough. Besides, you, no doubt, need to be asking them questions, so there would be little point in dispersing them in several different directions.'

'Thank you, that is very thoughtful of you,' Lennon said. 'Yes, we would like to talk to all seven of them. Often children notice things that grown-ups miss. We'll do that, I assure you, in a very non-threatening way.'

'I have every confidence that you will, Superintendent. I will, of course, sit in on these interviews – as a sort of a chaperon, to see that everything is – ah – as it should be.'

'I am afraid that won't be possible, Dr Fisher. A parent, certainly, but not a member of the school staff.'

Dr Fisher opened his eyes wide in well-bred surprise bordering on incredulity. He said, mildly enough, but firmly, 'Dear me. Are you telling me, Superintendent, that I and my staff are all under suspicion of having murdered poor Maurice Tyson?'

Lennon replied equally mildly and firmly. 'Well, without going that far, Dr Fisher, the presence of a member of the school staff might inhibit one or other boy from telling us something that we need to know. I do regret it if you see this as something hostile. It is not intended in that way, I do assure you.'

The headmaster said nothing, but made a gesture of surrender with his hands. Lennon felt that, in spite of his best intentions, he had offended the other man. There was an awkward silence, which the superintendent eventually broke.

'Dr Fisher, have you any inkling about what could have happened to Mr Tyson?'

'Well, somebody cut his throat, didn't they?'

'Well, yes, obviously, but have you any ideas about who that person might be?'

The headmaster was already shaking his head. He replied with a question of his own, showing the extent of his bewilderment and pain.

'Who could have done this terrible thing – to the most inoffensive man that God ever made?'

The superintendent and the sergeant spent the rest of the morning getting familiar with the buildings and grounds of the school. There was the castle, which accommodated some fine parlours and reception rooms on its ground floor, together with an oak-panelled library, a spacious computer room, a pocket-sized auditorium, some offices for the school administration, and Dr Fisher's study in its tower.

'What did you think of the occupant himself, Molly, the esteemed headmaster?'

'I didn't warm to him particularly, although he says a lot of the right things, like when he was going on about not punishing the naughty boys for their escapade. You could not fault him, so let's give him a chance. It may be just the surroundings. It must be difficult not to look like a bit of a gargoyle round here.'

The upper storeys of the castle were occupied by dormitories, private rooms, showering facilities and bathrooms, and also the infirmary where the barbecuers of the fatal night were finding temporary sanctuary pending preparation of a reasonably adequate junk room to accommodate them more permanently. As Dr Fisher had observed, the boys could not very well be expected to pass their nights in the room where their housemaster had been slaughtered like an animal.

The class rooms, laboratories, and study halls of the school, together with refectories and kitchens, changing rooms, laundry and services, were housed in modern buildings, cleverly designed so as not to take away from the full charms – or horrors, depending on one's point of view – of the original pile. There was also a gymnasium and a small indoor swimming pool, donated by a grateful and well-heeled alumnus. The headmaster moaned incessantly about the expense of maintaining the swimming pool. But not to do so would have been so unpopular as to lead to moral and political defenestration, if not literal flinging from the battlements. He grumbled, grinned, and bore it.

Dr Fisher and his wife lived in a cottage a few hundred yards away from the castle. There were no other married quarters on the campus, so teachers mostly came from outside by the day. Housemasters were usually young and mostly unmarried, or at least willing to restrict the attention they gave to their relationships to their meagre free time. There were seven housemasters in all for two hundred and fifty boys, five being in charge of houses and two rotating to replace the others on their days off. The housemasters, with the help of boy prefects, supervised studies, refectories and dormitories, and generally looked after the domestic, personal and spiritual welfare of all. This had been the exacting but strangely fulfilling task, and even vocation, of Maurice Tyson. He was good at it. If the boys did not particularly like him, they respected and trusted him and were already missing the quiet security, the moderation, and the sheer decency of his regime.

The police discovered the Fisher residence when they went for a stroll to get an overall impression of the various buildings on the campus. More quaint than charming, it was somebody else's concept of bijou and rustic. Molly had once seen a cottage just like it on the stage of the Gaiety Theatre in Dublin. It was the *pied-à-terre* of the Wicked Witch – when she was not flying around on her broomstick – in a performance of *Hänsel und Gretel* by Humperdinck. It eventually blew up spectacularly in the last act of the opera. Molly was never quite sure why this happened because the necessary explanations were warbled at length in German, of which she did not understand one word. The main thing was that Hänsel *und* Gretel did get to live happily ever after – which was made abundantly clear by their generally frolicsome demeanour in the closing stages of the performance.

Frau Fisher was known as George, which might even have been her real name. That much they had been told by the local police. Also that she wore trouser suits, smoked cheroots, bred bulls, and was quite useful as a veterinary surgeon in the locality. It seemed, too, that she and her husband were known jointly in the school to everyone except themselves as 'George and the Dragon'. She was in the bijou garden of their bijou residence, raking up leaves, when Denis and Molly broke from the cover of the shrubbery which lined the alley by which they had approached. Younger than her husband – perhaps in her late thirties – she was quite attractive in a *Star*

Trek mould. 'A bit of a surprise after Fisher,' Molly remarked later. 'He must have trouble keeping up, if you know what I mean.' Lennon grunted.

George saw them at once. 'Hi,' she called.

They began to explain who they were, but she cut them off with a wry smile.

'Oh, great heavens, I know who you must be. I am George – short for Georgina – Fisher, the head-master's devoted wife.'

She came up to the garden gate, quickly removing a rubber glove, and shook their hands.

'Come in, please, even if it's only for a few moments. Let's get acquainted.'

The police officers, to their surprise – so quickly did it happen – found themselves in a cosy sitting room with cups of coffee in front of them. 'The cottage is better inside than outside,' Lennon mused. Molly thought to herself, 'Boy, she sure takes the initiative.' It amused her to see Lennon, who was quite hard to shift, so effortlessly stage-managed.

Lennon said, when they had been through the milk and sugar ritual, 'A sad affair! Can you advise us?'

George looked at him with interest. 'Advise you! Dear me, what can I say? That will be more in my husband's line. I'm busy with my own work – I am a vet, you know – and I don't really get too involved in the school. A bit of driving, to the doctor, or the dentist, or whatever, that's about it. I knew Maurice Tyson, of course. We used to entertain him from time to time. My husband held him in high esteem. But speaking as an outsider – as I must – this whole thing has neither rhyme nor reason to it. My own guess is that it is the work of some deranged person. The uncomfortable part of that theory, of course, is that what happened once can certainly happen again. I'll be keeping the door locked when I am alone in the house from now on. That is why I spotted you so quickly when you came along this morning. I find myself frisking everybody mentally since this awful thing happened.'

'Where were you at the time?'

'In my bed, as far as I know.'

'Are you not sure?'

'Well, I am not sure what time it happened, so I am not sure whether I was still watching television, or whether I had already gone to bed. My husband was off at a dinner in Belfast. The first I heard of it was when they rang me from the school to find out where he could be contacted urgently. Then they told me the horrible news.'

'Who rang you?'

'It was one of the housemasters, Stan I think, or Billy. It will be easy to find out. I had been in a deep sleep – and then to be woken up to such an appalling announcement!'

'And what time was that?'

'Oh, the small hours. I don't know, I was so shocked. But, again, it will be easy to find out.'

'And your advice?' Lennon enquired, almost as if he had not heard what else she had been saying since he last asked that question.

'My advice,' she responded after a pause, 'is to do the same thing as me – frisk everybody.' She added, as if by way of an afterthought, and with the merest ghost of a smile, 'Why! You are doing that already, aren't you?'

As they walked back to the school, Molly said, 'What did you think of her?'

Lennon sucked his teeth, and replied, 'I sure wouldn't like to knock over her beer.'

Dr Fisher did not appear at lunch. A charming South African evangelical called Stan, who was spending a gap year as one of the rotating housemasters, shyly invited the police people into the refectory. Their presence created an almost embarrassing sensation, although Molly had the impression that the boys would have far preferred it if they had been in uniform, or even in battle fatigues. Lennon's stained anorak was clearly a disappointment. No sooner were they seated than the boy beside the superintendent demanded peremptorily: 'Have you got a gun?'

Lennon made a great show of rummaging in his pockets. Eventually, he announced: 'Do you know what? I think I left it at home on the television set. I was watching Chelsea and Arsenal last night.'

The boy stared at him with open-mouthed disgust. A few moments later Molly spotted the lad on his way back from self-service pausing with his tray at another table. He was saying indignantly: 'That pair couldn't even solve what time it is! I mean the stupid moron hasn't even got a gun.'

Meanwhile Stan the evangelical housemaster was giving his first impressions of the boys of Ireland.

'In one sense, there is no harm in them. They are very innocent. But their language is beyond belief, really atrocious – words I have never heard on any Christian tongue. I just don't know how they can be saved like that. The Catholic Church has really got a lot to answer for in this country.'

'Are they truthful?' Molly asked. 'I mean, will the boys tell the truth about Mr Tyson?'

'I am not sure what you mean by telling "the truth

about Mr Tyson"',' Stan answered. As Molly said nothing, he continued: 'If you mean the boys in the dormitory right next to Mr Tyson's rooms, they were out on an escapade – a midnight barbecue, if you please. It was they who found poor Mr Tyson on the floor of their dormitory when they returned.'

'Yes, they are famous,' Lennon remarked. 'Or infamous; even the newspapers had it. Of course, they stopped short of giving names.'

'Giving names,' Stan exclaimed heatedly, 'that would be outrageous!' He continued in a more even tone: 'Well anyhow, yes. Those boys will certainly tell you the truth, the whole truth, and nothing but the truth. They are deeply shocked, and they all know that this is, literally, a matter of life and death.'

'What can they tell us?' Molly asked.

'Well, for one thing, they may even have seen the murderer.'

'Are you serious?' Lennon was clearly astonished.

'Have you been through the castle yet?' Stan asked.

'Just a quick once over the course,' Molly answered.

'You have seen the spiral staircase leading to Tyson's tower?'

The officers both nodded.

'Well, just when the kids were approaching that on their way back from their barbecue, they saw a figure coming down the stairs. They thought it must be Mr Tyson – it was dark, of course – so they hid in a hurry, as best they could. But the guy, whoever he was, when he got to the bottom, headed off in the opposite direction. The lads couldn't believe their luck. Of course, when they got up the stairs themselves, they soon discovered that, no matter who else it was that they had seen, it certainly wasn't Mr Tyson – because he was lying on the floor with his throat cut.'

'So who was it?' Molly asked the obvious question.

Stan paused before replying. 'Actually, the boys discussed that a lot between themselves, and they didn't mind me hearing what they were saying. Still, I didn't like to question them too much myself, because I had strong views on some of the names that they were discussing, and I didn't think it would be right for me to, well, influence them one way or the other – you know what I am saying.'

Lennon was impressed. 'Young man, you would make a first-rate judge – or a referee.'

Stan smiled. Molly forged ahead. 'Tell us off the record.'

'I guess you'll hear it anyhow. You see, several of them were saying that it was Lady Macbeth that they saw on the stairs that night.'

Seeing their evident astonishment, Stan hurriedly explained about the school sleepwalker.

'And you don't agree?' Lennon probed.

'I wasn't there,' Stan pointed out, 'so it's not for me to agree or to disagree. I only know that that poor boy, Harry Lewins, wouldn't say boo to a goose. He may have been there but, surely, if there is justice in heaven or earth, he never put a finger near Mr Tyson. It is not in his nature.'

After lunch, when Dr Fisher had still not reappeared, Stan obligingly rounded up the barbecuers for Lennon. There were six of them. Lennon enquired about the seventh. Jim Higgins explained: 'That's Bertrand, the French chap. He's gone back to France. I think his parents freaked when they heard about the murder. He was only a little guy, you see, so they airlifted him out.'

Lennon and Molly sat in a club room with the boys around them and explained in plain and direct language what they hoped to achieve. Molly said: 'I am sure that you are very sorry about Mr Tyson. Dr Fisher has told us how brilliant you have all been with his family, and indeed how hard you are working to make the funeral really special when the body is released. Well, we want you to help us to get justice for Mr Tyson. After all, you guys were there, so we're really depending on you. I reckon you are pretty sharp observers. No, seriously, I'd say you don't miss much.'

Lennon was watching the boys closely. They were intent upon what Molly was saying, and they were clearly reassured by the way she was talking to them. Something important suddenly slipped into focus for him. He said it straight out: 'You boys have been feeling pretty guilty, haven't you?'

A shudder of recognition went through the group. They tensed up immediately.

'You feel that if only you had been good little boys, this terrible thing would never have happened. You think that you deserted poor Mr Tyson, and that if only you had been there to mind him, he would still be alive today.'

Two boys dropped their heads. Another was suddenly crying, tears flowing down his face. Jim Higgins said, 'That's it all right. I don't think we sort of knew before you said it, like, but yes, that's what's so awful. If only . . .'

Molly said gently, 'Listen, you guys, you mustn't

blame yourselves for Mr Tyson's death. How could you possibly know? You broke the school rules, that's all. Well, what else is new? You don't think we have come to arrest you for that, do you?'

It was the comical way she said it that finally broke the tension, and the boys laughed gratefully. Lennon went on to say that they would ask each boy to help with some simple questions. There would be no trick questions, no interrogation, no attempt to make them feel guilty or uncomfortable.

'We are all on the same side, and trying to help each other at this very sad time, okay?'

Molly promised the boys that there would be no tales out of school to the headmaster or to anybody else, and she explained that they were very welcome to have a parent present when they were being questioned.

When the police had finished, the boys came up spontaneously and shook hands solemnly with each of them. Then they left in silence.

Jim Higgins strolled down to the lake with Martin Wilson.

'What do you think?' Martin asked.

'Dead decent. I never thought they would be anything like that.'

'Are you going to bring your mother in on it, Jim?'

Jim's mother was a widow. She was friendly with Martin's parents.

'I don't think so. There's no need. She finds it hard to get away – with the young ones and all. Besides, she'll be coming for my birthday the week after next. That's enough.'

'I'm glad!'

Jim laughed, surprised. 'Glad? What are you glad about?'

'Because you'll have to tell the police about the bottle of wine I nicked from my dad's garage, and your mother, if she was there, might tell my parents. My father would skin me alive – or he wouldn't, actually. It'd be worse. He'd be totally disappointed and disgusted. He thinks I'm real honest and upright, and all that stuff.'

'My mother wouldn't repeat anything like that, and anyway, I don't have to tell them about the bottle of wine.'

'Jim, we have got to tell them everything, I mean *everything*, no matter how it hurts. We owe it to old Tyson.'

'Well, not to worry, I'll be on my own. What about your parents, Martin, are they coming?'

'No bleeding way! I won't even call them – just in case they might.'

Karl Hogan was on the phone to his mother.

'Pet lamb, I think I should be there.'

'Mummy, *don't* call me pet lamb. How often must I tell you? I'm the captain of the under-fifteens rugby team, for crying out loud!'

'Well you're still my own precious apple dumpling.'

'Agghh! There you go *again*!'

'I still think I should be there – to protect my little bundle of joy.'

'Your *what*? Oh my God! Listen, Mummy, if you dare to come, disgracing me, I'll never talk to you again . . . I'll emigrate to Australia.'

Chapter Four

In the afternoon Lennon studied preliminary reports
from Forensics and the State Pathologist. It was likely,
he read in the latter, that Tyson was attacked from
behind by a right-handed assailant who had tilted his
head backwards violently with his left hand and
severed both carotid arteries below the divide and a
principal jugular vein. There was no evidence of a
struggle. Tyson had obviously been taken totally by
surprise. Defenceless, off balance, he had probably
had to be held in a headlock for only a matter of
seconds before, buckling at the knees, he had slid to
the floor on his back where the boys were to find

him. The sudden closing down of the blood supply to the brain would have provoked a massive stroke and irreversible shock, leading to unconsciousness and death in a matter of minutes.

There would have been a lot of blood, spurting especially from the carotid arteries and drenching the little French boy's bed, but the murderer, standing behind his victim, would not necessarily have been soaked, except probably his left hand and forearm which were holding Tyson's head in position for what the report called 'the incision'. A long, straight and very sharp knife, with a good handle, was used. There was no evidence of sawing. One devastating slashing movement, the virtuoso stroke of a violinist playing *allegro vivace*, had cut that throat. Whoever had done the deed had known exactly what he was doing and was highly skilled.

Meanwhile Molly had been reading Des Tweedy's report. Des was the head of the Technical Branch. He was highly competent but had an annoying habit in conversation of trading vital information germane to an inquiry against willingness to hear at length his views on environmental topics, together with tirades against individuals and organizations who had incurred his ire – especially the Board of Works.

In the tower dormitory, it was not so much

environmental issues or even the Board of Works that were the object of Des Tweedy's righteous indignation: it was human hygiene and propriety. He seemed to have analysed all the dirty socks and other small garments that he had found under the beds and he was clearly dismayed by the results. He had also discovered some girlie magazines which seemed to confirm his gloomy expectations and merited three totally irrelevant paragraphs in his report.

'Is this guy Tweedy for real or what?' Molly exclaimed. 'This stuff is off the wall!'

Lennon nodded and grinned. 'He is ninety-seven per cent for real – with a fatal weakness for righteous indignation and the wrath of God. Thank your lucky stars you didn't bump into him in the Middle Ages. As Grand Inquisitor, he'd probably have left you for dead – which is not just a manner of speaking.'

About the murder itself, Tweedy had drawn a blank, or almost. This was eloquent in its own way. It was saying what the pathologist's report was saying independently: that Tyson had been killed by someone who knew what he was doing and did not intend to leave any trail behind him.

There was one clue none the less. A left-handed smudgy fingerprint in blood on the right lens of Tyson's spectacles. Incomplete and indistinct, it would hardly be enough to secure a conviction, but it would certainly be enough to narrow the field of suspects. The print was probably made when the assailant's left hand, which had been holding Tyson's head back under the chin, slipped upwards as the victim slumped heavily to the ground. By then, if not dead already, Tyson was probably deeply unconscious. His inert body would have slithered backwards down along the murderer's body to the floor.

In mid-afternoon Dr Fisher reappeared in his study. Lennon told him that he had had a preliminary interview with the six boys still in the school who had gone on the barbecue the night of the murder. Dr Fisher greeted this statement with a quiet 'Very well', which probably showed that he was still slightly miffed to be excluded from these colloquies. Too bad! Lennon pressed ahead.

'There was also a French boy.'

'Ah yes, Bertrand. A nice little fellow.'

'What happened to him?'

'Nothing happened to him, thank God.'

'Well, he's not here.'

'No, he went home.'

'Why?'

'Superintendent, Bertrand was only to be here for

a month or two, to improve his English. We do quite a lot of these exchanges. This boy was nearly two years younger than the average in that class. The murder must have been a great shock for him. The poor child's bed was literally drenched with Mr Tyson's blood. This was no place for him after that.'

'Was it not unusual to have a boy so young with lads so much older?'

'We are fairly flexible about that. Besides, the other boys were not that much older. Bertrand was well able to hold his own. Also, it is a particularly nice group. Boys like young Higgins and Martin Wilson are outstanding young men. There was also an element of self-interest in the arrangement, I must admit. These boys are in the third year. They have their junior certificate examination next June. The hope is that a French-speaker or a German in their midst will help them in their language oral examinations. So we try to arrange it like that.'

'Really? Did it work out?'

Dr Fisher laughed ruefully. 'Not very well in this case. Bertrand's English was very inventive, shall we say, and he really wanted to talk it all the time.'

'Was it you who decided to send him home in the aftermath of Mr Tyson's killing?'

'Well, I might well have done. Actually, it was not I. His parents telephoned me urgently the very next day.'

'How did they know about Mr Tyson?'

'Presumably the boy called them up.'

'Did he have a cellphone?'

'I have no idea. Even if he had not, he could easily have borrowed one. Besides, there are three card telephones at the disposal of students. But, to turn to a more serious matter, I should mention that it was, in fact, Bertrand's parents who had particularly asked for him to be in the tower dormitory.'

'Oh, and why did they ask for that?' Molly enquired.

'Security. Rightly or wrongly, Bertrand's parents thought that their son was a possible target for a kidnap attempt. They felt that he would be safest in the tower dormitory. It is the most inaccessible of all the dormitories.'

'This is very interesting.'

'Yes, isn't it, Superintendent? You asked me earlier today if I had any theories about who murdered Maurice Tyson. It was on the tip of my tongue to suggest the possibility of a kidnap attempt that went tragically wrong. I suppose I thought you would consider me naive to suggest such a melodramatic explanation. On reflection, maybe I should have mentioned it.'

'With respect, Dr Fisher, nothing could be more melodramatic than Mr Tyson's murder. I think that a kidnap attempt that went wrong is a very plausible explanation for that event. So don't be shy. Please tell me more.'

The headmaster stood up from his desk and began pacing the floor, his hands clasped behind his back.

'Monsieur Laporte, Bertrand's father, is a very wealthy man. Those people are very conscious all the time of the real threat of kidnap. We have had it several times before – not an actual kidnapping, you understand, but the fear of kidnap and the desire to take effective precautions. We even had one youth, the son of – ah, shall we say a prominent statesman of a country to the west of us – whose father required absolutely that he be accompanied at all times by a secret service bodyguard, armed to the teeth.'

'Good Lord!' Molly exclaimed. 'The poor child. That must have cramped his style unbearably.'

The headmaster gave a short laugh. 'Come to think of it, that might have been the whole purpose of the exercise. That boy was a tough nut.'

'Did you take him?' Lennon asked.

'No, no, he was quite unsuitable. Besides, I could not take the risk of one of my other pupils getting shot. They are a high-spirited lot, you know. They might have tried to kidnap the boy themselves – just for the hell of it.'

The headmaster and Lennon laughed. Molly smiled. Dr Fisher went on, 'This particular family – I mean the French boy's family – has major interests in Arab countries. They are in oil, in construction, and also in pharmaceuticals. That all adds up to very big money. Then again, a kidnap could also have a political dimension, as well as a financial one. The two elements are by no means mutually exclusive. Extremist organizations, even terrorist groups, need both money and to be able to exercise political leverage.'

'Al-Qaeda?'

'For instance, yes, I suppose, but we will have to leave it to the specialists to say who might or might not be involved. There are probably dozens of these radical groups in existence. One thing is clear. This assassin, whoever he was, or whatever organization he belonged to, knew exactly what he was doing, and he very obviously came prepared for any eventuality. Mr Tyson surprised him in a kidnap attempt, and he killed him.'

Molly was frowning like somebody who has bitten into something disagreeable.

'Well, that is one possible scenario, Dr Fisher.

But how can the supposed kidnapper have hoped to make off with this boy, with six other boys in his dormitory? They would have yelled blue murder.'

'I don't know the answer to that question,' the headmaster replied, pausing in his pacing up and down to face her. 'After all, I am not a policeman,' he added with just a hint of malice. He resumed his perambulations and trod in silence to the other end of the room. Turning to approach his interlocutors again, he continued: 'But these people are ruthless, and they are very resourceful. Normally speaking, children of that age sleep like dead men. A pad with chloroform on it, a knockout pill, or some other expedient, even another slit throat – God between us and all harm – would have been enough to neutralize any boy who stirred, especially Bertrand himself. Come to think of it, the dormitory in the middle of the night might well have been the softest target of all. Anywhere else, in broad daylight, the boys are always surrounded by chums and class-mates. At the very least, in the dormitory the risks are absolutely predictable and can be catered for.'

'All except one,' Molly said quietly.

'Namely?'

'Barbecues. Why, you didn't even predict that yourselves!'

Dr Fisher said very evenly, 'As you say, Sergeant, as you say.'

'What do you make of it, Molly?'

'The kidnap thing sounds outlandish and, at the same time, quite possible. Tyson wasn't murdered "for his own sake", so to speak. He got in the way of something or somebody.'

It was evening, and Molly was driving the car to Tralee where they had booked two rooms in a bed and breakfast before leaving Dublin. It had been a long day and they were both tired. After supper in a pleasant restaurant, where they had lightened up a bit and talked about their families, they continued their dissection of the murder in a pub, where their investigation widened to include two pints of Guinness.

'It's weird, Denis,' Molly went on. 'The killer has got to be an intruder – whether some crazy guy, or a botched attempt to kidnap the French kid. Everybody seems to take it for granted that Tyson himself could not have been the object of an assassination, and especially such a lurid one. He is like a guy who has stumbled into the wrong movie by mistake: dungeons and dragons, castles and cutthroats. That's just not *him*.'

'Yes, I agree. You'd swear that it had been done

for the tourist market, or for one of those murder mystery cruises, and that the blood was tomato ketchup – which, unfortunately, it wasn't.'

Later that evening Lennon made some telephone calls. The first was to Mary, his darling wife of thirty-five years. He was relieved to hear that his grandson's suspected appendicitis had been a false alarm, not so much because Lennon was dubious about surgery – a triple bypass had given him a new lease of life himself – but because he knew that the lad had just been selected for the under-thirteens rugby team in his school and was as keen as mustard. Grandad and grandson understood each other perfectly – everyone in the family said so – and Lennon, who was cracked about the boy, knew that, at that age, three months off games would be like a life sentence.

Then Lennon rang a psychiatrist friend to find out what were the chances of a sleepwalker's committing a serious crime requiring precision and skill.

'Practically nil,' said the medic, 'though it is surprising what people can do when they are asleep. They can even drive a car.'

'Don't I know,' was the rejoinder, 'aren't I meeting them all the time!'

He thanked the psychiatrist, then dialled the

number of a barrister friend who had a large criminal practice.

'Jerry, what happens if a person commits a serious crime when he is sleepwalking?'

'Are you serious, Denis? Well, I'll tell you what happens. No Irish jury would ever believe him. No way!'

'I could have such a case – just conceivably.'

'Look, Denis, there is case law on this in England, but it's inconclusive. None of my esteemed colleagues at the Irish criminal bar would be even remotely tempted by it. Irish juries and Irish judges would not give you the light of day on such a defence. Besides, as a cop, what do you care about the defence? Just pin your serious crime on the right guy. Leave the Supreme Court to get their knickers in a twist about the law. Do your job: let them do theirs.'

It was sound advice, if irreverently expressed. Lennon reflected that Jerry could be right up there with the finest of the fashionable lawyers if he could only couch his conclusions in more decorous language.

Planning the day ahead, Lennon thought that first he would have to have a chat with each of the boys in Tyson's tower, and with Lady Macbeth – though, of course, he would not call the poor boy that. Then he would see other boys, staff members – anyone who could have useful information. Lennon knew from experience that people were surprisingly diffident about coming forward, not because they were unwilling to help: on the contrary, it was because they did not want to seem officious or self-aggrandizing, or to be wasting his time. In almost every investigation, he knew, somebody fails to say something important, simply because he or she does not think it could be significant.

In the afternoon, he and Molly would have to revisit Tyson's tower, if only to remove the padlocks and give the school authorities free access again. There was only one stairway to the dormitory, which had been effectively isolated the morning after the murder by putting a padlock on the fire door at the base of the stairs. Tweedy and his forensics had been all over the tower with a fine comb. Neither Lennon nor Molly had paid more than a cursory visit there on the first day of their investigation. The real experts, Tweedy and his acolytes, had now completed their work. Mere mortals, like Denis and Molly, could visit it at their leisure – in Tweedy's view – for all the good it would do!

Molly had her own going-to-bed thoughts too. She remembered that, at one stage in the struggle against terrorism, the radical organizations were using medical professionals to do their dirty work. It was just another example of their exploitation of the facile psychology of Western cultures. Medical personnel were presumed to be exclusively inter- ested in healing – because that is what the Hippocratic Oath proclaims – and the developed countries were hungry for doctors, while the doctors were assumed to be hungry for well-paid jobs. All these factors added up to security checks bordering on the perfunctory when it came to medics. So, supposing that it was a doctor who had come to kidnap the little French boy, he would have known how to knock out his victim speedily, how to cope with any insomniac witnesses, and even, if push came to shove, how to slit a throat neatly. Far-fetched? Yes, but it is of the nature of terrorism to be far- fetched and, if necessary, to violate the norms of civilized living. What could be more far-fetched than 9/11?

Jan-Hein called on her mobile phone. Jan-Hein Van Zeebroeck, aged twenty-eight, from Maastricht, Holland, had been Molly's darling husband for the last two years. Sufficiently different to be each their own person, and both of them sensible and generous enough to allow it to be so, they were the best of friends and radiantly happy together. They looked forward to having children with equal excitement and trepidation. Their parents, all happily alive – though Jan-Hein's were considerably older than Molly's – were unanimous in assuring them that, when the time came, they would know exactly what to do. Molly's father joked, 'Musha, there is no fear that ye'll feed him on fillet steak for the first three months.'

Molly commented scornfully, 'Typical man. He assumes that the first baby has to be a boy.'

Her mother laughed. 'That's right, sweetheart, but just wait till you see. He'll be over the moon if it is a girl: she will always be *his* little girl.'

Molly and Jan-Hein had met in unusual circumstances. She was part of a team investigating the murder of a High Court judge who seemed to have less than savoury contacts in the world of art sales. One Saturday morning in July she was in the basement library of the National Gallery in Dublin trying to find out more about a Dutch Old Master by the name of van Honthorst, and not making much headway. She raised her head to seek inspiration and found herself looking straight into the green eyes of a young man standing directly opposite her at the librarian's desk. He had a good face, temperate and sensitive. To her consternation, they both blushed. It is a notorious cliché, of course, but it *was* love at first sight. Jan-Hein and Molly needed to meet each other. Which indeed was the more unlikely: that he should encounter the girl of his dreams, or that she should find the one person in Dublin that morning who was able to understand and answer her esoteric questions? He was, in fact, a specialist in seventeenth-century Dutch and Flemish painting. By the end of the year, Jan-Hein had gladly accepted a job as an assistant curator at the National Gallery, which gave him scope to continue his studies and to write – which he did superbly well. They were married six months later.

There is a lot of detective work in the exploration of the history of art, so the happy pair's interests and areas of competence were not as dissimilar as one might have thought. On the basis of his expertise, Jan-Hein was able to help the police in that first case about the High Court judge, and again, the following year, in a strange investigation about a young African man who had had his leg amputated and died. He was always interested in Molly's cases and willing to play any role she assigned him – expert witness, sounding board, Greek chorus, or devil's advocate.

They talked for over an hour that night.

'I am really impressed by St Isidore's, Jan-Hein – which I hadn't expected to be. The headmaster is a bit of a dry old stick. I think it is just a job for him. We met his wife. She keeps bulls.'

'Bulls! As pets?'

'Of course not, you dope. Commercially – she breeds them. She is a vet. Anyhow, she is a much livelier proposition than her husband. And then there is a young South African housemaster called Stan, a perfect gent – I mean in the real sense. He had to be drafted in to look after the boys whose housemaster was killed right in their own dormitory. He is doing a terrific job.'

'And how are the boys doing? It must have been tough on them.'

'Demons, I'd say, at one level – and absolute dotes. Full of honour, and decency, and fierce loyalty, and unassumingness – if that's a word – and stuff like that. That is what I find most impressive – not so much anything from the top down: it's the things that they bring out in each other!'

When they were about to ring off, Molly said, 'Well, what's your advice for me, Jan-Hein?'

He thought a moment, and then answered, 'Keep away from that South African dude.'

'Why? You don't think he did it, surely?'

'No, but he might want to run away with my little wifey!'

Molly laughed. 'Didn't I always say it? You are the original green-eyed monster!'

The rest of the call was an incoherent medley of audio-kisses.

Dr Fisher's wife had put on her face, which meant that she was not interested in entertaining him. She usually wasn't. So he ruminated instead. He reflected that, although he had not said so to the police, he had more reasons than the sensibilities of the boys to discontinue the use of the tower as a dormitory. Only a month before Tyson's death, he had been issued with a stern ultimatum from the fire department, to the effect that he must provide at least one alternative escape route from that tower or face compulsory closure of the dormitory.

Paradoxically, the same fire department that was prepared to close a dormitory was also partly responsible for keeping the swimming pool open. It insisted on an adequate body of water on site to cope with emergencies. It was not generally known in the school that the swimming pool was double-jobbing as a reservoir. Thus do headmasters make virtues of necessities.

Chapter Five

It was two o'clock in the morning. Night-time marks a truce except for those who have murdered sleep. Silence and darkness had brought, if not healing and understanding, at least rest from the tragedy that had overtaken St Isidore's School.

A figure detached itself from the margin of the forest and walked purposefully towards the castle. He – for it was indeed a man – entered the building by the same basement furnace room the barbecuers had used a few nights before. He advanced rapidly and noiselessly. Unlike the boys, he did not crouch, or dodge, or flit; there was nothing furtive about his movements. With a light step he climbed to the second floor, to the foot of Tyson's tower. Finding himself blocked from further progress by the padlock on the fire door at the base of the stairs, he paused a moment to think. Then, retracing his steps to the ground floor, he turned left along a corridor, and stopped in front of an old-fashioned hall stand, used in the school for lost or strayed outer garments: coats, anoraks, scarves, and a variety of headgear. It was an unwritten social contract that anyone who found such obviously orphaned items of clothing around the campus, particularly outdoors, would hang them on Gibson's gallows. Gibson was a former headmaster who had devised the system, which had proved itself remarkably effective down the years.

It was also true that youths found this piece of furniture particularly useful for *losing* items of apparel that their mothers had bought for them, and they found disgusting. Some of the more repulsive garments – as boys saw it – had actually been transferred directly from the store where they had been purchased, and where mother and son had probably had a stand-up row in front of shop assistants, to this white elephants' graveyard: castaways before even their maiden voyage.

Of course, where mothers had thoughtfully sewn a name tag on to the loathsome garment, it was important to pick it off again. Otherwise the owner could be traced and – some parents were prepared to sink even that low – the housemaster's authority could be invoked to force the unhappy camper to wear some degrading item of clothing from which neither his reputation nor his self-image would ever recover. Parents, so ignorant and so unteachable in the ways of the world, just did not seem to realize that a mere twenty-four hours in a sufficiently revolting jacket or pair of trousers was enough to have one branded for life as a nerd, a wanker, or – above all else to be feared in a boys' boarding school – any of the three dozen epithets for a homosexual.

The most remarkable case was an inoffensive tweed jacket which had cost somebody's mummy three hundred euro but had reduced the prospective wearer to paroxysms of rage. It had languished on the hall stand for five years until the same young man for whom it had been bought spotted it on a visit from university to his old school, decided that it was quite trendy after all, and – forgetting that his mother had bought it for him in the first place – stole it.

Without much difficulty, the man pulled this clothes rack towards him, revealing an ancillary door into the headmaster's study. It had not been used for years, being not nearly imposing enough. Besides, the immediate neighbourhood was not salubrious. The corridor was narrow at this point, the ventilation inadequate, the paintwork peeling. There was a pong, probably associated with an ill-concealed and dribbling urinal in the vicinity, which, to the headmaster's way of thinking, struck exactly the wrong note for parents and prospective parents. It had been assumed that the key for this door had been lost years ago. The truth was simpler. There was no key. The door was stiff but unlocked. The man opened it and stepped into the headmaster's study.

He went straight for the massive column to which all the Gothic arches of the ceiling plunged like five separate waterfalls, reflecting the five faces of the pentagonal centrepiece pillar. He walked all round this voluminous column, feature and focus, both architecturally and visually, for the entire room. Such a massive structure seemed excessive to accommodate one fireplace and one chimney, and even more than was needed to support the fine arches of the ceiling.

The man took a chair and put it against each of the mirrors enshrined in the faces of the column until he found the one he was looking for. He stood on the chair and, stretching an arm above his head, ran his fingers along the elaborate woodwork encasing the top of the mirror. At the third try, he found the lever. It was very reluctant to come out of retirement, but after several vain attempts the spring wheezed and clicked, and the mirror panel creaked open outwards. The pillar was so bulky because it had an inside.

A narrow stone stairway spiralled upwards against the inner circumference of the pentagonal column, winding itself round the chimney flue serving the fireplace in the headmaster's study. The steps of this stair were not even two feet wide. A fatter person than this man would have had a hard time ascending that corkscrew. The concealed stairway was an entirely gratuitous feature characteristic of the age, a conceit – indeed a folly – as was the whole castle. It had at least the redeeming feature of having been thought up to give employment for a desperate people during Black '47: 1847, the peak of the Great Famine, when the potato crop failed and a million people had died in Ireland – or trying to get out of it, to the Land of the Star-Spangled Banner.

After almost two centuries, the spiral stairway had rarely been used – or even discovered. Successive headmasters had told each other about it, of course, and each in his turn had gone up or down it a few times, to be able to say been there; done that. But even *saying* that much was not in their own interests from the point of view of security, so they said it rarely and did it even less. At last, the almost forgotten staircase had become important for someone. It went straight up through Tyson's tower, bypassing all fire doors and padlocks. In a matter of minutes, the intruder – if he was an intruder – was standing in Maurice Tyson's personal apartments. He knew about the stairs – and indeed about all the secrets of the castle – because he had lived there, man and boy, for longer than anyone else, alive or dead. He was Sir Neville Randler and he had come home for a purpose.

Denis Lennon was a methodical person. He believed in covering the ground, even if that meant making notes for himself that Molly scornfully described as 'blinding flashes of the obvious'. Lennon countered that some questions were so obvious that people forgot to ask them. So overnight he had listed a considerable number of obvious questions. These included: where Dr Fisher, and any other adults, were at the time of the murder; who could have known that a barbecue was to be held, so that Tyson would be alone in his tower that night; what, if anything, did the youthful sleepwalker known as Lady Macbeth remember or realize; who did each one of the seven boys, including the little French boy, think that the trespasser was whom they saw coming down the stairs from their own quarters minutes before they found Tyson's body. The police were to begin to work through these and similar questions on the second day of their inquiry.

On the night of the murder, Dr Fisher told them that he was in Belfast at a dinner to mark thirty years since he had left secondary school himself. It had been a convivial evening, prolonged into the night. Dr Fisher, normally a paragon of sobriety, had so far unwound as to give spirited renditions of 'The Ould Orange Flute' and, as an encore – which nobody had actually asked him for, but he did it anyhow – 'The Sash My Father Wore'.

All other adults on the St Isidore campus had been in bed, at the latest, by midnight, or said that they were. Few, if any, could, or were willing to, offer corroborative evidence in the shape of a partner to support their story. It was to Stan, the South African housemaster, that the boys who had discovered Tyson's body had come running in near panic on that terrible night. In the opinion of everyone, boys and adults alike, Stan had risen to the occasion superlatively. 'A marvel, a marvel' as the chairperson of the Board of Trustees had pronounced him next morning. When he said it once, it was already high praise. When he said it twice, it was his ultimate accolade.

Who could have known that a barbecue had been planned for that evening? The boys had some sense of what their elders call 'security'. Still, their operations were never too hard to infiltrate. Like young people everywhere, they were far too careless and far too trusting. This is part of the charm of the young, as also, fortunately or unfortunately, too often, of their undoing. Most of their classmates would have known about the plan. Boys from other classes too. The shop in the village was a principal security hazard. Purchase of sausages or burgers is a major giveaway, an early-warning sign of an impending barbecue. Someone who buys two pounds of sausages is almost certainly up to no good. Not that Madrigal – the unlikely name of the local shopkeeper – would sell the pass. Like the local innkeeper, she is not in the business of cutting off the branch she is sitting on. But there are often rivalries and resentments between classes, and in any school certain boys are sneaks, out of envy, spite, sadism, or simply because they are radically incontinent in the area of information.

There had been a moment of panic in the village shop on this occasion when George, the headmaster's wife, had suddenly appeared just as Bertrand, the French boy, was queueing up to pay for the sausages. The others let him do these transactions, which was deemed good for his English, and safer for the rest of them. George knew who he was because she had collected him at the airport when he arrived. She engaged him in conversation. How was he doing? *Fine.* How was the food succeeding with him? *Fine.* How was his English coming along? *Fine.* Even the weather, predictably, was *fine.*

Bertrand, who was nothing if not bright, had had the wit, when his turn came, to pay quickly for two small batteries for his flashlight and walk away leaving the sausages behind him on the counter. Fortunately, Madrigal realized what was happening and said nothing. Bertrand had accompanied the headmaster's wife out of the shop, saying *fine* six more times, and acting the part of a nice little frog to perfection. Meanwhile Karl Hogan scooped up the sausages. Later Gilhooly, who rarely said anything complimentary about anyone, described Bertrand as a 'devious bastard'. There was unstinting admiration in his voice.

About the question of Lady Macbeth, all six boys were eager to say that they had *not* positively recognized him as the person seen coming down the stairs from Tyson's tower on the night of the murder. To say so now, they all realized, would be tantamount to accusing the boy of killing a housemaster. Martin insisted – because it was he who had suggested the identification in the first place – that it was merely based on the fact that the figure seen on the night was shorter than Tyson and no one else was likely to be walking around at two o'clock in the morning.

'Only Harry Lewins – that's Lady Macbeth – would be coming down those stairs at that hour of the night for no reason. That's why I said it was him. But if there *was* a reason, and if that reason was to murder Mr Tyson, then all bets are off. Harry is the most harmless and inoffensive person in this whole school. He would never do a mean thing to anyone, let alone murder them.'

*   *   *

Driving over to St Isidore's that morning, Denis had said to Molly, 'Well, we have to check on Lady Macbeth today, give him the old one two.'

'Denis, you're too nice to give a schoolboy the old one two – especially one with an unfortunate handicap like that.'

Lennon was pleased that Molly thought of him that way. He even hoped that she was right. But he huffed and puffed a little bit. After all, cops are not meant to be soft hearted.

'Oh, I wouldn't make a universal principle out of that, if I were you. My bite is worse than my bark, if needs be.' He added, 'Incidentally, what is this boy's name? I forget. I can hardly call him Lady Macbeth, can I?'

'No, that would probably be deemed "torture" by the inevitable tribunal into Garda brutality. His name is Harry Lewins.'

Lennon sucked his gums for a while, an indication that he was thinking; then he said: 'Molly, this is a strange case. All the wrong people are up, and all the right people are in bed.'

'What does that mean?'

'I mean, all the adults are in bed – they are the *right* people for that kind of murder. But the schoolchildren are up and crawling all over the place – whether it be the barbecuers or Harry Lewins – and they are the *wrong* people to cut somebody's throat. You need to be cold blooded for that, and you need to have a strong, steady, and skilful hand.'

In the event, they drew a total blank with Harry Lewins. A shy boy with a stammer, he was transparently honest. He remembered nothing, to the point that he was practically certain that he had not been sleepwalking at all that night.

'Any-any-how,' he said, blushing, 'the do-oct-or says that I'm gro-ow-ing out of it.'

'Well good for you, Harry!' Lennon said encouragingly, and sent him on his way.

The kidnap theory was attractive. Any enterprising kidnapper could have found out where the French boy had been sleeping. It appeared on various lists on any of a number of noticeboards. Even the bed position was indicated.

A general appeal to staff and students about unusual requests for information from outside the school yielded meagre results. One senior boy admitted that he had photographed the captain of rugby with his cellphone in the shower room in a state of undress. This was, he said, for a girl who 'had the hots for Animal' – an affectionate soubriquet, apparently. The photographer added defensively, 'I didn't show her everything, like.'

Lennon was inclined to exclude the theory that the French boy was going to be kidnapped by a foreigner, especially one from the Middle East. Molly did her devil's advocate thing, a familiar role in this phase of an investigation.

'You're a terrible chauvinist, Denis. At all costs, you want to keep the murder at home. It's like the old radio ad, "If you want to sing a song, *do* sing an *Irish* song!" It's all right if Tyson was killed by an Irish Catholic, but a Muslim from the Middle East – no way! That is just not on.'

'Well, Molly, I do think that a Muslim from the Middle East is very unlikely. He would just not know his way around here, in a practical sense or, even more important, psychologically. Kidnap must be one of the most difficult crimes to commit or to conceal, unless there are masses of people out there who, at least tacitly, support what you are doing, like in Iraq. An Arab with a beard would not stand a chance with a quick-witted thirteen year old on his hands in rural Ireland.

'What *is* at least possible is that an Irish terrorist group did the job under contract – for money. They don't seem fussy about what they do for money – drugs, bank robberies, you name it. But even there, Molly, I doubt it very much. Even the very lunatic fringes of Irish terrorists have never targeted a child. The revulsion would be too great for even the most demented agenda.'

'So we just close our minds to the kidnap thing, and it will go away?'

'No, we can't do that either. I have already, between last night and this morning, launched three inquiries – or got three inquiries launched – into kidnap. First, we are going to get the French police to interview Bertrand and his parents, to assess the likelihood of kidnap, including how much money a kidnapper could realistically hope to receive. We will also get someone to chat up Bertrand about what he thinks, and what he noticed. He is one of the seven witnesses and, by all accounts, one of the liveliest.'

'Um, so far so good. I'm impressed!'

'Very civil of you, I'm sure. The second of the inquiries is one for the Gardaí. We are going to ask, in every division, for a check on lonely farmhouses or anywhere that seems to have been got ready for a kidnap operation. It is a bit like searching for a needle in a haystack, but it has proved surprisingly effective in previous cases.'

'Good, Superintendent, I really am impressed. And inquiry number three?'

'Well, that is for the real specialists in terrorism. We have excellent contacts in that world, and unrivalled experience ourselves, because we were fighting terrorism long before it became fashionable in most Western European countries and in the US. There are people who may be able to tell us useful things about what is happening in our own back yard. So let's try them too.'

Chapter Six

None of the parents had availed themselves of the option to be with their children when the police were questioning them. Perhaps more accurately, none of the children had offered their parents that option, except Karl Hogan, who bitterly regretted ever having mentioned the subject to his mother when he heard some of the horrendous things that she was likely to come out with. There was a general consensus among adolescents that parents had no idea how to behave on such occasions and would only succeed in embarrassing the hell out of their children, if they were let loose. Karl had had to threaten to run away to Australia and never to talk to his mother again before he could get her to back off.

Besides, Denis and Molly had been voted okay and even *dead decent*. Boys are fiercely loyal creatures, which is what makes their warfare and their team games so exciting and, not infrequently, so heartbreaking. These particular boys were determined to be absolutely candid with the police, so as to atone in some way to Mr Tyson for what they still saw as their desertion of him on the night he was murdered. They didn't want parents around – whose love they never doubted, of course, but whose lack of intelligence and catastrophic ignorance of the ways of the world might force them to be less than wholly truthful in what they said.

By the end of the morning, the boys, in their turn, had been voted by the police okay and dead decent. Their goodwill and concern to help had been manifest from the very start when, apropos of nothing at all, Martin Wilson, blushing furiously, had confessed to stealing a bottle of wine from his father's cellar, or at least from the garage where he kept his plonk.

'I didn't know whether to laugh or to cry,' Molly said afterwards. 'It was nothing to do with anything at all, and at the same time so touching.'

Lennon surprised her when he replied, 'I had to clear my throat myself. Dr Fisher was certainly right about one thing: that is one fine boy.'

In the set piece narratives, the police did not learn very much. It was the throwaway remarks, the afterthoughts, which were most revealing. For instance, the boy called Jack O'Toole told them that he did not think that the person seen coming down the stairs from Tyson's tower was Lady Macbeth because when he reached the foot of the stairs he had turned 'the wrong way'. Lady Macbeth was noted for his excellent sense of direction, even when fast asleep. Moreover, he was not in the habit of wandering around. He went some place and then he came back from there. His way back, the night of the murder, would have led him towards the group of boys crouching in the shadows, and not in the opposite direction.

'What lies in the opposite direction?' Lennon enquired of Karl Hogan. 'I mean, instead of coming towards you, Harry Lewins, or whoever it was, walked off in the opposite direction. So what is there in the opposite direction?'

'Nothing,' Karl answered. 'It's a dead end. Just a window. There is a bit of a corridor, with a dorm each side of it, and the window at the end of the corridor. That's it.'

'Two dormitories?'

'Yes, one each side.'

'Each with a door into that corridor?'

'Yes.'

'Is either of those two dormitories Lady . . . I mean Harry Lewins's dormitory?'

'No, he is in St Michael's, down at the other end.'

Molly asked Karl Hogan another question. 'What time did you do your shopping?'

'For the barbecue, miss, the sausages and things?'

Molly nodded.

'After class, about four o'clock. That's when we usually go down to the village, if we want to buy something.'

'On the same day as the barbecue?'

'Definitely. We couldn't keep sausages overnight. They'd go rotten – or we might be found with "incriminating evidence".'

Karl was clearly pleased with himself to be using the appropriate police expression, but he was also impressed that Lennon had bothered to learn Lady Macbeth's real name. He thought it showed respect for the whole class that the superintendent had corrected himself and not presumed to use a nickname which he must have known the entire class used freely.

*　*　*

It was the abrasive Eddie Gilhooly who provided the most intriguing piece of information.

'The next day, that window at the end of the corridor was open. I have never seen it open before. In fact, I didn't think it could open. I bet the murderer went out the window. He saw us. He knew that we had him cornered, so he went down that corridor – and out the window.'

'Did he run?'

'No, he didn't run, but he walked quickly. If he had run, the game would be up. So he walked. He probably guessed that we would think he was Tyson and that we would be in no hurry to come out of where we were hiding. So that gave him time to get out the window.'

Molly challenged him, 'But, Eddie, this is two storeys up, and there is a sheer drop on to tarmacadam below. Where could he go? If he jumped, he would probably have broken both legs or even killed himself.'

Gilhooly looked at her scornfully. 'I suppose where you come from they've never even heard of Spider-Man.'

At lunch the police sat with the six from Tyson's tower who, in spite of themselves, were beginning to enjoy the sheer awe in which they were held by the rest of the school. After all, they had survived a barbecue and *not* been suspended. That was because of the *awful* experience of finding their housemaster *dead* with his *throat cut from ear to ear* and *blood everywhere*. Then they had been *interrogated* by the Gardaí, who had ended up convinced that they didn't murder Tyson, but also that they were the *only* ones who could lead them to Tyson's killer. Therefore, they must be privy to all kinds of classified information and know exactly what leads the police were following and who the principal suspects were. Every boy in the school was green with envy of 'the Six' and would have cheerfully sacrificed his own housemaster for a share of their reflected glory.

After lunch, Denis said, 'Let's go up and take a closer look at this window.'

'What window?'

'The one that Spider-Man Eddie says that Lady Macbeth, or whoever it was, got out of, the night of the long knives.'

They climbed two floors to Tyson's kingdom and stood at the same spot where the boys had flattened themselves against the wall trying not to be seen on the night of the killing. Molly said what they were both thinking.

'Whoever was coming down that stair from Tyson's tower *must* have seen them. There is no way that he did not see seven boys plastered against this wall.'

Lennon agreed. 'So either it was the sleepwalker after all, oblivious of everything, or else it was somebody who did not want to meet the boys.'

'Because he had just murdered their house-master?'

'Well, it would be difficult to exchange pleasantries in the middle of the night about a subject like that!'

They continued in the direction taken by the presumed assassin, past the staircase leading to Tyson's tower, till they came to the corridor between two dormitories, with the window at its end.

'That is the window that Gilhooly says was open the next morning,' Molly said, and Lennon added, 'Which was very unusual, he also said. So let's see how Spider-Man could have managed it.'

The window was a single-pane casement, opening outwards. It was probably kept closed because it was very exposed and in the teeth of the prevailing south-westerly wind. Open, it would have made quite a wind tunnel of the corridor, rattling the doors of the dormitories and disturbing sleepers. The window was set quite high in the wall, but a reasonably agile person would have little trouble releasing the catch, hoisting himself to the sill, and passing through the opening. It was then that his problems would have begun. There was a fifty-foot sheer drop to the hard surface of the avenue below.

'Houdini might survive it, and even without serious injury,' Lennon said, 'but he would need to be awfully nimble and unbelievably lucky. I don't see how anyone in his right mind can have got out of that window – except Spider-Man, of course.'

Molly was already climbing on to the sill. She knelt there and opened the window. It had obviously been replaced in the past few years with double glazing in an aluminium frame and opened quite easily. She leant out, using the handle of the window to support her weight over the void.

'Molly, be careful,' Lennon exclaimed in alarm, 'or you'll end up as strawberry jam.'

She did nearly topple over, but because of surprise and excitement rather than mere carelessness.

'Denis, come up here, and just look for yourself!'

In her enthusiasm, Molly was forgetting that the superintendent was twice her age and had had major bypass surgery two years before. But her excitement was infectious. Lennon opened a dormitory door, glanced around the room, and commandeered a straight-backed chair. This he propped against the wall below the window and stood on. With much squirming and wriggling, he eventually managed to lay his chest on the sill and coax his head into position to look down the external wall immediately below the window.

'Good Lord, Molly, we are on to something. This is it all right.'

From four feet below the window to about six feet from the ground, there was a descending series of iron semicircles set into the stonework of the wall. Being quite slender, and of much the same colour as the red sandstone of the castle, these steps – which is what they manifestly were – would be almost invisible from the ground. Whether inserted before or after the castle became a school, this was patently a primitive form of fire escape, and could also have very well served as a rat run for whoever murdered Maurice Tyson.

The police spent the rest of the afternoon in a small library adjoining the staff common room, chatting to teachers, housemasters, and members of the domestic and administrative staff who had been invited to drop in 'when and if they could'. Once again, it was Stan de Witt, the South African housemaster, who had set up these encounters informally, almost casually, and therefore very effectively. The members of the various staffs, while they enjoyed cordial relations with each other, were not accustomed to sitting down together on an equal basis. For most of them, it was a new experience – and a pleasant and useful one, too. People who had been at St Isidore's for several years suddenly realized that they had much to learn about the school, about the boys, about each other, and even about themselves, simply by sharing their different perspectives.

The overall picture of Maurice Tyson that emerged from these various constituencies was of a man whom not everybody liked, but all without exception respected. With the boys, it was agreed, he had mellowed over the years, but even in his rigorist days he had always been scrupulously fair. In sudden tragedies especially, like the death of a parent, or a shock divorce, he could be surprisingly sensitive and supportive. It was particularly remarked that even boys who candidly did not like him – because he was certainly exigent – would turn to him spontaneously in such sad situations, as if they had always known that even troublesome boys like themselves could count on him absolutely if ever things went seriously wrong.

The police were treated for the first time to a mantra that they were to hear many times again: 'The boys are never wrong about a housemaster, a teacher, or another boy.' Molly thought about that a lot, wondering if it could possibly be right – especially the bit about other boys. Surely, she thought, boys do, at least sometimes, just gang up on one of their number. Nancy McGivern, the geography teacher, whom she had just met and taken to immediately, was to say to her when they discussed the topic later, 'They *always* have a reason.'

Nobody could suggest any reason why Maurice Tyson had been murdered. On the one hand, it was no accident. You do not slit somebody's throat in a fit of absent-mindedness or through mere carelessness. So was it a case of mistaken identity? But who else could somebody hope or expect to meet at midnight in Tyson's tower, if not Tyson himself? Robbery? What is there worth stealing and killing for, three storeys up in a boys' dormitory? A few pin-ups, a skateboard, a fishing rod, perhaps a contraband can of lukewarm beer!

Lennon mentioned the headmaster's theory about a kidnapping. People pursed their lips and shook their heads. They were sceptical. Thady Mulligan, who was one of Dr Fisher's mistakes, as he was both lazy and incompetent, jeered openly.

'Typical of our great leader! He would just love it. Imagine the buzz he'd get from being able to say: "Come to our snobby school – the boys are so filthy rich they even get kidnapped!"'

Polly Murphy, the cook, objected more soberly. 'Merciful hour, how could anyone carry a big lump like that down three flights of stairs, and no one the wiser?'

'Bertrand is quite a small lump, from what we hear,' Molly replied.

'Even a small lump of a boy is seven or eight stone,' Polly insisted. 'He is heavy. If any of the boys sounded the alarm, you could have forty or fifty little horrors milling around the stairs and the passages or running to banjax the getaway car. They are like a hornets' nest when they have got it in for someone – and absolutely fearless.'

Conversation changed to the figure that the boys had seen coming down the stairs from Tyson's tower. Lennon summarized: 'It was dark. There was no positive identification. A man about five foot eight inches, quite thin. Smaller than Mr Tyson – well, we know it wasn't him, unfortunately – but bigger than Harry Lewins, the sleepwalker. In fact, the boys think now that it was an outsider because they cannot think of anyone in the school with just that build or figure. And I need hardly add that whoever they did see is almost certainly our murderer.'

On the way back to Tralee on the second day, Lennon asked, 'Have we made progress?'

'Yes and no, or in which direction? On the one hand, the boys say the intruder doesn't look like anyone we know. And yet he cannot be some terrorist parachuted in from the Middle East by al-Qaeda. He was someone who knew the castle like the back of his hand. When he was confronted by the boys un-expectedly waiting for him at the foot of the stairs – remember they returned early from their barbecue – he was still able to take the ball on the hop. He just went in exactly the opposite direction to the one he had intended. He opened that window and climbed down the fire escape to the ground. It was a reflex action, second nature. He did it simply because he knew perfectly well that it was an option.'

'Molly, as soon as we get back to Tralee, let's ring for the powder-puff people to do an encore. I want Des Tweedy hanging upside down from those iron rings, doing his thing at first light. I want fingerprints, especially from outside the window or any place down along the wall. And I want anything else that the rag, bone, and bottle brigade can collect.

'God bless Gilhooly – even if he is a pain in the backside. It is thanks to him that, at last, we are motoring.'

Chapter Seven

'God bless Gilhooly,' Lennon had said, but sometimes Eddie Gilhooly was more than the others could
take. There was an awkward truth in what he said,
a quirky inconvenient integrity. Even his severest
critics conceded that he was straight as a die. You
could not imagine Gilhooly cheating or telling a lie.
But he seemed to have an inbuilt ineptitude when it
came to personal relationships. It almost looked as
if he was warning people off, getting in his rejec-
tion of the other person before that other person had
the chance to reject him.

Molly said, 'I feel sure that he has had some great

– what is the word? – some great disaster in his life-time, a betrayal even. It is as if he doesn't dare to be liked, still less loved, for fear of having to relive some very painful experience all over again. Sorry! I suppose that's a load of codswallop.'

Molly was chatting over a cup of coffee with Nancy McGivern in the teachers' common room. They were of an age and had struck up a spontane-ous friendship from Molly's first visit to the staffroom. Petite, vivacious, and quite pretty in a gypsy sort of way – bangle earrings, jet black hair, straight, with a fringe – she seemed just right for reading fortunes. Quite a number of boys had serious crushes on her, which she unashamedly enjoyed and used good-humouredly to their best advantage, academic and personal.

'If it helps the poor darlings to stop picking their noses, squeezing their pimples, and being completely absorbed in themselves, that has got to be good. But, Molly, you should have been a teacher yourself, not a policewoman.'

'Why?' Molly laughed, surprised and pleased. 'Do you think they'd stop squeezing their pimples for me?'

Nancy smiled. 'Definitely! But, seriously, Molly, you have the gift of seeing things from the point of view of the children. What you say about Eddie Gilhooly is not codswallop at all. It is just too true. You've hit the nail on the head.'

'What's the story?'

'It is sad, and it gets sadder. Eddie and his elder brother, Seán, were virtually orphans from birth. Seán was here in school too, five or six years ahead of Eddie. Their parents both died in a car crash when they were very young. I don't think that Eddie can have any memory of them at all, which is very sad. They got a lot of money from insurance because of the accident, so their schooling and university are provided for. But they have no real home, no close family at all – a grandmother who is an invalid, and an uncle who is nominally the guardian but has really shown no interest in them.

'Seán, the elder boy, was a delightful fellow, apparently, good-looking, bright, an all-round sportsman, and very popular. I didn't know him myself because he had left before I came to the school. Eddie, they say, hero-worshipped him. For God's sake, he was the only family he had.'

'Had? Wait a moment – you don't mean . . .'

'Yes, I'm afraid I do mean.'

'Oh, my God!'

'I suppose it was a delayed reaction to his parents'

death – what else could it be? – but at about the age of sixteen or seventeen, Seán began to turn in on himself. As one teacher described it to me, "he lost his magic". People could not believe that it was the same boy who had played so well, and with so much courage, the cruel hand that life had dealt him. But they were losing him. That was becoming as plain as a pikestaff. Several of his teachers tried to get through to him – especially Maurice Tyson, who had been his housemaster. He was the kind of boy that you would really make an effort for.

'I don't know the details, but nothing worked. Puberty is a difficult time for most boys, but this was something else. Seán grew moody – well, again, that is par for the course at that age – but then he became seriously depressed. The guardian and his wife were as useful as a hole in the head and, I'm told, just didn't want to know. As for Dr Fisher and Mr Tyson, well I suppose they didn't think it was their place to intervene.

'Seán staggered through his last two years here. He got some kind of Leaving Certificate result and went on to study something nondescript at university. I think this would have been his degree year. Last December, he offed himself.'

'Oh, sweet Jesus! Was he on drugs?'

'I don't know. I suppose that might have been it. Anyhow, that is probably what has got Eddie the way he is now. Not just the suicide – the whole history.' Nancy was silent for a few moments. Then she said, like an afterthought, 'You know the way we say that parents worry about their children, well, it is nothing to the extent that children worry about their parents. They don't show it, they don't even realize it themselves, but they worry terribly about their health, about their financial situation, and about their marriages.'

'You astonish me. I'll have to think about that – to see if I ever worried about my own old dears. I don't think so. I thought that most children were self-centred little monsters.'

Nancy laughed. 'Well, in a sense they are, and there is a good deal of self-interest even in the things that children worry about for their parents. But still I have had so many touching examples. Like the boy, a thirteen year old, who begged me to help him write a letter to persuade his mother not to leave his father. It would break your heart. Another time, we had a mother killed in a car accident coming to see her son. For weeks there were queues of boys calling their mummies, pleading with them: "Please, Mum, *don't* come to see me. I'm fine, Mum, really. I don't

need anything. Please, Mum, *please*, don't come!"
You would need a heart of stone not to be touched
by that.'

'Indeed you would, Nancy, I agree. But what is
your point, I mean in relation to Seán and Eddie
Gilhooly? After all, they didn't have any parents to
worry about.'

'Well, that *is* my point, Molly. They missed out
even on that. Perhaps that was why Seán offed
himself and why Eddie is the way he is now: they
didn't even have parents to worry about.'

'That is a bit convoluted, Nancy, don't you think?'

'Life is a bit convoluted, Molly, didn't you notice?'

Molly said on an impulse, 'Do you think that
this whole thing, the personal tragedy of Seán and
Eddie Gilhooly, has got anything to do with our
present inquiry – I mean with the investigation into
Mr Tyson's murder?'

Nancy did not answer immediately. When she did
reply, her words seemed to be carefully chosen. She
said, 'I cannot see how it could have.'

On the way back from her cup of coffee, Molly saw
Des Tweedy's mighty technicals at work halfway
up the castle wall where the intruder had supposedly
got out of the window and done his Spider-Man

routine. Tweedy insisted on referring to him pedantically as the 'extruder' because he had allegedly come *out* of the window instead of *in* at the window. In order not to contaminate surfaces which could have fingerprints or other telltale traces on them, the police were using a fireman's ladder, set practically vertical inches from the castle wall but not touching it.

Molly knew better than to holler to these trapeze artists, 'Guys, how are you doing? Any hoofprints, huh?' Tweedy was most particular that all infallible statements – and he dealt in none other – should emanate exclusively from the Holy Office in Beggarsbush. Lennon used to say, 'Tweedy is the nearest thing that the Presbyterians have got to a Pope.' Tweedy's uncompromising answer was, 'Yes, that's right. The only difference is: *I* really am infallible!'

As a result of Garda swoops on remote or abandoned farmsteads, in quest of a possible hiding place for a kidnap victim, the catch had not been negligible. One printing press for counterfeiting tickets for rugby and football matches, a poteen still, a unit for repackaging pirated CDs, and a love-nest where the happy couple were distinctly unhappy to be unearthed by the police pretty much as God made them.

But there was nothing like a holding cell for a fourteen-year-old French boy who had not yet been kidnapped. The trouble was, how would one identify such a facility, even if it existed? It would not necessarily be stockpiled with garlic and Gauloises, and volumes of *Astérix*.

Monsieur Laporte, Bertrand's father, telephoned Superintendent Lennon at the school. He had been contacted by the French police, who had suggested that he might call Lennon himself, as he spoke excellent English.

The Frenchman said that his wife was more nervous about the possibility of Bertrand's being kidnapped than either he or Bertrand himself. 'He is an only son,' he explained, 'and his *maman* adores him.' He spoke almost apologetically, as if there were tacit agreement, man to man, about the harmless weakness of motherly love. Lennon guessed shrewdly that Papa was just as crazy about the child himself.

'As for the actual prospect of a kidnap, we were very happy about Bertrand's being at school in Ireland. We regarded your country as "very low risk" for this kind of exercise, and the people who advise us were of the same opinion. Indeed, I have spoken since to some – how do you say – some very superior people in the *sûreté*, and they are raising the eyebrows at the very idea. They all say the same thing: why go to Ireland for a kidnap? It increases the imponderables.'

Without quite knowing what that was supposed to mean, Lennon felt it was quite an insightful way to describe Ireland: a place that 'increases the imponderables'. He was glad of the opportunity to ask a few questions.

'I understand that you asked especially for Bertrand to be in what they call the "tower dormitory" because it was considered to be particularly secure?'

Monsieur Laporte hesitated. 'Did I? I doubt it. I don't think that I knew what dormitory he was going to be in. Perhaps my wife made the request.' He laughed. 'You know, *she* thinks that *I* think that she makes the fusspot, so perhaps she did not tell me. Ah, the women!'

Lennon could picture him shrugging his shoulders while simultaneously raising hands to heaven in an archetypal gesture of Gallic resignation. He asked another question.

'How did you first hear of the murder?'

'Dr Fisher rang us urgently. He said that he was sending Bertrand home immediately because he had had a great shock, *vous voyez*, to be swimming in this unfortunate man's blood on his bed, in the dark, in the middle of the night. Besides, he said that the situation was generally unstable.'

'Wait a moment, I understood that Bertrand first called you with the news of the murder, and that you called Dr Fisher then.'

'No. I am sure that Dr Fisher called us first. This is fixed in my mind because we got a terrible shock. You see, my wife does not speak the English very well. She answered the telephone. She thought that Dr Fisher was saying that *Bertrand* had been murdered. Naturally, she went into hysterics – my wife is, how do you say, highly strung up, and she loves Bertrand so much. Fortunately, I was with her. When I at last managed to get the phone from her hand – because she was clutching it as if it was Bertrand himself – Dr Fisher explained to me what had really happened. But I assure you, we will not quickly forget the precise way we learned of this murder. It was a highly shocking and detestable way.'

'And what did Bertrand think?'

'Well, I'm sure that all those boys got a great shock.

But I must say that we were very impressed and deeply grateful for the skilful way that Bertrand was handled. First of all, a bigger boy in the dormitory succeeded in getting him out of there before he had seen the body. That was really good thinking, particularly when that lad himself must have been very shaken. They are all only fifteen years old, those boys. Then that nice young South African man lost no time in getting the blood-soaked pyjamas off Bertrand and fixing him up quickly with something else to wear. So his personal trauma was kept to a minimum.

'But you know, Superintendent, Bertrand is a real boy. Quite frankly, he was disgusted to be sent home. He was having a great time at St Isidore's. All his letters and his e-mails were radiantly happy, and he loved the company of the other boys. He is an only child, you see. His first words to me when we met at Charles de Gaulle were, "*Papa, c'est dégueulasse* – just when school is beginning to get really interesting – *on me fiche à la porte!* – they throw me out." I'd say he gave Dr Fisher a piece of his mind before he left. He is much too honest not to,' Monsieur Laporte added with obvious pride.

Molly had not been there when the Frenchman rang, so Lennon told her later what he had said. Her immediate comment was that she was disappointed not to have met Bertrand.

'He must have been quite a character. Even Dr Fisher seems to have been a bit in awe of him.'

'Yes,' Lennon agreed, 'a force to be reckoned with, I'd say. Both parents are clearly cracked about him. Incidentally, what do you make of the same Dr Fisher's insistence that Bertrand's parents contacted him after the murder and that they wanted him out? Laporte is quite definite that it was Fisher who called them up first.'

'Well, does it matter who called who?'

'Fisher seems to think that it does. I wonder why,' Lennon mused.

'Be fair, Denis,' Molly urged. 'That first twenty-four hours must have been horrific. One could easily make a mistake about a detail like who called who. Remember that Fisher, after what seems like quite a party in Belfast, was woken up in the small hours of the morning with the devastating news that one of his housemasters, and a friend, had had his throat cut in the middle of a dormitory, surrounded by the children. He has to get up immediately, after virtually no sleep, and drive at least four hours through the night, and then take charge of a school on the brink of hysteria. The poor devil cannot be blamed for getting some details not a hundred per cent right.'

'Maybe,' Lennon said.

'Denis, I hate the way you say *maybe!*'

'And how would you like me to say it?'

It was two days later that Des Tweedy rang Lennon to give a report on the Spider-Man operations of his team.

'I can't say that you are in luck, Denis, because we employ the exact sciences, where there is no room for luck, but in layman's language, yes, you're poxed with luck. Several good prints, including a two-hand, eight-finger print on the outside ledge of the windowsill. This would be where the chap was holding on with both hands until his feet were firmly set on the rungs of that makeshift ladder leading to the ground.'

'Fresh prints, Des?'

'They have to be. This window is directly in the teeth of the southwesterly. It would be washed clean any time it rains seriously. In that you are lucky too, to talk sub-scientifically. And guess what?'

'They match!'

'Yes, they match the print we already have on Tyson's glasses: a left hand, middle finger print.'

'Brilliant!'

Tweedy took it as a compliment, and no more than his due. 'Yes, isn't it? But I have a dessert for you, too.'

'Dessert? I hope it isn't fattening.'

'Well, you be the judge. It's blood, Denis, minute particles, but enough. It could be the murderer's, if he grazed his hand or something; in which case, between the fingerprints and that blood, you will have a very positive identification. But it could also be the victim's blood. I think I would like that even more. No way could Tyson's blood get halfway down that castle wall, except if the murderer carried it on his own hands or on his clothes. QED, as we used to say in maths class in days of old, *Quod erat demonstrandum*.'

'What is that, in the vernacular?'

'It's the Latin for *Bingo!*'

'When will we know definitely?'

'A week, ten days. DNA, so we have to queue.'

'You are a genius, Des!'

'I know. I sometimes wish I wasn't.'

'Why?'

'It's the morons I have to deal with . . .'

Chapter Eight

After most of a week of daily visits to St Isidore's School, the police felt that they had got as far as they were going to get by interviewing boys and teachers and visiting the scene of the crime. The matching fingerprints on Tyson's glasses and on the outside of the window through which the killer had exited seemed to confirm that the murderer was somebody who knew his way round the school. Confronted suddenly with a group of boys in the middle of the night, he had known exactly what to do. He had changed course, got out of that window, and climbed down the primitive fire ladder to the ground.

Lennon was reluctant to request mass fingerprinting of staff members. The teaching, administrative, and domestic staff were ahead of him and suggested it themselves spontaneously. As Nancy McGivern remarked, 'If the CIA and the FBI can have my fingerprints, just for the pleasure of arriving at JFK, I guess anyone can have them.'

A few eccentrics refused, and also some part-time champions of civil liberties – those whose interest in liberties in general was only activated by opportunities to be uncivil to somebody in particular.

The superintendent refused adamantly to have Lady Macbeth subjected to the ritual of fingerprinting.

'I am not in the business of frightening children, still less of making them feel guilty because of some unfortunate affliction.'

A consensus was emerging that the killing was the work of an adult who was well acquainted with the school but not currently on campus, because no match was found for the incriminating fingerprints among the present staff. In his last trip to the school during that first week Lennon asked Dr Fisher how long Mr Tyson had been at St Isidore's.

'Over twenty years.'

'And in that time, how many boys have gone through his hands?'

'Well, on average, forty leave each year. So twenty forties is eight hundred. He must have known about a thousand boys in all.'

'One or some of those might bear him a grudge?'

Fisher grimaced and nodded. 'That is school work for you. You cannot please all of the people all of the time. Maurice Tyson mellowed over the years. He was always straight and always just, but he was a disciplinarian, and even harsh in his early years. I was not here then, of course, but that is what I am told. So, yes, he may have bred resentments.'

'Is there anyone I could consult about his track record, someone who would know if there were specific cases where he had dealt severely – perhaps too severely – with a boy or boys who might have nurtured a deep resentment?'

The headmaster seemed to pray briefly for inspiration, seated deep in his desk armchair, head back, eyes closed, hands joined, with the tips of his fingers touching his lips. Lennon thought he did indeed look like Sherlock Holmes in that mode – with perhaps a tad too much opium on board.

'Yes,' Dr Fisher said, after a suitable interval, 'I would advise you to consult Blaise Pierce. He taught here for thirty years and only retired six months ago. Maurice and he were good friends. I think that if

113

there were something in the line of what you suggest, "a deep resentment", Blaise would probably be aware of it. He lives in Dublin. My secretary can give you the exact address. Yes, ask Blaise Pierce. He was a shrewd observer of the passions and the politics of school life over the years.'

While Lennon was talking to the headmaster, Molly had gone for a walk in the woods. It was one of those exquisite autumn days when the light is so pure, so subtle, that not even the best of Impressionist painters could ever quite capture it. She felt at peace with the world. This is the way it should be all the time, she thought to herself, if only we had antennae to capture the beauty of things and of people, and the perfect harmony of creation.

The path she was following turned sharply to the left. As she rounded the bend she collided with Eddie Gilhooly, who was coming the other way. The boy was mooching along, head down, shoulders slumped, his hands in his pockets, the picture of dejection. He scowled and did not excuse himself. But she had surprised him off his guard, and had discovered not somebody arrogant or cocksure of himself, but a lonely and miserable child. Suddenly, remembering her conversation with Nancy McGivern, Molly was filled with sudden pity for the boy. To her utter amazement, she heard herself saying: 'Eddie, tell me about your brother.'

His mouth fell open in blank astonishment. Then his whole body stiffened, defensive and aggressive at the same time.

'That is absolutely none of your bloody business,' he said fiercely.

Molly took the boy by the hand and led him to a felled trunk of a tree to the side of the path. 'Sit down, Eddie.'

He was so surprised that he sat down. They sat close together.

'Did you ever talk to anyone about Seán's death?' she asked him gently.

He was totally shocked, almost panic-stricken that his formidable defences could so easily be overrun. He had to get this interfering bitch off his back!

'What is there to talk about, for fuck's sake?' he replied savagely. Gilhooly virtually never used strong language, but he knew from experience that saying *fuck* to someone in authority usually created a satisfactory diversion. But Molly said nothing, and her question still hung there in mid-air. After an awkward silence the boy said: 'Look, they gave me a bereavement counsellor, okay? She cost a bomb – and it was *my* money they were spending, nobody else's. But they didn't mind because it made *them* feel better, not *me*. That fat bitch of a counsellor had bad breath and BO, and I'm not surprised because I never met anyone so full of shit in my entire life.'

That surely should be enough, he thought, to shake the prying bitch off. How *dare* she barge her way into something so intimate, and so unbearable! He said out loud, 'I didn't know you were mind-police too. You must have great fun with all that power to really *hurt* people.'

'Why are you so angry, Eddie? You are very angry. Do you realize that? I wonder who you are so angry with?'

He did not reply. So she said 'Hm?' several times, coaxing him, and not going away. Eventually he said, 'I'm angry at that cow.'

'I don't think you are. She was doing her best. You are too intelligent not to know that.'

He glanced at her with a flicker of interest. He was not accustomed to receiving compliments, even oblique ones.

'Okay,' he said vehemently, 'I am angry with God. Seán was the only . . .'

He gulped and could go no further. They sat

together in silence for a while. Then Molly said very softly, 'Are you angry with Seán, Eddie?'

There was a deadly silence. Molly could hear her own heart beating, like the countdown to some unimaginable calamity. Slowly, and quickening, the boy was making an ugly sound deep in his throat, like the rasping of a rusty iron door that has not been opened for centuries. It had never been seen or heard before: Eddie Gilhooly was crying. She took him in her arms. He went rigid for a split second, then yielded to her, and cried as if his heart would break.

When at last the storm had passed, he unwound himself gently from her embrace and sat beside her, elbows propped on his thighs, his head bowed in his hands. In a small quiet voice he asked with sad bewilderment, 'Why did he do it? Why? Why?'

'I don't know, Eddie, but you must forgive him. He was not himself. He was very sick.'

There was another silence. Then the boy said almost in a whisper, 'Do you know how he did it?'

'No, but I'm sure it's not important.'

'Oh, it is,' he said gently, 'it is. This is not known in the school. Our lawyers managed to keep it out of the newspapers. Please don't tell anyone.'

He paused, as if to dredge up the courage to say

what she knew intuitively he had never said to anyone
– out of loyalty to Seán, and from sheer horror of
the words he would have to say. Then he continued
very deliberately.

'Seán was alone in his flat in Dublin. He took
a knife and he casterated himself, or whatever the
word is – listen, I don't know how to say this –
not crudely like – he cut off his balls with a knife.
The doctor said that it must have taken him three
days to die – in agony, I guess. There was blood
all over the place. You see, he made a right mess
of the job. He half-disembowelled himself. I
suppose it was just like when Mr Tyson died – a
butcher's yard.'

Molly had been in the murder squad for six years.
She had seen and heard more than her fair share of
harrowing sights and accounts. None of it had had
the impact of this heartbroken narrative. She closed
her eyes and thought she was going to faint.

Several moments passed. When she opened her
eyes again, he was standing over her. His face, no
longer sardonic and sneering, had become the face
of a bewildered child, grave, and almost beautiful.

'Can I kiss you?' he said.

Molly smiled and nodded. He kissed her
awkwardly below the left ear.

'I'm sorry. I am not good at this.'

'That was a most beautiful kiss,' she said.

'Really?' he said, in wonder. There were tears in his eyes but he was smiling. Then he turned quickly and was gone.

Molly was glad that Lennon slept the whole way back to Dublin in the car. She did not feel ready to tell him about Eddie Gilhooly. First, she would need to reflect deeply on what had been an intense experience for her and, undoubtedly, for the boy as well.

It was in the arms of her loving and lovely young husband that evening that she began to unravel what had happened between them.

'Jan-Hein, I was astonished at myself. I mean, to be asking him such intimate questions. From one point of view, it was bordering on child abuse. If it had not come off, I could have been in deep trouble.'

'So why did you take the risk?'

'Somebody had to take the risk for that child. No, it was not prurience or voyeurism, or whatever you call it, and I certainly didn't plan it. It just came out. I seemed to know what to say, what I *had* to say.'

'Well, God sent you, my lovely angel.'

'In a strange way, Jan-Hein, I think he did too.'

'I am certain of it. From what you tell me, that boy has probably never been held close by any woman, never been kissed, or hugged, or cuddled, since before he can remember.'

'Oh, God, I suppose you're right. Isn't that awful?'

'Awful? It is unimaginable.'

Chapter Nine

As it had been progressing, the police inquiry into Maurice Tyson's death had been more and more informed by a received wisdom, an orthodoxy, which consisted of two dogmas. Dogma number one: the housemaster had been killed by an adult, skilled in cutting other people's throats. Dogma number two: the housemaster had been killed by somebody who was no stranger to the geography of the school. As in most dogmatic systems, those two propositions did not hang too comfortably together.

On the one hand, it was possible to believe that Tyson had been murdered by a skilled cut-throat in a botched attempt to kidnap Bertrand Laporte. On the other hand, it was hard to conceive of any such criminal being familiar with the castle to the point of effortlessly changing his escape route in the middle of the night when suddenly confronted by a gaggle of schoolboys.

St Isidore's School had recruited its fair share of weirdos over the years, in the ranks both of its student body and of its staff. Some of these – a very small number, of course – had been during their subsequent careers, or were even now, guests of the nation in various custodial institutions or homes for the bewildered. All of them, to the extent that they noticed such details, had been familiar with their surroundings during the months or years that they had spent at St Isidore's. But nobody could imagine any of them, except perhaps one – who was detained in a very safe place at all material times – either murdering a housemaster or, still less, being retained by al-Qaeda or any other serious terrorist organization to capture a French boy.

Lennon had dutifully fed into the Interpol network details of Tyson's murder and the possibility that there might be a terrorist involvement. This supposition was centred on the theory that the real purpose of the exercise was to kidnap Bertrand Laporte, whose father was well known to have major interests in Arab countries. Subsequently, Lennon had filed a report saying that he and his colleagues were now satisfed that there was no terrorist involvement. This was on the basis of his telephone conversation with Monsieur Laporte, and because the investigation showed that the murderer must have been somebody who knew St Isidore's intimately.

Lennon's report was immediately rejected by a caustic communication, not to Lennon himself but to his superior officers. This was signed, appropriately enough, with the initials A.X. There was no indication of the identity, the nationality, the rank, or the service in which this *axeman or woman* was employed. Upon enquiring, Lennon was told that, for security reasons, he could not have access to this information. It was all part of the international struggle against terrorism, he was assured, and therefore a matter of faith and morals to be accepted with bowed head and bended knee, and acted on immediately by all the faithful.

The anonymous and, clearly, highly placed international struggler against terrorism was, in effect, admonishing Lennon for dismissing so lightly the possibility that Tyson's death had been the work of terrorists. There was more than a suggestion that any officer who, in this day and age, was capable of making such a cavalier judgement must be long past his sell-by date or living on the moon. It was pointed out with tiresome emphasis that terrorists nowadays plan their coups with meticulous care and attention. Examples of this were said to be the incredible cunning with which the unthinkable attack on the twin towers of the World Trade Center in New York was carried out in 2001, the frightening and wholly unexpected capacity of Hezbollah to wage war on Israel from Southern Lebanon in 2006, and, in the same year, the plans to carry the seemingly harmless ingredients for explosives on to as many as a dozen aeroplanes and to mix them into lethal cocktails on board.

There was no way, it was suggested, that an accomplished terrorist would venture into a terrain like Tyson's tower without detailed knowledge of all the alternative means of getting in and out. The suggestion that the assailant must be someone who previously knew his way around the castle was condemned out of hand as 'naive' and 'hopelessly out of date'. Any self-respecting terrorist, it was said, would make it his business to get this information and to be thoroughly versed in it when the moment came to make his move.

The words of wisdom issuing from A.X. ended with an ABC, presumably for slow learners like Lennon, about the strategy of terrorists which, it was said, consisted in continuously changing their tactics. There was even a ponderous paragraph about the difference between strategy and tactics and a solemn initiation into the concept of psychological warfare which the writer seemed to believe had been invented single-handedly by him or herself. From the terrorist's point of view, it was explained, the important thing was to keep the good fairies guessing about where the bad fairies were going to strike next: poison gas, aviation, nuclear reactors, kidnapping soldiers, and – why not? – kidnapping the children of French fat cats with substantial interests in Arab countries.

It was true, the interminable peroration continued, that established terrorist networks with unlimited budgets from the governments of various states did not need to stoop to such sordid means of finance. However, on the one hand, new and ever more radical groups were appearing all the time which might welcome such doubtful sources of income; and, on the other hand, even established terrorist groups with no money problems might perpetrate a few kidnappings for the psychological instability and sheer misery that they could be relied upon to create.

125

Denis Lennon was a mild man, one open to suggestions and advice. This document annoyed him exceedingly.

'Some smartass watching his own ass,' he snorted, as he threw it into the rubbish bin.

Everything about the document exasperated him. It was anonymous, a glorified poison-pen letter, which had been sent to his superiors and not to himself. That was no way to treat a colleague. Besides, Lennon was convinced that no police person had written that letter. It contained too many dismissive, even contemptuous phrases which simply brushed aside careful analyses and judgements that he had made, and it did not include a single concrete suggestion or counter-proposal to add to what had already been done. It was the kind of letter that had been written by somebody's handler to keep his boss safe from censure, if things ever took an unexpected turn: a form of communication that was becoming familiar within a worldwide bureaucracy. For instance, Lennon could think of similar letters that had been written about child safety, another very emotive issue. They were couched in sanctimonious and self-righteous language but they meant: *Dear Sir, If anything ever happens, it is your fault and not ours, and don't say we didn't warn you. Ha! Ha! Yours, Joe.*

'Pre-emptive buck-passing,' Lennon snorted once again to himself, but at the same time he retrieved the offensive screed from the rubbish bin – 'just in case'.

Dr Fisher had also received a letter, not from A.X., but from a firm of solicitors in Dublin. He had read this letter twice, once quickly and once very slowly. He paused for several minutes, doing his impersonation of a praying mantis. Then, opening his eyes and unjoining his hands, he reached for the telephone and rang the number of the school's attorneys.

'Clarence, Fisher here. What do you know about solictors called Purley and Flint?'

The answer came unhesitatingly. 'Less than salubrious. Chancers who sail close to the wind. Why do you ask?'

'Because they are threatening to sue us for child abuse.'

'Oh, God, I suppose it was bound to happen, sooner or later.'

'I beg your pardon. It was certainly *not* bound to happen at St Isidore's.'

The attorney changed the subject. 'Who is the alleged victim?'

'A fellow called Percy Dandy. He left about fifteen years ago, so he must be in his middle or late thirties now. I didn't know him, obviously, because I have only been here for a few years, but I think I remember hearing that he was expelled.'

'For what?'

'I have forgotten. I'll look it up.'

'Are the police involved? You know that any prosecution has to come before a civil action.'

'There won't be a prosecution.'

'Why not?'

'Because the abuser – or the alleged abuser, I should say – is dead.'

'Fifteen years ago, of course. Can I know who it is?'

'I am telling you this in the strictest confidence. The alleged abuser is Maurice Tyson, who is not yet cold in his grave.'

Chapter Ten

Inspector Jim Quilligan was of the purest itinerant stock: a tinker. It showed. He was large, ruddy faced, and flaxen haired. He had spent the early years of his life, until his teens, criss-crossing the length and breadth of Ireland with his family in a series of caravans and jalopies, stopping briefly at designated halting sites – in effect, open-air ghettos – or camping on the long acre that borders the roadsides in rural Ireland. He was happiest riding bareback on one of those wild piebald ponies known to settled folk, disparagingly and apprehensively, as 'tinkers' horses'.

When Quilligan was thirteen, his father, concerned

for his wife's declining health, and also to give his children a better start in life, decided to settle down. The change was excruciating for all the family. It takes at least three generations to get the wanderlust out of the system.

Quilligan had another string to his bow. Three or four generations back, during the Civil War in the nineteen twenties, and again during the Economic War in the nineteen thirties, big houses were being sold in the Irish countryside as their gentlefolk proprietors retired to England to continue or resume civilized living. An enormous quantity of good furniture, paintings, and antiques came on the market during those years. That is when the Quilligans became dealers. Jim Quilligan's great-grandfather and grandfather were clever men who learned their trade fast. By his father's time, representatives of the family were regularly to be seen in the fashionable fine art auction rooms of Dublin, Limerick, Cork, and even London, where, in spite of their somewhat rustic accents and allure, they inspired a healthy respect for their integrity, their competence, and their business acumen.

It was not entirely surprising that, with this background, and as he had elected to become a member of the Irish police force, Jim Quilligan should find himself one day heading up the Garda Art Crime Squad, with the rank of inspector. The GACS was somebody's beautiful delusion of grandeur. It consisted essentially of Quilligan himself, with untrained extras who were grudgingly lent if absolutely necessary. He got miserly funding from the state's Horn of Plenty – it being understood, of course, that if ever the Book of Kells were stolen from Trinity College or the Caravaggio from the National Gallery, the squad would qualify for an instant allocation. Anne, his wife, suggested brightly that he should steal one of these items himself, then spend the entire allocation working out whodunnit.

His superiors would have had fits of the vapours at the thought of anyone saying such dangerous things to Quilligan. They genuinely esteemed him, but were also in dread of what he might do next. That tinkers are unstable and volatile seems to be written into the genetic code of most Irish people, apart from the tinkers themselves.

In the meantime, while waiting for someone to steal the Book of Kells, Quilligan was employed in a variety of maverick operations which did not fit into any precise category. That suited him fine because he did not fit into any precise category himself. He cut corners. Everybody knew that.

But he was intelligent, too; he did believe in the rule of law – at least in the non-academic sense of fair play; and above all, he always knew – as the French say – 'how far not to go too far'.

Jim Quilligan had worked with Denis Lennon and Molly Power on several cases. They were always glad to see him coming. He was invariably in good humour, had a delightful sense of his own worth, and possessed in abundance those most precious of qualities – common sense and simple decency.

Lennon and Molly called to see 'the Great Bear', as some felon had aptly dubbed him, at his offices in Store Street. His offices consisted of one vast Aladdin's Cave, large enough to accommodate both himself and a copious library of outsize art books, magazines, and fine art catalogues of exhibitions and auctions. Quilligan had himself acquired a small and exquisite collection of paintings, which he called his 'investment for a rainy day'. In fact, it would probably have required precipitation on the scale of Noah's Flood to induce him to part with any of his pictures.

At the sight of his visitors, Quilligan boomed heartily: 'Ah! The assassins. To what must I attribute this honour – and indeed this pleasure? You are very welcome. A nourishing cup of tea?'

Quilligan was famous for his tea, which he was

reputed to make in a storm kettle, with water 'from the river'. To somebody who, taking this literally, asked him nervously, 'What river?' – no doubt worried because there is scarcely a river in the Western world that is not polluted – Quilligan gave the uncomfortable answer, 'Arrah, sure the boiling takes most of the bad things out of it, and anyhow, when you've lived for years in your bare feet, doing all your things in the river, doesn't that work wonders for the antibodies?'

When Quilligan had his visitors seated comfortably and had fed them some tea, he enquired, 'So what's new?'

'The Tyson murder,' Lennon answered. 'You've heard of it?'

'Just what it says in the papers, and the media generally. Something to do with a kidnap that went wrong. Al-Qaeda, Ali Baba and the Forty Thieves. Aren't you living exotic, Denis? Up there with the jet set!'

'Maybe. Kidnap is one theory, and I'm getting pressure from Europe, or from God knows where, to go with it.'

'Why not?'

'I'll answer that when I'm being wise after the event. In the meantime, there is another possibility. The headmaster – it's a school, you know, a boarding school – well, the headmaster tells me that they have just got a letter from some solicitor, saying that Tyson was a sex-abuser, and . . . well, you know how it goes.'

'So what's the solicitor-guy's point? Is he claiming the prize for his client as having cut Tyson's throat?'

'Of course not. He is just looking for money for one of Tyson's alleged victims. But if Tyson was a sex-abuser, he almost certainly had other victims – and one of these may have given him what he had coming to him. Molly and I think that all this Arabian Nights stuff – kidnaps and so on – is a bit far-fetched. So there may be something in this child-abuse scenario.

'Now the point is that this crazy old castle, where the school is, looks like something out of Harry Potter. It seems certain that whoever did the killing knew the place like the back of his hand. I cannot believe that it was some blow-in El Hadji who did the job.'

'Do you read Harry Potter, Denis? Well, wonders will never cease.'

'I read it to my grandchildren.'

Molly gave a yelp of laughter. 'Will you listen to him, Jim! He keeps the poor children up half the night so that he can get to read *The Prisoner of Alcatraz* or whatever it is.'

*   *   *

When the detectives parted company with Quilligan, he had been commissioned to investigate Percy Dandy, who was making allegations of sex-abuse against his former housemaster. Quilligan had been warned that neither Dandy nor his solicitors would be winning Nobel prizes for anything. But Lennon also pointed out that Dandy at least could legitimately attribute deficiencies in his character to the fact that he had been abused. Indeed, he could expect more compensation, rather than less, on foot of those very deficiencies. That is, if he ever *was* abused.

Quilligan had also been charged with interviewing Blaise Pierce, who had retired within the last six months, after thirty years teaching at St Isidore's. Dr Fisher had said that Pierce knew Tyson better than anyone and would probably know of any boys who had particular grudges against the deceased housemaster.

As, with Molly at the helm, they crawled through rush-hour traffic – an absurd contradiction in terms – Lennon mused, 'I don't suppose that Pierce will know of any boys who had particular grudges against Tyson because he was, er, interfering with them. And even if he does know about such boys, he may not be willing to say so.'

'Don't you worry,' Molly replied. 'Jim Quilligan

is just the man who won't forget to ask him that very question, at point-blank range, and in the most explicit terms. I meant to ask you, what was Fisher's attitude when he was telling you about the solicitor's letter and the accusations against Tyson? I mean, did he ever have any inkling, or any suspicions, about any such thing?'

Lennon thought for a few moments before he answered. 'He was strangely dispassionate – that is the precise word. Almost judicial, in the sense of not taking sides. He did say that he had never heard any whisper or suggestion that Tyson was a sex-abuser. On the other hand, he did *not* jump to his defence, hotly denying the accusations, or suggesting that Percy Dandy and his shyster solicitor were nothing but a pair of sleazy gold-diggers. I suppose his attitude was correct for a headmaster. He does have a certain duty to keep a level pitch, no matter what he thinks himself. Still, I thought he was very unemotional about it – even icy.'

'Do you think that Fisher believes that Tyson did abuse children?'

'Maybe. But it is uncommonly difficult to know what Dr Fisher believes. He keeps his cards very close to his chest.'

Chapter Eleven

Next morning, Superintendent Lennon was woken up at 7 a.m. to be told that Bertrand Laporte, who had been spending a long weekend with school companions in a youth hostel at Chartres, south of Paris, had been kidnapped.

Inspector Hervé Quesnel arrived on the first plane from Paris later in the morning. He had been delegated to research the Irish prelude to the Chartres kidnapping. The French media, which, at the time, had given modest coverage to the story that Bertrand Laporte had possibly been the target of a kidnap attempt in Ireland, went fully agog at the revelation that not only had there been an earlier attempt less than a month before to kidnap this child in Ireland, but he had actually ended up, on that occasion, 'drenched in the blood of the victim who had sacrificed his life for him'. The story, told in that way, had all the ingredients of what the moralists call *delectatio morosa*, which is what sells tabloid newspapers: money, murder, blood, terror, and a sweet little boy up to his neck in all of them.

By and large, the French media were not finding fault with the Irish police, who had promptly signalled to the appropriate authorities the possible involvement of terrorists in the earlier incident. Besides, the essential fact was that Bertrand had returned from Ireland safe and sound, and it was down to the French authorities to take such precautions as they saw fit from that point on.

The French police had not taken any particular precautions because, in the first place, Bertrand's family had not invited them to take any such measures. In the second place, they knew that the Irish police were sceptical about the suggestion that the boy had been involved in a failed kidnap attempt, whether by terrorists or by 'ordinary' criminals. Now they immediately swung into action, deploying a nation-wide hunt for Bertrand and despatching Inspector

Quesnel to Ireland to discover whatever light the Irish episode could cast on their own inquiry.

A.X., the anonymous writer of letters to Lennon's superiors, saw things with a different eye from the French media. He must have stayed up all night exulting with indecent glee and writing another letter to Lennon's superiors, this one addressed care of Inspector Quesnel. It poured scorn on the Garda investigation to date. The Gardaí had recklessly failed, this jeremiad declared, to heed the clear warning that this boy was a target for kidnap by international terrorism.

Invited to comment, Lennon was succinct. 'I am paid to investigate murders within the Irish jurisdiction. I have no mandate to provide security cover for anyone in any jurisdiction and, still less, to patrol the streets of Chartres.' But he was deeply troubled. The very vividness of his reaction showed just how much he was shaken. He felt that his whole investigation so far was unravelling. Had it been a waste of time? Was it possible that he had missed something or neglected some aspect of the inquiry? Above all, had he decided prematurely that Tyson's murder was not a kidnap attempt that had gone wrong? He said to Molly, 'I am a father and a grandfather myself, Molly. I can tell you, I will never forgive myself if this little guy comes to any harm because of anything that I did or did not do.'

She replied as reassuringly as she could. 'Denis, what more could you have done? The fact is that he was not kidnapped on our watch. Dr Fisher was right to send him home once there was any hint of danger to him. For the rest, well, Bertrand's parents are fully aware that he is always at some risk. This could have happened anywhere and at any time.'

For three days Denis and Molly gave their full attention to Inspector Quesnel. They discussed every aspect of their own case with him and gave him full access to all the evidence: statements, fingerprints, technical reports. They spent two whole days with him at St Isidore's, where he was at liberty to visit every corner of the castle and estate, and to question any of the staff or students. Dr Fisher gave his full cooperation and, moreover, seemed to espouse enthusiastically the theory that Tyson had been killed in the course of a kidnap bid that went wrong. He seemed to have forgotten his earlier statement that it was the French boy's parents who had wanted him home in the aftermath of Tyson's murder, claiming credit robustly for himself for the decision to repatriate him.

Quesnel was a rather solemn man, soft spoken and courteous. Probably in his early fifties, he looked like a sympathetic funeral director. He managed well in English, which was fortunate because neither of the Gardaí had much French. Whatever he might have thought privately, he never voiced the slightest criticism of the Garda investigation; indeed, on the contrary, he several times expressed appreciation for various aspects of his Irish colleagues' work. When Molly tackled him directly on the subject of the letter from A.X. which he had delivered, he professed complete ignorance of the contents. When she enlightened him – not moderating her language unduly – he coloured slightly and replied: 'I do not know who Monsieur Astérix is. What I do know is that he does not speak for the French police.' He added in his vernacular, '*C'est de la connerie pure!*' which Molly was gratified to learn later meant, translated dynamically, 'That's total bullshit!'

It was Quesnel, too, who gave his Irish colleagues factual details of the kidnap. Bertrand had been staying at a youth hostel in Chartres with ten of his classmates, doing an architectural project on the famous cathedral. It was supper time. The boys were queueing up for their meal. One of the kitchen staff had come looking for 'Bertrand Laporte'.

A policeman, he said, wanted to see him because he had found his *carte d'identité* and needed to be sure that he was giving it to the right person. Bertrand was not sure where his identity card was supposed to be. Had he brought it on the trip? Was it in his overnight bag, or had he given it to the teacher who was in charge of the group? This teacher had not yet come into the dining room. In fact it later transpired that he was grabbing a quick apéritif in the nearest bistrot.

Bertrand went out with the kitchen boy. He had not come back after one hour, nor after two hours, nor after six hours. The tippling teacher, who had finally arrived for his supper, first of all acted cool, saying that Bertrand would 'turn up'. Then he went on the defensive, blaming the boys, the youth hostel authorities, anybody and everybody except himself. Towards midnight, he suddenly buckled, and more or less went to pieces. He sobbed piteously throughout the night, which was not reassuring for the rest of the frightened youngsters, who had to try to console *him*. Finally, when the trail had gone stone cold, it fell to a boy to ring the police and the *directeur* of his *lycée*. 'Not leadership material!' Quesnel commented mildly.

It emerged next day that the kitchen staff member was a phoney. No such person was working in the youth hostel. He had probably walked the boy to a car where he was quickly overpowered by a drug, an anaesthetic, or brute force. The phoney kitchen boy had probably got into the same car and been driven away to God knows where. The police had already decided in the small hours of the morning that this was a kidnap and had swung into action accordingly. The one or two boys who had noticed the scene between Bertrand and the fake employee, when asked, said that he looked like 'a Moroccan – or something like that'.

By the time Inspector Quesnel left Ireland, he had received an e-mail informing him that the kidnappers were demanding a ransom of ten million euro. There was no indication as to who they were or how the ransom was to be paid. The police presumed that Monsieur Laporte had received further information, with warnings of what would happen to Bertrand if he were to divulge it to the police or in any way try to pull a fast one. Everybody knows that the authorities are always against paying ransom money, whereas families are in favour of it, if they have or can get the required cash. Ten million was well within Monsieur Laporte's reach, but it would take a few days. The police had no doubt that he had already communicated that to the criminals.

'How did the kidnappers know that Bertrand was going to be in the youth hostel in Chartres on that particular weekend?' Molly asked the inspector.

'We don't know for sure. But, assuming that they had decided to kidnap him in advance – which is almost certainly the case – they would have been looking out for an opportunity. Bertrand was delivered to school each day by limo, and collected again in the evening, because, precisely, of the danger of kidnap. We speculate that there was somebody in the school – like the kitchen boy at the youth hostel – who was commissioned to watch out for an occasion when the boy would be vulnerable. The trip to Chartres was well advertised. People had to sign up on a list posted on the noticeboard, and pay in advance. If there was a mole in the school – and for ten million euro, the kidnappers could well afford one – it is indeed frightening to think how simple it would have been to know when this boy could be picked up as easy as *bonjour*.'

'Check your Moroccans,' Molly said.

Quesnel replied soberly, 'Ethnic profiling can produce great injustices.'

Lennon, who had remained quiet during this exchange, remarked reflectively, 'If it was really so simple to kidnap this boy in France, what in the name of God were these people thinking of when they had already tried to kidnap him in Ireland? I mean, why complicate things for yourself?'

Quesnel nodded. 'Indeed, I agree; having seen all the evidence that you have so painstakingly assembled, it is by no means certain that what happened in Ireland was, in fact, a kidnap attempt that went wrong. And even assuming that there *was* also a kidnap attempt in Ireland, it need not have been the same people who made the two attempts. This more recent incident may have been a copycat operation. The publicity that the first event attracted may have drawn attention to Bertrand as a possible target.

'I think that there are three possibilities. First, that the same people tried twice to kidnap this boy, once in Ireland which failed, and once in France which has succeeded. The second possibility is that nobody tried to kidnap Bertrand in Ireland – in which case you still have to solve the mystery of who murdered your Monsieur Tyson – and that somebody succeeded in kidnapping the young man in France, which was, how do you say? in the cards anyhow.'

'And the third possibility?' Molly prompted.

'The third possibility is a combination of the other two. Whether there was or was not a first kidnap attempt in Ireland, the media talked of such an event.

Alors, this put the idea into the heads of some gang in France, whether of terrorists or of common criminals, that Bertrand would be an attractive target for kidnap, in view of his father's great wealth. So, it was a copycat-kidnap thing.'

Inspector Quesnel eventually went back to France, expressing himself *ravi* about the cooperation he had received from the Irish police. He kissed Lennon on two cheeks, somewhat to the superintendent's surprise. He kissed Molly on four, as he came round for second helpings. Quilligan, whom he had briefly met on his last day in Ireland, he did not kiss at all, no doubt sensing, rightly, that Quilligan was not the same-sex kissing type.

Chapter Twelve

Jim Quilligan meanwhile was ploughing his lonely
furrow and acting as if the French interlude were
the merest distraction from the real task of finding
out who had killed Maurice Tyson. He had been
commissioned to interview Blaise Pierce, who was
reputed to be the man who knew Maurice Tyson
best. He had also been asked to 'look into' Percy
Dandy, who had posthumously accused Tyson of
sexual abuse. Denis Lennon was not sure what
Quilligan would do about Dandy. He preferred not
to ask.

Blaise Pierce lived in a comfortable modern house

in Leeson Village. He looked like Mr Pickwick, as Quilligan would have imagined him: rosy, rotund, and amiable. He wasn't sure if Mr Pickwick had been married, but if he had – Quilligan surmised – he and Mr Pierce would have had in common no real need of a wife, except perhaps to tell them what to wear and whether or not they were hungry. Apart from that, they would probably have had difficulty remembering the good woman's name and in what circumstances she had got into their house in the first instance – let alone into their bed. Mr Pierce was not in any sense a misogynist. Indeed he quite understood that many men had a passion for matrimony, just as others could not survive without fox-hunting, fishing, golf or cricket. He was nevertheless of the opinion that such pursuits consumed an inordinate amount of time and attention. Meanwhile numerous married women found him quaint, old worldly, and really quite soothing.

The small house was full of books. Pierce had taught history all his life. He had been effectively subversive in a culture where tradesmen's subjects monopolize far too much of young people's time. He had taught boys to think – which is quite unusual in these days where so many topics are best, or at any rate more comfortably, left alone. The boys liked and trusted him. They were sure that there was no price to be paid – emotionally or intellectually – for what he could ignite in them. Like grace, it was free, and it left them free also. Consequently, Mr Pierce had whole generations of disciples who never outgrew their esteem and affection for him.

'Come in, come in!'

He started to boom encouragingly when, seemingly, at the remotest outpost of his not very extensive kingdom. There is a traditional Irish greeting, *Cead mile failte*, which means 'a hundred thousand welcomes'. That may be because the ancient Irish took an inordinately long time to get to their hall doors. Mr Pierce had certainly welcomed Quilligan very comprehensively by the time he actually opened the door.

'Oh, are you the plumber?' he asked expectantly. 'No.'

'Aha! I *knew* you were not the plumber because I have not rung for him yet.' Taking this brilliant piece of deduction in his stride, Pierce thrust the door open wider and invited the inspector in. 'Well, whoever you are: coffee time. Come in.'

Quilligan explained who he was and what was his business. Pierce nodded his head approvingly.

'Ah yes, poor Maurice! You had better come in.'

He settled the inspector at the kitchen table, did something clever with an unlikely apparatus, and produced delicious coffee, so strong you could trot a mouse on it. Then he came to sit opposite Quilligan. He sipped his coffee a few times, then put down his cup.

'Maurice Tyson was a dear friend. I shall miss him very much. Who killed him?'

Quilligan shrugged. 'What do you think?' he asked.

Pierce mimicked the shrugging gesture. 'I have been trying to work it out. I can't see that he has been murdered for his own sake, so to speak. Tyson was not the kind of man who gets murdered for his own sake. So, tragically, he must have simply got in the way.'

'Of kidnappers?'

'Perhaps, or it may have been a case of mistaken identity.'

'Hardly, surely! Who else could murderers be hoping to meet up with in that tower at that hour of the night?'

Pierce did not know the answer to that one. He raised his arms in perplexed surrender. Quilligan pressed his advantage.

'So maybe, just maybe, Tyson *was* murdered for

his own sake – for instance, by a former pupil of the school who, let's suppose, had a grudge against him.'

Pierce rolled coffee about his mouth, reserving judgement for all of fifteen seconds. Already after ten seconds, the jury was in and shaking its head. He swallowed and said: 'Inspector, even the most popular teachers and housemasters do have some youngsters in their charge who cannot abide them. Often it is just a matter of chemistry – oil and water – they just can't get on with each other. That's a fact of life. Then, sometimes, it is something that the authority figure has done, a harsh decision, some perceived injustice, even a wounding word. The toughest-seeming adolescent can be hypersensitive to a rebuke or a taunt. Again, frequently, it is a question of envy or resentment, that this particular master seems to like or admire certain boys, to have time for them, whereas he manifestly dislikes another, whom he regards as annoying, tiresome, or even contemptible. Perhaps that is largely in their own heads – the boys' heads I mean – but they feel it keenly and are so easily discouraged, when all the time they so need to be affirmed.'

Quilligan was nodding his head, as if keen to believe the worst of Tyson the tyrant. He added fuel to the fire.

'I am told that, particularly in his earlier days, Tyson was a tough disciplinarian.'

'Yes, that is true, he was. But he was never unfair, in the sense that everyone got the same; he was evenhanded – especially when it came to disembowelling people.'

'That's nice to know. But can you think of anyone who really detested Maurice Tyson?'

'Well, that is what I was leading up to in my peroration: can I think of anyone who really detested Tyson, to the point of murdering him – or at least rejoicing that he was dead? Frankly, and unhesitatingly, no. And, on the contrary, I can think of large numbers who venerated him, even if he tore strips off them. You know, boys are very fair minded. They do see the total picture.'

'Do you remember a boy called Dandy, Percy Dandy?'

'Dandy? Yes, I remember him. A nasty piece of work: a liar, a thief, and a cheat. But he did not murder Maurice Tyson either. He was sneaky and sly, but not violent. He wouldn't have had the guts to cut the throat of a chicken.'

'Was Tyson involved in Dandy's expulsion?'

'Well, he was his housemaster, and he set a trap for him, a hidden camera, which proved conclusively that Dandy was stealing from his own companions on an outrageous scale. He wasn't expelled exactly. His parents – decent people, God knows. I don't know what they did to deserve him – well, they accepted that his position had become untenable in the school. He was an unpopular fellow anyhow. That finished him off. He just didn't come back after the Christmas holidays – or was it Easter? I forget.'

'Was Tyson gay?'

'Well, you couldn't say that he was exactly gay: he was a serious man. But he was usually in good humour.'

'I mean, was he a homosexual?'

Pierce was so shocked at the question, fired off at point-blank range, as Molly had said it would be, that he knocked over his coffee cup.

'Inspector, Inspector,' he expostulated. 'First, I have not the faintest idea as to whether Mr Tyson was, er, as you have insinuated; and in the second place, what has that got to do with anything?'

'Are you serious, Mr Pierce? You knew Tyson for twenty years or more, and you never knew whether or not he was gay?'

'Inspector, people of my generation and of Mr Tyson's breeding would never have discussed such an intimate matter. I am, of course, aware that nowadays young people have no shame about talking about these things – "coming out", I believe they call it. I am saying to you categorically that Maurice Tyson never discussed any such question with me. I have no idea what his sexual orientation was – and I don't really believe in sexual orientation anyhow. Some people get into certain unpleasant habits. That is all. But if the drift of what you are asking me is to imply that Mr Tyson ever behaved in an unseemly manner with one or other of his charges, I am absolutely certain that this is not the case. I repeat: it never happened.'

Quilligan pulled his ear several times, as if to stimulate his meditative faculties. When he spoke again, he did so gently.

'Dandy has made such allegations about Tyson.'

Pierce's mouth fell open in shocked disbelief. When he had recovered his voice, all trace of his customary courtly language had temporarily deserted him.

'If anyone in the world was having sex with that Dandy creature – well! That has to be the queerest queer I ever heard of. That boy was a revolting little git!'

He coloured suddenly, as if he had been shocked into showing his own hand, and he was too intelligent not to know that Quilligan had spotted it. There was an awkward pause. Then Quilligan said: 'I agree with you when you say that Dandy is unlikely to have killed Tyson. But, in view of Dandy's present accusations, we must at least think about the possibility that whoever *did* kill Tyson was getting his own back for sexual abuse – perhaps long years ago.'

Chapter Thirteen

'Okay, let's suppose that there *was* some terrorist involvement in Tyson's murder – a kidnap effort that went wrong, the little French boy, and so on.'

This was Lennon thinking out loud. He and Molly Power were driving down to the Garda training college at Templemore for a session with the rookies about the Garda murder squad. They both enjoyed these encounters. The two officers would make a presentation, tell some hair-raising stories – and some malicious ones too, mainly about Tweedy and his mighty technicals – then take questions and discuss. The recruits were as keen as mustard, and such good fun. 'We must be doing something right after all,' Lennon mused.

Meanwhile Molly knew the difference between Lennon's throwaway remarks and when he was on to something solid. His seeming, if still grudging, conversion to the idea of a terrorist involvement in Tyson's murder interested her. She tried to second-guess him. It was one of their spontaneous work methods.

'Terrorist involvement! You don't really believe that, Denis, do you? It just suits you to play the Brussels sprouts game for the moment. Why?'

He cocked an eye at her, and said nothing.

'Come on, Denis, what are you up to? Out with it!'

'Perhaps I've seen the light,' he replied sanctimoniously.

Molly said something coarse, a sure way to get Lennon to hurry up. He disliked coarseness, especially in the mouth of a young woman.

'All right, all right! Well, see here. We are one fingerprint away from solving this crime. Do you realize that? We have a print on Tyson's glasses, and one or two prints on the window and on the wall where it seems certain that the murderer exited.'

'That is all correct, but so what? We cannot match that fingerprint.'

'So the anti-terrorist crowd have the vastest data-bases in the world when it comes to fingerprints.'

'Well, can't you access these databases routinely when you work through Interpol?'

'I don't think so. Convicted criminals, maybe – but listen, let me tell you how it happens. Mary and I went to the US in the summer, a respectable middle-aged couple, one of them a cop. We were both photographed and both fingerprinted at Immigration. Who gets those records? The CIA, the FBI, Disney World? I haven't a clue. But that must be on its way to becoming the most comprehensive database of fingerprints on the entire planet. Well, that's the one I want to get into – and if that means pretending that I think this was a terrorist plot that went wrong, okay, I'm your man, delighted to play ball!'

Molly laughed outright. 'Machiavelli,' she exclaimed.

'I'll take that as a compliment.'

'It could be – taken in context, of course.'

'Besides,' Lennon conceded, 'it *might* even be a terrorist thing all the time, and I *might* be wrong – it's just I so hate these anonymous, faceless mandarins from outer space, or wherever they come from – we don't even know that. But still

I might be wrong, and if the murder was in fact a terrorist cock-up, well, we need to know that too, don't we?'

'We do,' Molly agreed, 'but now that you have come at last, with much huffing and puffing, to admit the kidnap scenario as a viable possibility, I have something else that I need to tell you.'

'Don't tell me! Gilhooly did it?'

Molly, who was driving, fumbled her gears. She was startled.

'Denis, I declare to God, you are psychic! No, Gilhooly did not do it. He has the perfect alibi – out on the barbecue with the others, and being an absolute pain in the arse, for fear they would forget him for two seconds. But it is amazing that you should mention Gilhooly just now.'

'Why?'

'Because he is exactly who I want to talk to you about just now, he and his brother.'

Molly wondered where to begin: with her conversation in the staffroom with Nancy McGivern, with her intense exchange with Eddie Gilhooly himself down in the woods, or indeed with the talk that she had had with Jan-Hein in bed that night. Each of these conversations seemed to be confidential in its own way. She made a start, realizing that she was going to find it difficult to talk to Denis Lennon about these emotive and intimate topics.

'I think that you will have picked up that Eddie Gilhooly is an orphan. He has had a very sad life. His parents were killed outright in a car crash when he was so little that he has not even the faintest memory of them. The only close relative remaining was Seán, a brother, whom he hero-worshipped. Seán was a sort of Renaissance man. Handsome, charming, clever, an all-round sportsman, madly popular, the life and soul of the St Isidore's party. You've probably heard that much.'

'Yes, more or less, I think.'

'Well, here is the tragic bit.'

'God, I thought we'd had the tragic bit, with the parents being killed.'

'Wait for it! In senior school, when he was seventeen, Seán began to change.'

'They all do, Molly, they all do – pimples, beards. It goes with the territory.'

'No, Denis, no, something much more radical. To cut a long story short, his whole character, or personality, or whatever you call his *self* just went belly up. For his last two years at school, and for two or three years of university, nobody could reach him. Last Christmas, he offed himself.'

'God between us and all harm! I didn't know that. Drugs again, I suppose. What are we coming to at all in this country?'

'It wasn't drugs, Denis, or not only drugs. Let me get this over with. Alone in his flat, he castrated himself and half-disembowelled himself in the process. They estimate that it took him three days to die.'

There was a stunned silence in the car. Even Molly was shocked all over again merely hearing herself saying the words. Eventually, Lennon asked quietly, 'How do you know all this?'

'Nancy McGivern, the geography teacher, told me some of it. But it was Eddie Gilhooly himself who told me the rest, particularly the way that Seán died. I had an extraordinary conversation with him, the last day we were at St Isidore's. I had gone for a walk and I bumped into him in the woods. He was looking miserable. You know, his whole manner – cocksure, brash – well, it is only a front. Nancy had told me that already. He is one very sad, lonely little boy. He told me the whole thing. He cried as if his heart would break – which I think did him a lot of good. He hasn't had too many people in his life who he could cry with. Incidentally, he made me promise that I would not tell anyone how Seán had died.'

'Is that why you didn't tell me?'

'Yes it is.'

Lennon took a few moments to absorb that. Then he said simply: 'Good for you, Molly.'

'Anyhow, it didn't seem to have anything to do with Tyson's death, so why mention it?' Molly paused, then went on. 'It was something that Jan-Hein said only last night in bed – that's where we discuss everything – well, this thing really made me think. Jan-Hein said, "I bet you, Molly, that your Seán guy was abused, I mean sexually abused." I said, "How do you know that, Monsieur Maigret?" – I call him that when he comes poaching on my territory – but actually, he is not a complete fool.'

Lennon chuckled. 'Jan-Hein is no fool at all. Tell me more.'

'He talked about a big scandal in Belgium a few years ago, or Holland – that's where he comes from.'

'I know.'

'Of course you do. Well, Jan-Hein said that one of the things that they have learned from these big scandals is that sudden changes in a child's personality – I mean deep changes – can often be explained by the fact that somebody has been molesting that child sexually. You see, the child knows that what is going on is evil, and she or he is bewildered and

163

scared, especially if it is a parent or a member of the family that is doing the abuse, or some other authority figure that the child is meant to obey and look up to.'

'Hum. I think we know that, in a general way, but I also think that it has mostly got to do with small children, not "Renaissance man" or all-round sportsmen.'

'Nancy McGivern says that the change was just unbelievable. He may have been Renaissance man, but some teenagers can be very fragile psychologically. Seán, obviously, had been making a heroic effort to overcome the terrible handicap of losing both his parents. He was certainly putting his best foot forward. But he must have been so brittle underneath. If something else really traumatic happened to him then – such as abuse – yes, I am sure he would easily have caved in.

Lennon brooded a while. When he spoke, it was as if reluctantly. 'I think I'd nearly prefer terrorism to child abuse. Come to think of it, they are the same thing. Child abuse is simply terrorism against the softest of soft targets, though you say that Sean was seventeen: not exactly a child! We do have already one explicit accusation of sex-abuse against Tyson – I wonder how Quilligan is getting on with that

164

one – and, of course, there may be more. There usually are, once somebody has broken the ice.'

'But Denis, what clinches it is the awful way that Seán died. He cut off his own sexual organs! That has got to have some terrible meaning.'

'I suppose it is one of these "cry for help" things.'

'No, Denis, it is not a cry for help. It's the very opposite. It is a plea of guilty, a self-condemnation, a recoiling in horror from what has been done to him and, no doubt, what he has done himself under the influence of somebody really evil or totally deranged. You know, the worst part of this abuse thing – what is really unforgivable – is the unbearable burden of guilt that it lays on a young person's shoulders. I had no idea, no idea at all, before I came face to face with this nightmare. It's too horrible.'

Molly suddenly pulled into the hard shoulder of the road and stopped the car. She closed her eyes and leant her forehead against the steering wheel. She sat there in silence for several minutes. Lennon did not utter a word. When Molly eventually opened her eyes and started the car again, she sketched a sidelong grimace at the superintendent and said simply, 'Thanks.'

'You have been through the mill about this thing, haven't you?'

'You better believe it, Denis. The more I think of the stuff that has probably happened here, the more heartbroken I am for those two orphan boys – both of them.'

A few seconds later, Lennon's cellphone sounded its inane jingle. He reached for it in its cradle. He said 'Hello', listened, made a half-gasp-half-exclamation, listened some more, said 'We'll be right there' and clicked out. He sat motionless for five seconds, then said: 'Molly, turn the car, will you? We need to go straight to St Isidore's, or close by.'

'Why?'

'Because Sir Neville Randler has been murdered.'

Chapter Fourteen

Bertrand Laporte had lived since before he could remember with the prospect that, some day, he might be kidnapped. He knew that the kidnappers would be ruthless men, playing for very high stakes, that they would not hesitate to kill him if things did not go according to their plans, that they would be prepared to torture and mutilate him in order to put pressure on his parents, and that he would probably be forced by all kinds of terror and cruelty to plead with his own parents, who had given him life, for a second chance, begging them not to walk away from him, never to say that his life was worth only so much and no more and that – regretfully, of course – they had to retire from the bidding. If that ever happened, he thought – because he did think sometimes about these things – he would not want to live. He could not bear to face his parents again, if he knew, and they knew, that a price tag had come between them.

Such, or some equivalent anguish, are the hidden terrors of youth for even the happiest of happy princes. Bertrand was a very happy prince and a contented child. But there is always that twilight touch.

So it had happened. How long ago? A week – could it be two weeks? How had it happened? He remembered getting a message in the youth hostel at Chartres about police and a lost *carte d'identité*. It had made him feel like a grown-up – that the police wanted to talk to him man to man. He remembered going out to a car. What kind of car? colour? size? He did not remember. There were people in the car. How many? Three or four, he did not know exactly. He had stood at the window of the front passenger seat, where there was sitting the man whom he had called 'Snake-Eyes' in his mind from the first moment he saw him. The man had smiled at him – a smile without warmth or reassurance.

He had got out of the car. He had struck like a snake, so fast that Bertrand did not know what hit him – a bolt from the blue, a knock-out pad, a pill, or a punch? He did not know. He had blacked out immediately. And now he was here.

Where was *here*? Quite a large room, unfurnished except for the bed that he was lying on. There was a big window, blanked out with something like black plastic sheeting, and closed. Which accounted for the stink in the room: the closed window, and the fact that he had to piss and shit in a big iron bucket beside the bed. He had begged them to empty the bucket. They had only done so once when it was more than half full, including vomit, when he had been sick, probably from what they gave him to knock him out the first day in Chartres. He was tethered to the bed by an iron chain to his ankle, which left him four feet in which to manoeuvre, just enough to reach the bucket, not enough to approach the window. He had not been able to wash himself or change his clothes since his arrival. His underwear was in such a disgusting state that he ached to peel it off, but he was too cold all the time, and especially at night because there was no heating, there were no blankets on the bed, and he had only the clothes that he was wearing when he was captured: underwear, short socks, jeans, a T-shirt, and a light sweater.

The food was basic: cornflakes with milk some-times, but more usually with water, bananas, apples, yoghurt, bread and cheese; no sugar, nothing cooked except an occasional wedge of bought-in pizza. He heard the delivery boy at the door once – definitely a Parisian, the clipped accent was unmistakable. Bertrand guessed that he had been brought back to Paris from Chartres. From the sounds of traffic in the street, he was fairly sure that he was in an apartment three or four floors up in what was evidently a rather old building in a residential area. There was not much traffic in the immediate surroundings, but he noted that cars approaching tended to make a lot of noise from a long way off. That meant that they were being driven hard in a very low gear up a long slow hill. Farther away, he could hear a low steady hum of busy traffic, day and night.

It came to him suddenly on the fourth day: Montmartre – of course! That was the only place in Paris that he knew which would fit exactly what he was hearing. The steep ascent to a place where traffic was rarer but from where, at the same time, he could hear the unceasing growl of movement along both banks of the River Seine. Curiously, it was only after he had convinced himself on the evidence of traffic noises that he had begun to hear the bells of the Sacré Coeur basilica, which had been distinctly audible all the time. He knew then where he was. Suddenly his problems were not indefinable any more: they were merely insoluble. That had to be progress.

Bertrand's captors were a complete enigma. If he had expected them to be wearing black beards and speaking Arabic, he was disappointed. They spoke French to him – the few words that they had to say – and what they spoke between themselves was anyone's guess, because they didn't. There were three of them, that he saw, but he had the impression that there were one or two more who came and went to the apartment, including at least one woman, who did speak French, with the accent of the Midi.

When any or all of the three men whom he did see were with him, they did not answer questions. Their visits were purely functional, to assure themselves that he was still there, to feed him minimally, and to check that he had not undone his chain. For the rest, they had him where they wanted him, showed him neither compassion nor overt cruelty, and pretty well ignored him as a living breathing person.

There was the man that he had called Snake-Eyes from their first encounter in the car park outside the youth hostel in Chartres. He was clearly the leader of the two others. Unsmiling, expressionless, apparently devoid of feelings – and, at the same time, totally focused on what he wanted. Bertrand sensed that this man would be ruthless in punishing bad behaviour on his part, without, on the other hand, considering that he deserved even the smallest show of pity in return for meek subjection.

There were the other two men, those who usually brought him his food and routinely ignored his pleas for a change of clothes, blankets, an opportunity to wash, something to read, news of his family, any clue about why he had been kidnapped, by whom, and the terms or prospects of an early or even an eventual release. One of these men looked exactly like a comic strip hoodlum: thick-set, with no neck to speak of, his head seemingly stuck directly on to buffalo shoulders. Bertrand labelled him Bullet-Head in his mind. He actually thought that Bullet-Head was a genuine deaf-mute, but when he asked him one day for a radio, the zombie was shocked into speech, exclaiming, '*Merde – NON!*' Presumably, the boy reckoned, he was not meant to hear any news bulletins about how near or far the police were to finding him. They had taken his watch, so that he would not know what time it was – or possibly because they guessed that his parents had given him that watch, which they had, the previous Christmas, and that he would find its loss demoralizing, which he did, until he made a conscious decision not to.

The third man was the only one who showed the boy some small humanity. At least he knew his name, Jacques. Jacques would squeeze his arm, or pat his shoulder in passing, or even whisper a few words of encouragement, *Ça ira* or something vague like that; but it helped. The thing that meant most to the captive was that, on one occasion when they were alone together in the apartment, Jacques helped the boy to take a hurried sponge-bath and gave him clean underwear – his own, obviously, because it was several sizes too big, and warmer too.

Bertrand's enforced idleness by day meant that he slept poorly at night. Those nights of total blackness seemed to stretch to infinity, a hell from which there was no redemption. That is when his wretched state really got to him: the squalor, the cold, the hunger, the unrelieved darkness by day and by night, the long slow hours of mind-numbing inactivity, for a boy who normally just about managed to squeeze into twenty-four hours all that he wanted to do.

Above all, there was the loneliness, and the fear that he would never see *Papa* and his *maman* again. Sometimes he sobbed secretly in the small hours of these endless nights and, once or twice, his courage failed him completely. Then he wept like the child which, after all, he was.

One morning when he was doing press-ups on the floor – just to get some kind of exercise – he discovered under the bed what he knew was some kind of recording apparatus, the kind that trips in when there is some significant sound. He realized that they were recording him crying during the night. Having thought about it a good deal, he reckoned that the probable purpose of the recordings was to play them over the telephone to his mother. He was so angry at the sheer cruelty and meanness of this that he did not eat all day. When Bullet-Head approached him with a dish of food, he kicked it out of his hand. The zombie beat him viciously with his fists. Tethered by his chain, he took the full brunt of the apeman's rage.

Bertrand knew that his mother could not bear to listen to him crying, and that, equally, she could not bear not to, if that was the only noise he was making. From that moment on, he began to hate his captors. He hardened his heart with hate, because he knew that this was the only way he could manage never to cry again during the night.

In the third week of his captivity, Bertrand began to have a nightmare which further disturbed his fitful sleep. He dreamt that he was alone in Tyson's tower. It was the middle of the night and very dark. All the other boys had gone out on a barbecue and left him on his own. He was very afraid. He was also very cold. He heard Eddie Gilhooly saying to him repeatedly, 'We're going to take the heating with us, we're going to take it with us. You are going to be so cold! You are only a frog, *sang froid*, cold blood, cold blood. HA, HA!'

Eventually, in his dream, Bertrand got up and started to creep down the stairs. Suddenly, he heard angry voices coming from where the boys had crouched on the night when Mr Tyson was killed. They were shouting, 'Bertrand did it; Bertrand did it. He is all blood. He is all blood. Cold blood! Cold blood!'

He knew that they meant that he had killed Mr Tyson.

Chapter Fifteen

When Sir Neville Randler had been forced by
financial circumstances to sell his castle, he took
refuge in a large manor house on a hundred acres
of land, which he let for grazing on the *eleven month*.
According to the arcane mysteries of Irish land law,
this ensured that none of his grazing tenants could
acquire a prescriptive title merely by 'squatting' long
enough. He never married, but did settle down to
the life of a reasonably provident country gentleman
of leisure. His domestic needs were simple and were
catered for admirably by a local woman of indeter-
minate age called Hannah. No whisper of slander

or scandal ever adhered to Sir Neville and/or Hannah. One would not wish to be ungallant, but Hannah's personal appearance was very reassuring on this point. It included features like huge ears, leathery skin, and – well, if one said a moustache, it would really be a bit of a euphemism.

Sir Neville was a dedicated sportsman. He rode to hounds, and was a good horseman. He fished ardently – fly-fishing, of course: he would have regarded spinners as something that came in with the Bolsheviks. He was a crack shot, who observed all the times, seasons, and holy days in the wildlife calendar. If Sir Neville mourned the setting of the sun on the British Empire, so close to home and as near to the bone as Ireland, this was largely a matter of *cricket*. As far as he was concerned, you could take the rest, including the monarchy, the House of Lords, and the Church of England. He *did* miss the cricket.

The Lord never closes one door but he opens another. Sir Neville discovered with joy the whole world of Gaelic games, football and hurling – not camogie, however, which he described as 'a bridge too far'. Perhaps he associated it with 'strong' girls like Hannah – which is manifestly groundless. He was a regular at Croke Park and at a wide selection of provincial venues too. The somewhat bathetic element in Irish nationalism which he discovered on these occasions, he shrugged off with well-bred detachment. 'Well, they have got to do their thing, haven't they?' he would say, in the teeth of even the most virulent displays of synthetic patriotism. Another expression of his for such performances was, 'They are just acting the *Fír Bolg*!' Needless to say, he had no idea what *Fír* – or even a *Fear* – *Bolg* was. It was just an expression he had heard which seemed and, in fact, was right for the occasion.

Heatherside Manor – a name which Sir Neville disliked but never got round to changing – was only twenty minutes away by car from his ancestral chateau, which had become, together with other disasters – like the demise of cricket – St Isidore's School. He never darkened the door, or even the gate, of his former residence for at least a decade. Then one evening he encountered a young man in his local pub who engaged him in pleasant conversation. O'Hara's pub was that kind of place, where everybody knew everybody else. A single room with a Liscannor-flagged floor, a sturdy wooden counter, and an open turf fire, with a kettle singing suspended from an iron, ever ready to make whiskey or poteen grogs. Sir Neville had enjoyed that first chat.

The young man was Maurice Tyson. He explained that he had newly arrived to take up a job as a house-master in the new school.

Within a few weeks the two men had become firm friends and Tyson had coaxed Sir Neville to revisit the scenes of his childhood and early manhood. To his surprise, he enjoyed himself immensely. He found the boys mannerly and great fun. He was touched to recognize himself in their pride and pleasure in the castle. He was even glad that he had moved aside and allowed so many youngsters to share and enjoy the experiences that he had had himself growing up.

From then on Randler visited several times a year, mostly to meet Maurice Tyson, but he also enjoyed chatting to whatever boys he encountered from time to time and feeding them up with exciting stories about the castle – some of them outrageously un-believable. He didn't mind, because he knew that the boys didn't mind either. They *wanted* to believe his stories. Young people have a different kind of truth. In many respects, Sir Neville was the youngest of them all.

The baronet spent the nights alone. Hannah prepared an evening meal for him and chastely withdrew. After supper, two or three nights a week, he would visit O'Hara's pub for two pints of

Guinness, never more, never less. He would chat to neighbours or play cards, usually twenty-five, bridge sometimes, rarely poker. Tyson attended the pub less regularly, but when he did they usually chatted to each other. Other nights, Sir Neville stayed home and read or watched television. He was not the nervous type and generally left the doors unlocked, whether or not he was in the house. It would certainly have been easy for someone to enter through the kitchen and approach his chair from the back without his being aware of it, particularly if he was watching television at the time.

It was well known in the staffroom that Maurice Tyson and Sir Neville Randler were good friends. When Sir Neville died a mere few weeks after Maurice Tyson – and in exactly the same manner – nobody thought that it was just a coincidence. The only difference between the two cases was that whereas Tyson was very probably standing when his assailant had taken him from behind, Sir Neville was sitting watching television, blessedly unaware of his peril until the attacker had suddenly jerked his head backwards and slit his throat. The television set was still on when the faithful Hannah had found her employer slaughtered in the morning.

Nobody had bothered to tell the police about the

close friendship between Tyson and Sir Neville, simply because it was only the second murder – manifestly done by the same person as the first – that made the relationship so obviously relevant. It was then that the police checked telephone records to see if the two men had been in contact shortly before Tyson died. Surprisingly, they found that Tyson had only a house telephone in his room, and that he did not even possess a cellphone. There was, however, a staff telephone in a booth beside the staff common room. Significantly, it was discovered that somebody, on the very night that Tyson had been murdered, had dialled Sir Neville's number from that booth. It was very likely to have been Tyson, first of all because he was the person who was most friendly with the baronet, and second, because the teaching staff would all have gone home by the time the call was made.

That was when Denis Lennon got lucky. Sir Neville did not receive many telephone calls, and he was not diligent about erasing his voicemail. Lennon checked and, sure enough, Maurice Tyson had indeed called him on the night he died. He did not get through, so he left a message. And that message was still on the answer machine weeks later: 'Neville, this is Maurice. Listen, I will call over tomorrow afternoon after class. I need your advice as never before – about a letter I received a few days ago. It is absolutely devastating! I don't want to talk about it on the phone. I'd really appreciate it if you can be there. Bye!'

Lennon shook his head in annoyance. 'Well, we never approached Sir Neville, because nobody told us that the two men even knew each other, let alone that they were friends. The irony is that I was looking forward to meeting him again after all those years since P. J. Connolly and myself had that famous booze-up with him. I just didn't think that it was important enough to waste an afternoon on a courtesy call. Perhaps if we had gone over to see him, he could have told us something that we badly needed to know.'

Molly exclaimed, equally exasperated: 'Why the hell didn't he come over to see us? He *must* have known that this telephone call from Tyson the night before he died was a vital clue. Tyson had just received a "devastating" letter. What was that about?'

Lennon shook his head. 'We just don't know. It might have been about the Percy Dandy affair. Perhaps Tyson had already confided in Randler about that, and Randler guessed that the devastating letter had something to do with that sordid business. Perhaps he just said to himself, when Tyson died the same night, that Tyson was dead, and there was no point in shaming his friend by dragging all that unsavoury mess up.'

'Another thing is,' Molly said thoughtfully, 'some people never listen to their messages. Sir Neville actually sounds as if he might well have been one of those. He might never have listened to the message.'

'Oh, it was listened to, all right, though perhaps not by Randler. But I have a further theory for you. Perhaps Sir Neville *did* know more than we know, about Dandy or about something else, and perhaps he decided to do his own sleuthing, and perhaps he got too close for comfort, and perhaps somebody took him out – as a sort of a left-handed compliment.'

There was one significant lead. It seemed clear that the assailant, having murdered Randler, had then begun to ransack the house in search of something. Drawers were pulled out, presses opened, seat cushions displaced from armchairs and sofas – not only in the sitting room, but all round the house. Even the mattresses on the beds seemed to have been lifted and dropped back. The airing cupboard in the bathroom had been sifted through, and Randler's dirty laundry had been emptied from its basket on to the floor of his bedroom. Cash did not seem to have been the objective of this rigorous search, because not only was Sir Neville's wallet in his pocket left untouched, but an unlocked drawer in his desk, containing several hundred euro scattered loose, was also undisturbed.

'Did the murderer find what he was looking for?' Molly wondered.

'The chances are, no, he did not,' Lennon replied.

'How do you work that out?' Molly enquired.

'We can assume that the killer took his victim by surprise, and cut his throat as he was watching television in the sitting room. We can also assume that he started his search there. But he had to continue searching, through all the reception rooms, then upstairs, from one bedroom to all the others, the closets and cupboards, even the hot press in the bathroom – and finally, in desperation no doubt, he turned out Sir Neville's dirty linen on the floor. He was really scraping the bottom of the barrel at that stage, wasn't he? So, no, I don't think he found what he was looking for.'

'And, the fundamental question' – Molly asked it – '*what* was he looking for? Could it be the "devastating letter" that Tyson was talking about in his message on the voicemail?'

'How could it be?' Lennon replied. 'Tyson was murdered before he had a chance to show that letter to Randler. He said that he would do so "tomorrow" – and, of course, tomorrow never came.'

'Well then,' Molly said, 'at least let us go through Randler's place with a fine comb, to see what the murderer can have been looking for – if it is still there. And let us also ransack Tyson's pad to find the letter that he so badly wanted to consult Randler about on the very night when he was murdered. In one or the other place, we must surely find *something*.'

Molly undertook to do the ransacking of Tyson's rooms at St Isidore's. She spent five hours on it. Tyson was an orderly man. He had box files for correspondence, marked clearly on the spine with the year in which a letter had been received, and the letters in each file were in strict chronological sequence. One could be sure that if Tyson wrote 1999 on a box file, it contained all and only the correspondence from that year. Even so, Molly went through all the files without exception. Her reasoning was that if Tyson had received a highly sensitive letter, he might have concealed it deliberately in a file to which it did not belong, so as to escape prying eyes. She also flicked rapidly through every book on Tyson's shelves for the same reason. Mercifully, there were not too many books – not that Tyson was not a reader: he was, but he hated clutter and he believed that the proper place for storing books was in a library.

There had been, certainly, sensitive letters over the years, letters from parents about family problems, health, money, or a marriage in difficulties. These letters typically would be asking the housemaster to look out for Tommy or Jack who was worried sick about a secret sorrow at home. There would also be letters complaining about teachers – 'Robert is really quite bright, but that horrible Miss Sweeney shouts at him, and the poor little fellow freezes up' etc. etc. – or about food ('Robert is getting too fat/thin/greasy/farts too much') or about Robert himself ('his nails are dirty, or he bites them, or he doesn't say "please" or "thanks", or his language is foul, or he never writes home') – 'and we don't do this e-mail thing, or still less that *texting* business – the very essence of analphabetism.' Which, of course, it is.

But there was nothing in the correspondence that could be described as so alarming that Tyson would

need to see Sir Neville urgently about it, and certainly
not received within the last three months.

In the days that lay ahead, Molly did have one
significant breakthrough. Rummaging in Sir
Neville's dustbin, outside the house, for either a
'devastating letter' or some other unknown object
that might have fired the murderer's passion to turn
the house upside down, she came across a slightly
unusual green folder with gold tips on all four
corners. It was empty and had nothing written on it.
There was nothing really remarkable about this
folder, except that Molly was sure that she had seen
it somewhere before.

The folder was sent for fingerprinting and, sure
enough, it bore Maurice Tyson's fingerprints. That,
in itself, was not very strange. The two men were
friendly. They had surely exchanged books, papers,
and documents of all sorts. But how could Molly
have seen this folder before, since she had never
been in St Isidore's before Tyson was murdered and
she had never been in Randler's house before he,
too, had gone the same way? The question of the
green folder niggled away at her to a surprising
degree.

'I hope I'm not getting obsessive,' she said
anxiously to Jan-Hein, who replied, 'Only about

potatoes,' which was intended as a discreet hint about certain features of her Irish cuisine. He had put on five pounds since their marriage.

It was at three o'clock the next morning that she awoke with a jolt and a cry, knocking Jan-Hein half out of the marriage bed, and remembering where she had seen the green folder before.

'It's impossible but it's true, Jan-Hein.'

'Whatever you say yourself, O great seer,' Jan-Hein replied, clinging to the edge of the mattress.

'Listen, Jan-Hein, this is so weird. I saw that folder in the photographs taken in Tyson's room the morning after his death. It was in there, or one very like it. It caught my attention. It is a bit unusual. I am nearly sure that, by the time Denis and I visited Tyson's room two days later, that folder simply was not in it any more. That is most unusual. By the time the photographs were taken Tyson's tower was under padlocks. Nobody could enter and, certainly, nobody could remove anything without express permission. That is standard police procedure. So how could this green folder walk out of Tyson's room very shortly after he was murdered, and when the room was already sealed, and how could the same green folder be found at Sir Neville's house after *he* was murdered?'

'Molly, what you are really saying is that both men were murdered for that green folder – or for the contents of the green folder, which has now been found empty, in a dustbin. No doubt the murderer has got the contents now and will, presumably, live happy ever after.'

Chapter Sixteen

For a third time Bertrand had his nightmare. As on the other two occasions, he was alone in the dormitory, because all the others had gone out for a barbecue. He was cold, lonely, and afraid. Then he was creeping down the stairs, presumably trying to join his companions. But those very companions were all shouting that he was the murderer, because he was covered from head to toe in Mr Tyson's blood.

At that point he woke up with a start and sat up. He could hear himself saying out loud and quite distinctly, 'Very well, I will tell you who the *real* murderer is.'

He was astounded to hear himself saying these words – and so confidently. He was even more astonished to know with quiet certainty that he would never have that nightmare again. His own words had had the effect of a self-exorcism, a healing.

At first, and for two or three days after that, Bertrand did not focus on the undertaking he had given, on the threshold of a dream, to name Tyson's killer. Surely that would not be possible for him, he reasoned, and anyhow, it was probably not necessary because the Irish police would have solved the mystery in the intervening weeks. So he was simply grateful for the fact that he could find once again in sleep some relief from the misery of his captivity.

But gradually Bertrand found that, in spite of himself, he was revisiting memories of that horrible night when Mr Tyson was killed. He realized that he had not wanted to do this. It was too frightening; indeed, by far the most scary thing that had ever happened to him in his entire life – well, until he was kidnapped. Perhaps there was a difference between an acute terror, like that of the night when Mr Tyson was murdered, and a chronic terror, like his present ongoing situation of being kidnapped. All his instinct had been to put the acute terror behind him, to suppress it, to get beyond it. Now it seemed to be precisely the chronic terror of his present situation that was forcing him to face up to, and giving him the courage to re-run in slow motion his mental video of, the events of that terrifying night. He was amazed to find that he had near perfect recall of those events, once he chose to exercise it.

He remembered that, coming in from the barbecue, at their first sight of the castle suddenly looming out of the darkness, he had been scared. He had even said so, and Martin Wilson had held him and made some comforting reply. Why had he been afraid? Was it a premonition, a feeling of something evil that was stirring?

Then, as they scuttled through the boiler house, they had all seemed to sense it – something inhuman, cruel, and implacable.

When they had got to the base of the staircase to their tower dormitory, they had heard someone coming down that stair. They had recoiled, terrified. Was this just the instinctive reaction of schoolboys, not wanting to be caught doing something naughty? Or was there something else, something more sinister? They knew that the person on the stairs was bound to see them, so the game was up. Yet every one of them, even the bravest, drew back in something like horror.

Finally, Bertrand forced himself to remember exactly what it had been like to lie in Mr Tyson's life's blood, to feel it seeping through his pyjamas, cold and wet against his skin. Instinctively, convulsively, he had rolled over on his bed, and lost all sense of coordination. He was soaked front and back. His head had plunged forward, his face, his mouth; he could even taste blood, Tyson's blood! He forced himself to think about these things exactly as they had happened. Hidden memories stirred.

Bertrand had said many prayers since his ordeal had begun, the simple and very powerful prayers of a child. He felt now that this was a decisive moment. He had made up his mind, or rather he had been *led*, gently but firmly, to confront a great and powerful evil. He knew in his heart that the battle had already begun. He was utterly alone, starved, filthy, and cold. He would have to be very, very brave. 'God help me,' he prayed, 'God help me.'

It was night. For once, Bertrand was sleeping. Someone came into the room and turned on the light. Instinctively, the boy twisted his face away and buried it in the pillow. He had become used to semi-darkness by day and total blackness by night. After several weeks, perhaps as much as a month, without ever seeing the light of day, he was well on his way to turning into a human mole. He had never seen the electric light on in this room since his arrival there.

His visitor was Snake-Eyes, unaccompanied. He closed the door behind him. The boy was suddenly fully awake. He smelled danger. He also smelled drink, a lot of drink, prevailing over even the pong of his own unwashed body and clothes. He sat up. The man advanced unsteadily into the room, drawing cruel lips back from yellow fangs in a grin with all the warmth of a crocodile contemplating a tasty supper.

'Bertrand, you are free. Get up! Your papa has paid the ransom – five million of the best!'

So his father had paid all that money! He felt tears of gratitude and love welling up in his eyes.

'But don't worry. Papa can well afford it,' Snake-Eyes continued. 'Besides, I went light on him.'

He paused, then went on very deliberately, 'Because I'm sweet on you, Bertrand. You're a nice little fellow – brave too. So, before I let you go, I want you to be nice to me. Hum? Let's have a little fun!'

He made an obscene gesture that Bertrand had never seen before but instantly understood in a flush of shame and horror.

Suddenly it all came together for the boy with terrible clarity. This devil-man, whom he had instinctively loathed from the very start, would never let him go home to his parents. How could he have hoped that he ever would? Bertrand would recognize him anywhere in the world, and his two accomplices. The police had loads of mugshots of terrorists and of common criminals. He would certainly be able to lead them to the gang, or at least to one or other member of it.

Besides, this monster, utterly devoid of pity or feelings, had no further use for his captive, now that he had his papa's money safely in his greedy claws. He would never let him go home. Fun! The mention of fun sealed his doom. This animal's concept of fun would be to rob him of his nascent manhood, to humiliate him utterly, to take his pleasure in a child's pain and desperation, then to kill him. It came to the boy overwhelmingly that he was certainly going to die, not just because he could identify his kidnappers, but because if Papa ever heard of what was happening in this room at this very moment, he would follow his son's rapist to hell and kill him with his bare hands.

How would Snake-Eyes kill him? Would he strangle him, suffocate him, stab him, drown him?

Did it matter? Before this night was out, he would end up in the Seine with a bag of cement around his neck.

Bertrand slid off the bed quickly. Snake-Eyes stumbled towards him, the sour smell of drink mingling with the acrid stench of violent sexual arousal. Through his greasy clothing, the boy could even *see* his bloated passion. He shuddered in terror.

The man was on his knees now to unlock the chain holding Bertrand to the bed.

'There now, you are free, so be nice to me,' he snarled, grasping the boy's ankle in a grip of steel, making it plain to him that the only freedom was to be Snake-Eyes's own freedom to manoeuvre and manipulate his victim according to the whims of his depavity.

Bertrand was no match for this hardened criminal but, even in his extreme terror, he was fully deter-mined to go down fighting. Necessity is the mother of invention, they say, and this boy, whose need was desperate, had suddenly invented something to do, something defiant and even grotesquely funny, something that would be outrageous in any other situation, and something that, against all the odds, did make him feel sublimely *free* – no doubt for the last time.

While the man was still on his knees clutching his victim's ankle, Bertrand slewed to one side, bent from the waist, and hauled up the heavy bucket containing at least two weeks' urine and excrement. Swivelling again to face his tormentor, he crashed the bucket down with all his force over the monster's head.

Uttering a strangled cry, Snake-Eyes staggered to his feet, shit, piss, vomit, and smeared soggy papers cascading down his whole body as from some surreal cornucopia. He took two frantic steps forward, slipped on the scum and slime, toppled from his full height and, still with the bucket jammed on his head, crashed with all his weight on to the iron fender of the fireplace.

The percussion of his fall, bucket helmet striking iron fender – though muted somewhat by excrement past its best – yielded three mellow notes of a tonality, Bertrand thought, reminiscent of Beethoven's Pastoral Symphony.

He waited to be murdered. Seconds passed. Nothing happened. Snake-Eyes did not stir. After a month's captivity, culminating in the imminent prospect of sexual violation and death, the boy had to catch himself up. In the twinkling of an eye, his situation had utterly changed. For a minute, which is a very long time, he stood with his hands hanging, not knowing what to do. Then, as if somebody had thrown a switch, he spun into action. Racing towards the door, already noting how creaky his whole body had become because of his enforced immobility, he flung it open and was through in a flash, and already on tiptoe. Was there anyone else in the apartment? What time of the night was it? He had no idea.

There seemed to be about six rooms in the unit. Two doors were open, a toilet and a kitchen. There was a pencil of light under a door at the farthest end of the hallway. Halfway down was the hall door. It was locked but it was not difficult to work out how to open it. He did so and scampered through.

Exhilaration hit him like a tsunami. *Free!* He wanted to whoop, to slide down the banisters, to turn somersaults, to punch the air, to fall on his knees. Most of all he wanted to shout the news so loud that his parents would hear it immediately. He knew that they had been thinking of him, praying for him, worried out of their minds every single second since he had been kidnapped. He wanted to give them the biggest hugs, the most enormous kisses that he ever could manage – like a vacuum cleaner, he thought delightedly, and he laughed out loud for the first time in a month. He was sure this was by far the longest time in his whole life that he had *not* laughed.

He began to take the stairs four by four, and promptly collapsed in a heap. He laughed again. He was definitely out of training for steeplechasing. He contented himself with two by two. He whizzed round a corner, and collided violently with Bullet-Head, who fell back on his substantial rump.

'What the fuck are you doing out here?' he bellowed.

Bertrand, all engines suddenly thrown into reverse, was already beating a hasty retreat, pounding randomly on doors that he met in flight. As he ran he thought frantically of his options. Would he race back to the apartment where he had been imprisoned and lock the door against Bullet-Head? But the other kidnapper was more than likely in there, and Snake-Eyes must have revived in the interval and would show him no mercy. He would certainly add torture to his list of rape and murder.

By the time he drew level with the apartment door his options had been reduced to one – to continue upstairs, to God knows what or where. Even with the disadvantage of cramped muscles and sinews, the younger man fared better running up stairs. So he had widened the gap between himself and his pursuer. But if once he let himself be cornered, he knew he would be easy meat.

The next floor was the uppermost, an afterthought, where some enterprising developer had created a mansard space behind a shallow parapet that fronted the roof on two sides. The gable ends of the adjoining buildings at each end were higher and rose as solid blank walls. At the top of the stairs, Bertrand was confronted with a door, on which he pounded, with no result. Behind him there was a mansard window on to the roof, through which he scrambled. This was to be the battleground for his last stand. He summed it up at a glance. A channel behind the parapet to catch the rainwater, front and back of the building. These two trenches, extending the full length of the building, were separated by a ridge-roof, punctuated by mansard windows. All the windows were barred.

Bullet-Head scrambled on to the roof. Bertrand immediately went over the ridge and dropped into the trench on the other side. An interminable game of cat and mouse began. Bertrand was trying to lure his pursuer sufficiently far from the window at the top of the stairs to enable him to steal back across the ridge and in that window. Once on the stairs, he would make a supreme effort to run, tumble and, if necessary, fall down them like a bolt of greased lightning. Bullet-Head fully understood the boy's strategy. He made successive vicious thrusts to take Bertrand off his guard or to keep him pinned down, but he never left his flank exposed. The window to a possible escape remained inaccessible.

It promised to be a long night, and it was cold. Bertrand heard a clock somewhere sounding two solemn chimes. He had been right, they were on Montmartre. He could not see the river but he could hear the growl of traffic along its banks and he could see the basilica to the southwest. Sleep was the enemy. He must stay awake. He must do things. He tried shouting – things like *Au secours!* or *À moi!* – but his voice was weak and, at two o'clock in the morning, nobody seemed to be listening. Besides, he did not want this gorilla to hear the terror that he felt sure his voice was betraying. So he changed his mind about shouting. Instead he broke a window with a loose slate between the bars, in the hope that this might trigger a burglar alarm. No joy there.

He *must* stay awake, alert, he *must*! But Bertrand was exhausted. He had been starved for a month. The intense emotions and the sheer physical efforts of the last hour had drained his last reserves. He crept from his trench to the summit of the roof to force himself to do something. From this position he could see over the parapet and into the street, five storeys down. Abruptly he felt dizzy. His stomach heaved. Shaking violently, sweating, he broke wind uncontrollably and filthied himself. He thought confusedly, as in a dream, that perhaps that would persuade Snake-Eyes to just want to kill him, and not to do anything else. He sank to his knees, lowered his head to the ridge of the roof, and simply lay there.

Bertrand had grown his hair long in Ireland – for fun, or just to experiment. When he got back to France, his Jesuit *préfet des études* was more than dubious. Was this a prelude to a lethal attack of free-thinking and fornication? Actually, both Papa and Maman rather liked his hair that way. It was flaxen – so unusual in a French boy – and silken. In his parents' view, it made him look more angelic than ever. After a month in captivity, in which he had never been able to wash his hair, it looked neither flaxen nor silken, not to speak of angelic. It was matted and greasy, a nest of vipers, Medusa-like, a wild jungle of rats' tails.

Bullet-Head had bided his time, seething with vicious anger, but never losing contact with his quarry. At last, he saw his opportunity and pounced.

In seconds he was dragging the boy by the hair over to his own side of the roof, then down into the gutter, where he propped him against the parapet and beat him with closed fists: his eyes, his nose and mouth, then savage jabs at his stomach, and under the belt where it hurts. Then he dragged him, again by the hair, bent double and staggering, down the flight of stairs and into the same apartment he had left so joyfully earlier in the evening.

Chapter Seventeen

Blaise Pierce had been deeply shocked by Inspector Quilligan's insinuation that Maurice Tyson might have behaved 'inappropriately' with some of the boys in his charge. The inspector seemed to believe that this misbehaviour had even been so gross that, years afterwards, one or other of these boys would actually want to cut Tyson's throat.

It was true, as Pierce had told the inspector, that he and Tyson had never discussed such questions as homosexuality or pederasty, or at least never in personal terms. He would have assumed that Tyson was as fully committed as he himself was never to take advantage in even the slightest way of any youth in his charge. That was one of the reasons why he himself had never considered applying for employment as a housemaster. Frankly, he was not sure that he could take all that closeness – physical and emotional – to boys in dormitories, showers, changing rooms and, above all, in the inner space of his psyche and theirs. He was quite lucid about the possibility that teenaged boys, bewildered about their own sexuality, might attempt to lead him into an emotional, and even a physical, relationship. He knew that such things did happen. His housemaster colleagues laughed them off, but he knew that they themselves had to be vigilant and of total integrity in such situations. He was not certain that he would have that virtue.

In his young days Pierce had read – in French of course – *La Nausée* by Jean-Paul Sartre. This was the first book he had read that dealt with what is now commonly called child abuse. It is not the main theme of the book, which is concerned with more abstruse philosophical topics, but it was Pierce's most vivid memory of it. He identified with one of the characters in that book, the *Autodidacte*, a lonely man of humble origins and limited education. The centre of this man's life was the public library in the small town where he lived. He had set himself to read every book in the library from A to Z, and so to become wise, knowing at last the meaning of the universe and of his own existence in it. It was probably quite a small library because at the end of a few years the *Autodidacte* had got as far as the letter B, or perhaps C, or even D. He probably did not understand much of all that he was reading, but he pressed ahead doggedly with his project, counting on the cumulative effect of all his laborious study.

There was, however, a distraction to this work of the spirit in the shape of two boys, perhaps in their early teens, who also frequented the library. These youngsters were not exactly dedicated scholars. They attended the library for want of other entertainments and derived such amusement as they could from the books and from their fellow patrons. The *Autodidacte* found these boys strangely troubling and exciting – their vivaciouness, their looks, their innocence. They in their turn – not so completely innocent as they looked – sensed his excitement and were excited by it. They sniffed a powerful chemistry in the air, and they knew that in some mysterious way, it was they who had been given power over this adult. Breathless with anticipation – of what? They had no distinct idea – they loitered, and lingered, and trailed their coats. Knowingly, and at the same time largely ignorant, they led him on, and on. At last he did it, he dropped his hand, he invaded their private space, in some way; in whatever way – he went too far!

Suddenly there was pandemonium. The *Autodidacte* had done something frightful, unimaginable – and in the very middle of the reading room in the public library, in broad daylight. Cries of outrage. He was cast into exterior darkness where there would indeed be weeping and gnashing of teeth. Never to be permitted to enter the library again, he was condemned to wander like a lost soul until the day he died. The tenuous meaning of his life was extinguished by that one impulsive gesture.

Blaise Pierce was never going to allow himself to stray or to be betrayed into a situation like that. He was sure that he was neither homosexual nor a paedophile, in the sense that neither grown men nor pre-pubertal children, of either gender, had any sexual attraction for him. But he recognized that – as the ancient Greeks had so well understood – pedagogy and ephebophilia can often go hand in hand, and that he himself was not insensitive to the charms of winsome youths who had not yet had all the female hormones boiled out of them.

He admired Maurice Tyson who, unmarried like himself, still had the strength of character and the integrity to be around teenaged boys. He also understood very well the relative harshness of Tyson's early years as a housemaster. This was quite simply a defence mechanism by which Tyson kept his charges at a safe distance. But he was a kind man at heart. As he learned self-confidence and to trust in his charisma, he became less defensive and more able to show affection.

The more Pierce thought about Percy Dandy's allegations, the less credible did they seem to be. But Dandy was alive and saying these things, and Tyson was dead and unable to defend himself. Besides, Dandy's version did have the merit that it provided a possible motive for Tyson's killing: revenge for depraved acts at the expense of defenceless children. The only other motive that had been suggested was that Tyson had got in the way of a kidnap attempt. That, too, seemed fairly unlikely.

One night, a few days after Inspector Quilligan's visit, Pierce was lying awake endlessly circling around these confusing and conflicting issues. It suddenly occurred to him to consult the school almanac, to see who had been Dandy's contemporaries in the school, particularly those who had been in the same class. It is a truism that a boy's own companions know him best. Teachers and housemasters do not actually believe this, because they think that they have superior rights and X-ray vision to read all their charges like open books – witness the fatuities written in school reports. But, very occasionally, they will concede that the truism is probably, in some sense, also true.

Pierce got up out of his bed and went in search of the almanac, which was not published quite yearly but, when it did appear, contained useful final year lists of all the classes back to the foundation of the school. Taking into account that Dandy had left early, Pierce had to calculate which group he had belonged to. Once he had resituated Dandy with his actual contemporaries, the rest was easy. There had been thirty-five of them. Two were dead – predictably for men so young – one as a result of a road accident, the other from an overdose of heroin. Nine were living abroad, and three had sunk without trace. That left twenty-one. It did not take Pierce too long to establish a short list of three. There was Niall Fitzsimons, who was a lawyer, and a good one; Michael Murray, an accountant, reputed to be both honest and brilliant; and Mossy McLysaght, a nightclub owner, which was undoubtedly a strange occupation for an alumnus of St Isidore's.

Returning to bed, to his surprise he had already decided that McLysaght was his man. 'Horses for courses,' he said to himself sleepily, and slept soundly.

In the morning, he had not changed his mind. He telephoned Quilligan.

'Inspector, we left things, when last we met, suspended from a question mark.'

Quilligan still had mild difficulties with that kind of English, so he said 'Yes', leaving room for it to be, 'Yes?' Blaise Pierce explained the evolution in his thought since that first evening.

'I really think you should talk to Mossy McLysaght. He is the most likely person to still be in touch with Percy Dandy, and indeed to be able to give you the measure of the man.'

So Quilligan called to see McLysaght at his nightclub, spelt Nite Klub, and called Pieces-of-Eight, in Mary Street in Dublin's inner city. He left his visit until late afternoon on the assumption that 'nite-klub' proprietors are not early risers. He was surprised to find a handsome, smiling man, manifestly fit, who told him that he went jogging almost every day in the Phoenix Park for forty minutes from 8.20 a.m. When within seconds of being apprised of the topic for conversation, McLysaght had described Percy Dandy as 'a little fart' and, on further information being supplied, as 'a complete bollocks', Quilligan felt that they did indeed talk the same language and could do business together.

McLysaght did not have particularly sweet memories of either St Isidore's or Mr Tyson, who would still have been in his martinet mode in those days. He described St Isidore's as 'a bit of a concentration camp' and Tyson as 'a fierce bastard'. He further expressed himself totally incredulous that any boy, 'no matter how weird', could find Tyson sexually attractive. 'It would have taken more than two Mars bars and a bag of crisps, I can tell you!' He continued, 'Look, I didn't like Tyson. As far as I was concerned, he was full of shit, like punctuality, tidiness, hard work, a real nerd. But to give the fellow his due, he was completely fair. Everyone got the same crap; just, I suppose, some of us were more house trained than others. Actually, I'm sorry we never met in later life. We would probably have got on very well. When I heard he was dead I didn't particularly care. Now, when you talk to me about him, I realize that I did respect him. Perhaps I was just at that age – I guess I still am! Listen, warts and all, Tyson was a – what do you call it? I mean he wasn't in it for himself. I just don't believe he ever messed around with any of the kids. He was Mr Integrity, what's the adjective for that? Hey, I guess that means that I actually respected him a lot. I must really reopen his case!'

Quilligan and the 'nite-klub' owner talked some more. They did indeed speak the same language. Eventually McLysaght said: 'Look, I do know Dandy quite well, to my sorrow – too well. He's always scrounging money off me. I think I'll set up a commission of inquiry, like as to where he is going with this shit.'

'Commission of inquiry?' Quilligan raised an eyebrow.

'Just me, and some of the other cardinals who know old Dandybones well, and who are used to his little ways. Well, we'll just use gentle persuasion to get him to empty out his sack – just to see what he has at the bottom of it. Nothing smelly, I hope. If he is on the level, okay, Tyson deserves it, or his reputation, or St Isidore's. The damages will be astronomical, and it will be the first serious money Dandy has ever earned in his whole life.'

'If he is not on the level . . . ?'

'If he is not on the level – Do you really need to know?'

Quilligan did not answer the question. McLysaght laughed out loud. He said, 'Don't worry, no violence or anything like that. Just counselling, earnest counselling. I owe old Tyson at least that much – the old bastard!'

Chapter Eighteen

When Bullet-Head had dragged the boy into the apartment, he hit him a few more times but, this time, more open-hand slaps than fists. In the light, he could see the cumulative effects of what this small creature had suffered during a month's captivity, and especially as a result of his own handiwork that night: a half-closed eye, a cut lip, a broken tooth, a bloody nose, and more, no doubt, under the surface. He felt a flicker of shame, or at least something like sympathy, when he thought about what Snake-Eyes would probably be doing to the boy in a few minutes. He had seen him with others – and it had not been easy to watch, even for a certified psychopath like himself.

Bertrand was swaying on his feet. He half tottered, half crawled into the toilet he had seen earlier and sank to his knees. He vomited into the bowl the meagre contents of his stomach, then continued retching miserably. Bullet-Head almost went over to help him, but hardened his heart, and didn't. That failure in humanity and basic decency probably saved Bertrand's life.

Gradually the retching subsided. He felt very weak, but better, and more lucid. The germ of an idea was forming. Could it be that he was not finished yet? He stood up slowly, walked haltingly to the door, towards Bullet-Head. He even sketched a grotesque grin, and Bullet-Head, incredibly, grinned back. It was the beginning and the end of a beautiful relationship. Suddenly, Bertrand slammed that door, locked, and bolted it. A split-second later, but too late, the psychopath splattered himself against the wood. It was solid oak, the jambs firmly set into the walls. The lock and the bolt were of pre-war quality, from an era when evacuation of the bowels was regarded as a state secret. No way could that door be breached or removed except by serious tools and loud hammering – unthinkable in the middle of the night unless they wanted to set the whole house-hold and neighbourhood on the alert. They would have to wait until morning. Within the timescales that Bertrand had been facing during that night, 'until morning' seemed like a very handsome remission. The boy lay on the hard, cold tiles and fell fast asleep.

There had been a few complaints about loud knocking on various doors in the same apartment building during the night. That had been when Bertrand was running back up the stairs, pursued by Bullet-Head, and desperate to get in any door to safety. People had been afraid to open their doors, but they did telephone the police to protest, as if the whole disgraceful episode had been meticulously planned in the *gendarmerie*. The most popular adjectives to describe the events of the night were *inouï, inadmissible, déplorable, dégueulasse* and *insupportable*. The callers described themselves and their families unto the third and fourth generations as *désespéré(e)(s), effaré(e)(s)*, and even *effarouché(e)(s)*.

The duty officer, who was used to this kind of thing – because the French love to complain and to use all those lovely adjectives – believed that these good citizens should just roll over and go to sleep again. So he promised the imminent arrival of the French Foreign Legion, the CRS, and *Les Pompiers*, which is the fire brigade, and did nothing whatsoever about it.

It was at about two o'clock in the morning that an insomniac, who was standing in his pyjamas at a fifth-floor window, smoking a cigarette, became aware of an unusual piece of theatre on the roof of a building opposite. At first, it seemed that a full-grown man and a small boy were playing some sort of chasing game – in the small hours of the morning, by the light of a silvery moon, *bon sang!* When the grown man suddenly sprang up the roof and dragged the boy down by the hairs of his head, the observer knew that this was anything but a game, *nom d'un chien!* When the man then proceeded to bash the child with his closed fists, *merde alors, NON!* He waited no longer: he called the police

All France and most of Europe had heard about the kidnap. Bertrand's photograph had been in all the media. *Adorable!* was the unanimous verdict. *You could eat him!* Everyone's idea of *un gentil garçon*, he had captured the imagination of a whole nation. Could it be? the midnight watcher asked himself. Could it be? the police telephonist asked himself. He put the

call through to the special headquarters in the *préfec-*
ture on the Île de la Cité, which was monitoring the
case day and night. Inspecteur Banet, who took
the call, exclaimed, *C'y est*, That's it! Earlier in the
day, they had identified a stolen car believed to
have been used in the kidnap, but now abandoned
in the vicinity of Saint-Eustache and Les Halles. This
at least seemed to indicate that the kidnappers could
be holed up somewhere on *la rive droite*.

Banet sent a team immediately to infiltrate the
target building and to liaise with some of those who
had made indignant phone calls earlier in the night.
He himself would follow within the hour with a strong
contingent of anti-terrorist specialists, equipped for
every conceivable scenario.

By 4 a.m. marksmen were covering the main entrance
of the target building. Banet had the option of closing
the road and evacuating neighbouring buildings. He
decided not to do either before getting up to speed
with the best intelligence available to him. His
advance team had made contact with a Dr Courbet
and his wife who lived on the third floor. Courbet
was a retired military doctor who had called up the
police earlier in the night to complain about wild
pounding on his and other doors. He was feeling

distinctly abashed now at the possibility that what he had taken for a drunken prank had in fact been the desperate act of a child in danger and in distress. He and his wife were eager to cooperate in any way. By the time Banet had climbed to the third floor, his team had already established a sort of base camp in the Courbet apartment.

Dr Courbet and his wife knew all about the other tenants in their building. There was a Greek couple with two small children on the ground floor. He was a journalist with one of the Athens dailies and she was a chiropodist. An ageing star of stage and screen and her current toy-boy conducted a turbulent love-hate relationship on the second floor. The Courbets and their grown-up son, Jean-Claude, who was doing his National Service, occupied the third floor. On the fifth floor the mansard apartment was unoccupied by night and, in fact, used as a depot for antiques destined for a fashionable but minuscule boutique in the heart of Montmartre. Hence the bars on the windows.

That left the fourth floor. The apartment on that floor had been occupied for the entire summer by as many as nine or ten Polish students who had various holiday jobs around the city. They had been surprisingly quiet aand refreshingly mannerly.

Shortly after the students had left in mid-October to return to their various academies, three rather tough characters had moved in. They did not fraternize with the other tenants but, to the extent that they had to run the gauntlet of determined cross-examiners like Madame Courbet, it had been ascertained that they had a two-month lease, with an option for an extra month. They were working, it was understood, on *un projet technique* which would not take too long. Curiously, they did not move out of the apartment very much, to advance their *projet*, and they did not seem to do any serious cooking, being content with a diet of takeaways or bought-in meals. With the wisdom of hindsight, it figured that their *projet technique* was to keep a twenty-four-hour watch over a kidnap victim.

It had been noted, too, that the window of their front bedroom had been blacked out by day and by night. Once again, people had wondered in an unfocused way what this might be all about. The police reasoned, perfectly correctly, that it meant that Bertrand was being kept in that room. The purpose of the screening was to keep people from seeing into the room, Bertrand from seeing out of the room, and anyone at all, in or out of the room, from seeing eye to eye.

At half past five exactly, Inspecteur Banet pounded on the door of the apartment, loud-hailing an introduction, *Police*, adding a pressing invitation to come out with one's hands up. Twice he repeated this ritual. Then they sledgehammered the door, bullets being considered too dangerous in the circumstances.

Bullet-Head, whose neat and naive plans for the next morning had been so rudely interrupted by the police action, was feeling very put out. He had envisaged knifing Jacques, strangling Bertrand, and emigrating to South America with five million euro. He could not be described as the adaptable sort. On the contrary, he had an abnormally low threshold for frustration of any kind, as the few luckless women who had consented to live with him soon discovered. His average time span for intimate relationships was four days, or a weekend, whichever was the shorter.

He had had a major row with Jacques during the night about the necessity of strangling Bertrand which, of course, they both knew that Snake-Eyes had fully intended to do, once the ransom had been paid. Disliking arguments – and to that extent a man of peace – Bullet-Head had resolved to murder both man and boy and to take all the money for himself. This was made possible, of course, by the untimely death of Snake-Eyes, whom the two had discovered together – to their great surprise but without any great sense of grief – when they went looking for him to seek instructions. Neither of them could work out why their chief had ended up with his head stuck in a bucket of excrement. They speculated whether this might be one of his less socially acceptable perversions – of which he had not a few – which had got too exciting for him, inducing heart failure.

But Bullet-Head was a pragmatist, and Snake-Eyes could now best be described as 'a fact on the ground'. He decided to run with it. Accordingly, he had devoted the remaining hours of the night to laying plans for an orderly withdrawal. He must first secure tools to open the lavatory door. Before opening it, he would kill Jacques. He had a very neat and effective way to do that. True, he would have preferred a firearm, but the sound of a shot would have been a complete no-no in an apartment house where everyone stuck their noses into everybody else's business. Second, he would dispose of the boy, without regret. He was a damn nuisance. Third, he would transport the ransom money, which was surprisingly bulky, to a safe address. Last, he would simulate an electrical fire which would conveniently destroy the apartment and all the evidence it contained without consuming too much of Paris at the same time.

In other words, Bullet-Head was stark, raving mad. If Snake-Eyes was the more vicious, his side-kick was much more dangerous when deprived of his boss's criminal intelligence. Then he was simply a rabid dog.

The sudden interruption of the police at the door of the apartment drove him quite berserk. It meant that he had to cancel all his plans for the coming day, and probably for the rest of his life too. He was not going to collect the tools. He was not going to kill Jacques and the boy – which meant that they had made a fool of him. He was not going to transport five million euro anywhere. He was not going to torch the apartment. He was never going to travel to South America, and he was never going to live happily ever after. *Instead* . . . The instead did not bear thinking of.

As the sledgehammers stove in the door, Bullet-Head levelled his revolver. Jacques, taking his life in his hands, shouted, 'Look out! He has a gun.'

Bullet-Head swivelled his gun on him, took aim, then decided that Jacques could wait. There were priorities.

Banet called up a sharp-shooter, then shouted to the sledgehammer-wielders, 'Use a drill. Get me a hole, two metres from the floor.'

They pierced a hole about five feet up in the door. Whether or not Bullet-Head read accurately what was going to happen next, he suddenly released a burst of rapid fire in the direction of the police which did not hit anybody but could just as well have killed everybody. Banet threw a quick glance through the peephole.

'You got him,' he rapped. 'Shoot. That's an order.'

The sharp-shooter looked once, shot him in the face, one bullet. He spun like a top, and half his skull flew off. Jacques shouted again, 'There's only me left. I'm coming out.'

He was surrendering. Banet shouted, 'Step forward where I can see you.'

Jacques came forward with his hands up. The sledge-hammerers completed their work. The kidnapper stood in the doorway, still with arms raised. A cop frisked him thoroughly.

'Clean,' he reported.

'Where is the kid?' Banet asked.

The man gestured with his head to the lavatory in the apartment behind him. 'In the john. He locked himself in.'

Banet pushed him ahead of himself and two policemen with machine guns at the ready. They entered the apartment cautiously, using Jacques as a shield. If this was a terrorist job, there could still be a suicide fireworks display to round it off. A booby trap: the sting in the tail of the scorpion. Jacques could be even more dangerous than his recently deceased melodramatic companion.

They advanced to the door indicated.

'Bertrand,' Banet called, 'you are safe. We are the police, come to set you free. Open the door. Don't be afraid.'

There was a pause. They heard the key turning, the bolt being drawn back. Then the door opened slowly. The boy stood there with all the shy self-consciousness of Lazarus emerging from the tomb. Indeed, the resemblance to the Biblical model was surreal. At some stage during the night, in an effort to keep himself warm, Bertrand had swathed his arms and his legs in yards of toilet paper. He was looking like anyone's mummy out for a stroll.

Banet lunged forward and engulfed the boy in a bear-hug. Before they rushed him out of the room – still regarded as potentially a minefield – Bertrand bowed ever so slightly to Jacques. Without a trace of irony he said, 'Well, goodbye. Thanks for the things that you did for me. You were the best. Good luck. I hope that things work out for you in the end.'

They brought him down to the Courbet apartment, where the doctor and his wife smothered him with hugs and kisses. They fed him, and scrubbed him in a hot bath – two hot baths actually: he was so dirty that they had to change the water halfway through. They cut his toenails and fingernails – but not his nice hair – and dressed him in clothes which had belonged to their own son when he was growing up, an approximate fit, to be sure, but the clothes were soft, clean, and warm. Bertrand thought that he had never been more comfortable in his entire life.

The boy's parents arrived back in Paris by mid-morning. On hearing the joyous news of their son's release, they had rushed back by private plane from Marseille, where they also had a house. They found him sleeping peacefully on the sofa in the Courbet sitting room. He woke in his mother's arms, and thought that he had indeed died and gone to heaven. Practically the first thing he said to his father was, 'Papa, did Toulouse beat Ulster?'

His father replied: '*Hélas, mon vieux: trente à trois en faveur d'Ulster!*'

To which Bertrand responded with feeling, '*Zut alors! Quelle catastrophe!*'

Later in the day, Inspector Quesnel telephoned Superintendent Lennon. The news of Bertrand's release had been flashed round the world within minutes of the event, based on a police statement that, acting on intelligence reports, officers of a specialist unit had stormed an address in central Paris. Bertrand Laporte had been liberated unharmed. One man had opened fire on the security forces and had been shot dead. Another body had been recovered from the scene. A third man had been taken into custody. Further arrests were not excluded. A large sum of money, believed to have been paid as ransom, had also been recovered from the house. The statement added that Bertrand Laporte would be reunited with his parents as soon as they had arrived from Marseille and that, in the meantime, he was being cared for by friends.

Lennon and Molly were intrigued by this statement, for what it said, what it omitted, and what it left ambiguous. Who or what was the 'specialist unit'? Did the presence of that unit, or the mention of 'intelligence reports', imply that there was a terrorist dimension to the kidnap? What was the significance of 'another body' which had been recovered from the scene? Above all, what relevance, if any, had the kidnap of the French boy to the murder of Maurice Tyson – and/or even of Sir Neville Randler?

Inspector Quesnel's telephone call was eagerly awaited. When it eventually came through, Molly was with Lennon so he put his telephone on loud-speaker so that she could share in the conversation. Quesnel got straight to the point.

'There does not seem to be a link to any terrorist group. The three men involved – of whom two are already dead – are, or were, well known to the police as hardened criminals. They were not such as would be employed, directly or indirectly, by any terrorist organization. Terrorists are dangerous fanatics, but they are also dangerous idealists.

'The simple fact seems to be that the publicity generated by the Irish episode drew the attention of these men to Bertrand, and, more precisely, to the wealth of his father. So they kidnapped him. They collected the ransom eventually, five million euro in cash, in spite of our best efforts to prevent the boy's father from paying anything – and then they intended to kill the boy, one of them having buggered him in advance.'

'Good God! Why?'

'He had peculiar tastes, and a motto: waste not, want not.'

'That is disgusting,' Molly exclaimed.

'A man called Singe,' Quesnel resumed, 'which means monkey in French.'

'How perfect!' Molly said. 'The French have a word for everything.'

'Bertrand up-ended his chamber pot on Monsieur Singe's head,' the inspector continued. 'It was the only thing he could do to defend himself.'

'Well, good for him!' Lennon said approvingly.

'To his extreme surprise, he killed the guy outright.'

'To my extreme surprise too!' Lennon said.

'Whatever did the scumbag die of?' Molly enquired.

'A cracked skull – he fell with the pot on his head – and inhaling shit.'

'Not a nice way to go!' Lennon commented.

Quesnel thought about that for a moment and replied: 'No, but poetic justice none the less.'

'What do you mean?' Molly asked.

'Work it out,' was the answer.

On the day that Bertrand was liberated, Dr Fisher received a handwritten letter from Percy Dandy.

Neither the handwriting nor the epistolary style reflected much credit on St Isidore's as his former academy. One might almost have said that the writer's heart was not really in that letter. It began with the statement that whereas he, Percival Dandy, had instituted legal proceedings against St Isidore's School on foot of allegations of sexual abuse by the late Maurice Tyson, he wished it to be known that:

The said proceedings were discontinued, terminated, withdrawn (and several more past participles meaning the same thing).

No such sexual abuse – nor any other abuse (physical, verbal, or et cetera) – had ever taken place since the dawn of history in St Isidore's.

The aforesaid Percival Dandy was prostrate with grief and wanted to apologize abjectly for having made these FALSE allegations.

The firm of Purley and Flint had been discontinued, terminated, withdrawn, and dumped in the rubbish bin of forensic history, as solicitors for the said Percy Dandy.

Quilligan telephoned Lennon to report on these developments, which he had in turn learned about from McLysaght.

'How in blazes kate do you do it, Jim?' Lennon asked. Quilligan had known better than to ask McLysaght the same question.

'I just appeal to their better nature,' Quilligan replied sanctimoniously, confident that he would not be believed.

Molly's comment was: 'At this stage, we were almost counting on Tyson abusing Dandy, so that we could say that he abused Seán Gilhooly too – and that with all this abusing, no wonder that somebody murdered Tyson. Well, now we are back at square one, meaning terrorism, only now we've got to make it explain how Tyson *and* Sir Neville got murdered. I suppose Sir Neville got in the way of *another* kidnap. This must be the kidnap capital of the world.'

'It makes you proud,' Lennon quipped, 'don't it?'

'Hardly, because the very same morning that we receive news from France that Bertrand's abduction had nothing to do with terrorism, we also receive news that Tyson's murder had nothing to do with child abuse.'

Chapter Nineteen

Stan de Witt, the young South African assistant housemaster, had been nominated by Dr Fisher the morning after Maurice Tyson was murdered to take charge of the Middle House 'on a temporary basis'. He was the one to whom Tyson's boys had gone running in terror on the previous night. From the word go, he had done so well from everyone's point of view that nobody was in any hurry to replace him. Not only in the first twenty-four hours, when the whole school was on the brink of hysteria, but also in the long aftermath of such a tragedy, Stan had proved himself a rock of good sense, and, indeed, of real wisdom. For the six boys in Tyson's tower, his concern, understanding, and support had been enormously helpful in bringing them through a horrific experience relatively unscathed.

The police, too, had appreciated Stan. He it was who had invited them into the refectory on the first day of their inquiry. He had facilitated the preliminary contacts with the six boys most immediately concerned with that inquiry, making sure – in the measure that this was possible – that they were not intimidated or apprehensive. Once again, it was Stan who had organized the relaxed and very useful exchanges between all sections of the school staff and the police in the staff library.

When the preliminary stage of the investigation was completed, Denis and Molly had asked Stan to exchange cellphone numbers with them so that they could stay in contact with each other. Initially, the South African was not too comfortable with that proposal. He explained that, while he was anxious to cooperate in every way, he did not want to become a sort of undercover agent for the Garda at St Isidore's; in effect, a police spy.

'You know, where I come from, we used to have a lot of that kind of thing. I don't want to go down that road. It's not – not straight!'

Lennon reassured him. 'No, Stan, it's not like that at all. We certainly don't want you to be a spy or to do anything sneaky. But the point is that you are a sort of outsider, almost like a referee on the field, a fair-minded, independent witness, with no axe to grind. Quite frankly, we have found you easily the most helpful and the most reliable person to deal with round here, precisely because you *are* straight.

'You happen, too, to be in charge now of the boys who, for better or for worse, are closest to this tragedy. You understand them. They trust you, and we trust you. That is not flattery. I'm telling it like it is. We would like you to stay in contact. That's all.'

Stan shrugged and said, 'Okay.'

In fact, the police did ring Stan a few times. Usually it was for some detail that needed to be clarified, like, 'Please ask Jim Higgins what did he mean in his statement when he said . . . (this or that).'

Or it could be, 'There is a reference in our notes to the "cricket pavilion". Where exactly is the pavilion? Neither of us can remember seeing it.'

So it was a convenient arrangement from the point of view of the police; and it did also have the advantage of keeping them in the background and maintaining things as near normal as possible for the boys. The sight of the police forever sniffing round in a school is not a good idea.

Towards the end of the Christmas term, for the first time, Stan phoned the police. He got through to Denis Lennon.

'Superintendent, I have got something perhaps really important to tell you.'

'Okay, Stan, shoot! I'm all ears.'

'I think it would be better if we could meet. We probably need to discuss. Anyhow, I don't want to talk about it over the phone.'

The superintendent immediately agreed. In fact, he was glad of a meeting. Some things had come up in the police inquiry that he and Molly would be happy to bounce off Stan.

As next day was the housemaster's day off, he agreed to come to Dublin, and Lennon offered to pay his expenses. The journey involved eight hours in a train for the round trip from Tralee, which allowed for a four-hour interval between trains in Dublin. Lennon and Molly met him at Heuston station shortly after eleven o'clock in the morning. They spent nearly two hours in discussion and speculation, one hour eating, during which the talk continued, and Stan was back in plenty of time for his train to Tralee at three o'clock in the afternoon. Lennon was generous with the expenses. He remarked to Molly: 'I'm sure Fisher doesn't pay that chap one tenth of what he is really worth.'

She agreed, adding, 'Besides, he is a dish. He must have the Kerry girls' hearts broken.'

'Not necessarily!' Lennon retorted, which was about as near as he ever went to a risqué remark.

'Oh, necessarily,' Molly replied. 'Nancy tells me that he has a true love in South Africa, whom he is missing terribly – and that he is very *moral*.' She pronounced the word as if it were a rare and interesting disease.

As soon as they were sitting round a table in a quiet office, Stan had begun to speak.

'I have had an e-mail from Bertrand, the French boy.'

'Oh, the little dote!' Molly enthused. 'How is he, after his terrible ordeal?'

'Dangerously well!' Stan laughed. 'That kid is as tough as old boots. Actually, the e-mail was not important. It was just to ask me to telephone him any evening at his number in Paris, which he gave me. So I did that. We talked for more than an hour. Fortunately, his English is terrific – not very orthodox sometimes, but so adventurous! He can find a way to say absolutely anything!'

'Did he tell you who he thought he saw coming down the stairs the night that Tyson was murdered? We have waited six weeks to ask him that question.'

'Well, yes. That is exactly what I want to tell you. Bertrand has had more than a month in solitary confinement, with not much else to think about. He says that he is certain *now* that it was Mrs Fisher – George, the headmaster's wife – that he saw. He said that he recognized her by the way she walked.'

Molly laughed. 'French men – even French boys, it seems – notice how women walk.'

Stan continued, 'Bertrand said that he told Dr Fisher the next morning that he had seen his wife on the stairs the previous night. Dr Fisher seemed taken aback, but then he said that this was impossible because his wife had been with him in Belfast the previous evening. So Bertrand believed him and thought that he must have been mistaken. He also believed Fisher when he said that his parents wanted him to return to Paris immediately.'

Molly exclaimed: 'Well, that is a brace of bare-faced lies for openers. If George was sighted in the village shop at four p.m., which she was – when

Bertrand was buying his sausages for the barbecue
– she certainly was not in time for dinner the same
day in Belfast. Secondly, as Denis found out from
Bertrand's dad, it was not Bertrand's parents who
asked for him to be sent back to France: it was Dr
Fisher who called them up and more or less insisted
on it.'

'Well, the fact is,' Stan resumed, 'that no one in
the school ever saw Bertrand again, not his friends
– even to say goodbye – not his housemaster, by
then myself, who had cleaned him up on the previous
night. He was kept in the Fisher residence until the
time of his plane. Dr Fisher himself drove him to
the airport. Mrs Fisher collected his things and
packed them – she can't have packed much, because
half of his stuff was in the dormitory, which had
been cordoned off by the police. It must have been
sent after him later.

'Things were so totally chaotic that morning that
nobody quite noticed the strangeness of Bertrand's
departure. Mind you, I remember thinking that it
was odd that Dr Fisher drove the boy to the airport
himself. Anybody would have been glad to do it,
and the headmaster should really have been around
in the aftermath of such a tragedy.'

Lennon and Molly both nodded encouragingly.

Neither said anything. As Lennon remarked when Stan had left again for Tralee, 'It was a day for listening and not for speaking.'

Stan had gone on, 'As I say, Bertrand has had plenty of time during his enforced captivity to work it all out, and he is bright. Quite simply, he became convinced that it *was* Mrs Fisher that he had seen on the stairs that night and that Dr Fisher was lying. He is equally convinced that he was bundled out of the country with indecent haste because there was a danger that he was going to point the finger at the headmaster's wife. He even worked out that the fact that Mrs Fisher is a vet meant that she could be a good candidate for slitting throats.

'Also, he remembered that Mrs Fisher had come into the village shop just when he was buying sausages for their barbecue. He thought at the time that she had not noticed what was going on, but, apparently, she had. What clinched it for him was the fact that Mrs Fisher knew that he was in the only dormitory that is in Tyson's tower. She knew that because she had collected him at the airport at the beginning of term and had helped him up with his cases to his dormitory.'

'Why do you think that that is so significant?' Molly asked.

'Because if there was going to be a midnight barbecue involving the kids in Tyson's tower, that meant that Mr Tyson was going to be absolutely alone up there that night – and Mrs Fisher knew that fact from mid-afternoon. She knew that the coast would be clear and she had time to psych herself up.'

'Exactly!' Molly assented.

'Did Bertrand really work all that out by himself?' Lennon enquired admiringly. 'We knew about the vet thing – that George, theoretically at least, could have done the job. We also knew that she often wears trouser suits, so that she could have been mistaken for a man in the dark. We did *not* know that she actually knew that Bertrand was in the only dormitory in Tyson's tower. That, too, is very significant for the reason that you have just mentioned. And do you tell me that this little fellow really worked out all of this for himself?'

'Yes, he did,' Stan answered. 'After a week or two of enforced idleness during his imprisonment, he began to have bad dreams about the night of the murder. He found that it helped if he faced the thing head-on, and really thought about all that had happened that night, remembering even things that he would probably have much preferred to forget. Well, you can see, he did some pretty good thinking.'

Stan then filled in for the superintendent and the sergeant – a sympathetic and even tender-hearted audience – details of the conditions in which the boy had been held, together with some of the more hair-raising events and near-misses of his captivity. Lennon punctuated this narrative with one or two 'Oh my God!'s, and Molly with heartfelt counterpoint of 'The poor little mite!' and 'The lousy bastards!'

During lunch they discussed motive, and what possible reason George Fisher could have had to murder either Maurice Tyson or Sir Neville Randler. Stan shrugged his shoulders and said simply, 'Search me.' He had only met Randler once, he said – not enough to give him any real impression of the man. He had no idea what relations were like between Sir Neville and the Fishers, though he had never heard anything negative on that subject. Between Tyson and the Fishers, he had always assumed that contacts were cordial and normal.

Lennon and Molly told Stan about Tyson's last telephone call to Randler, when he had left the message about a 'devastating letter' that he had received and wanted to discuss with his friend on the next day. For Tyson, that next day had never come, and no letter answering to that description had been found either in Tyson's rooms or in Randler's house.

'This mysterious letter may provide us with a motive for one or for both murders,' Lennon said. 'We have an uncomfortable feeling that the murderer might have grabbed it. If so, he might have destroyed it – and certainly will destroy it if we make any overt move in his – or I'm afraid that we have to say in her – direction.'

'Have you any idea what this mysterious letter contains?' Stan asked.

'If you had asked me that a week ago, I would have said an accusation of child abuse against Tyson – and, mind you, it could still be that. There was such an accusation made after his death – please, don't repeat this – but we had it investigated, and it seems to be entirely groundless.'

'I would certainly think so,' Stan said fervently.

'A sleazy attempt at gold-digging,' Molly added, 'and the gold-digger came out with his hands up.'

'Praise God!' Stan the evangelical said, even more fervently.

On the way to the train station, Stan had asked, 'Well, what is your next move?'

'We have got enough on George to arrest her right away,' Lennon answered, 'but we want to arrest the two of them at exactly the same time. The worst scenario for us would be to arrest the headmaster's wife, and to leave the headmaster himself as a loose cannon, able to destoy evidence – and especially that bloody letter, if indeed it hasn't been destroyed already.'

Molly continued, 'You see, with George arrested, we could probably get a search warrant for their house. But we might not get one for his study in the school – and the letter may be there.'

'Why couldn't you get a search warrant for his study? I would have thought—'

'Ah,' Lennon cut in, 'because our great leaders in politics don't think as you think. They think that a man's home is his castle – literally, in this case – and they are reluctant to depart from the Queensberry Rules, to mix my metaphors.'

'And,' Molly appended, 'our great leaders in the Gardaí have got to watch their own precious asses.'

'So what are you going to do?' Stan asked.

'We think that we may get George's fingerprints from the US anti-terrorist people – she passed through JFK within the last year. If we get those prints, without arousing the Fishers' suspicions, and if they are incriminating, we think that our bosses will be sufficiently confident that she is the killer, and that he is an accomplice, to give us all the warrants we need for both of them at the same time. That's the name of the game!'

The morning after Stan got back from Dublin, he was in the teachers' common room struggling to assign tennis courts as equitably as he could for games time. There were eight courts at St Isidore's and there was ongoing warfare about their allocation. The courts varied in quality on a scale from near perfect down to lunar landscape, and those who drew the short straws were always wrathful and some-times tearful. At least Stan did not get accused of taking backhanders, as one of his predecessors in office did, and probably had. But he had to endure predictable and inevitable displeasure, even to the point of letters from irate parents accusing him of ruining their fat, lazy, flat-footed, tuck-guzzling, and slow-moving offspring's chances of ever appearing at Wimbledon.

There was a light knock on the door, and Stan opened it. Martin Wilson and Jim Higgins were standing in the corridor.

'Hey,' he greeted them. 'Are you guys not meant to be in class?'

'Sir, it's urgent,' Jim said.

The boys, who would never have dreamed of

calling Mr Tyson by his first name – to his face anyhow – called Stan interchangeably 'sir' or simply 'Stan'. 'Mr de Witt' would have been a non-starter: it lent itself to too many silly puns. 'Sir' was for the more solemn occasions.

Martin craned his head round the door and saw that there were no other teachers inside.

'Can we come in, sir? It's urgent, and it's private.'

The boys looked around uneasily, as if the walls had ears. Stan knew who he was dealing with and he did not need to be asked a second time.

'Of course, Jim, Martin. Come in.'

He stood back to let them enter, closed the door, and led the way to a cluster of easy chairs. They sat down together.

'So, guys, what's the big deal?' Stan said lightly. He knew that they were uptight about something and he was trying to put them at their ease.

'Sir,' Jim began. That was three 'sir's in a row, Stan thought. No doubt about it: this was a solemn occasion!

'Sir, yesterday when you were away, a junior came to us – to me and Martin – we can't tell you his name. He made us promise not to. He is very afraid. He told us that a few days before Sir Neville Randler was killed, he was sent to the headmaster for something or other – a form he had to fill in, I think. He was half in the door when he heard somebody talking, real angry like, to Dr Fisher.'

'They were having a flaming row,' Martin interjected, 'and the other person was Sir Neville.'

'Did he see Sir Neville?'

Martin answered, 'I don't think so, but you'd easily know him. He has this real posh accent, West Brit like, and he talks real loud, I mean, all the time. Well, he was really blowing his top this time.'

'Did your little guy hear what they were saying?'

Jim replied, 'Not really. You feel nervous every time you have to go to the headmaster's office. It's as if you have done something wrong, even though you know you haven't. You just want to do your business and get out. Then to hear two adults going for each other like crazy, that's pretty scary for a little chap. You almost want to stop your ears.'

Martin added, 'The only thing the kid remembered was something about "better have a good explanation by the weekend". That was from Sir Neville. Anyhow, the kid didn't go any further. He skedaddled out of there as fast as he could.'

'Why?'

'Listen, Stan, if you hear two adults having a bad row – one of them your own headmaster – you sure don't want them to know that you heard it. It's dangerous.'

'How – dangerous?'

Jim came in again. 'Look, Stan, this young chap is really scared. First, Mr Tyson gets his throat cut. Then, a day or two after the kid overheard that row, Sir Neville gets his throat sliced. The guy doesn't want to be next. That's why he didn't breathe a word to anyone.'

'In the end,' Martin said, 'he knew that he had to say something to someone. But he was nearly crying when he was asking us not to give his name.'

'Still, perhaps you really should tell me.'

Both boys answered together, 'No way!'

Jim Higgins added reluctantly, 'Look, Stan, to be honest, we are pretty scared too. Just for knowing stuff about this lousy business, next thing you end up with your own throat slit. Well, my dad is dead, and my mother really needs me—'

He broke off. Stan realized that they really were scared and that, to his surprise, if he was as honest with himself as Jim Higgins, he himself was beginning to be scared too. He asked, 'Why did that junior come to you?'

The boys looked at each other. Martin said, 'Most of the school think that the guys in Tyson's tower know all about this investigation and that we have all kinds of secret knowledge. And then, I suppose, as he sees the world, we rate as big boys!' He laughed.

Stan smiled. 'That is all true. But I reckon he told you two because he was really scared and he trusted you – literally with his life. That is some compliment. Okay?'

Martin blushed and said, 'I guess.'

Jim laughed self-deprecatingly and said, 'Ah, well.'

Stan said, 'Well done, you guys, and thanks. I'll pass it on to the police – and tell them that no way are they getting the name until they have arrested the throat-slitter.'

Eddie Gilhooly sent Molly a Christmas card. It was well intentioned, but garish, and the Magi's camels did indeed look like horses designed by a committee. He signed it in red Biro and added two large Xs. Molly was touched, as indeed was Jan-Hein, who did not seem to mind the blatant competition for his wife's affections.

Molly rang Stan to get Eddie's address. He gave it to her, and then he said: 'Next autumn, Eddie's class have a period of work experience during their transition year. You know the kind of thing: someone takes them on for a few weeks, an auctioneer maybe, or a landscape gardener, whatever, so that they can see what a real job is like. Well, Eddie wanted to ask you to take him on – solving murders! But he was too shy to mention it. Actually, I have noticed that asking for something for himself is the one thing that Eddie is shy about.'

When Jan-Hein heard, he laughed. 'I don't suppose the Gardaí do that kind of thing, do they?'

Molly shook her head. 'Well, there are so many aspects of our work which are either dangerous or just not suitable for youngsters. I don't think so.'

Jan-Hein thought a moment and said what Molly was hoping that he would say. 'Suppose I could fix him up with a job in the National Gallery? It is quite interesting work, arranging exhibitions, cleaning paintings, everything that goes on in the restoration laboratories, and endless carrying of large canvases from one place to another. Obviously, he would need to be able to follow instructions to the letter. There is only one right way to do all those things. Above all, he must not attempt to do anything which he has not been specifically told to. There are tens of thousands, sometimes millions, at stake!'

Molly smiled. 'I think that Eddie is the kind of guy for whom once you get his loyalty, it will be a question of pride to do exactly what you expect of him.' She paused, then asked, 'Do you think that, if you can succeed in getting him a job in the gallery, he could possibly stay with us for that few weeks?'

'Of course, my darling. He seems to be quite a guy.'

'Oh, yes,' Molly said, taking Jan-Hein's hand in her own and kissing it, 'I really think that he is quite some guy.'

The day before term ended for the Christmas holidays, Superintendent Lennon rang Stan on his cellphone.

'Good news for some people, and bad for others: the US mandarins have come through on the finger-prints. They are unmistakably those of Mrs or Ms George or Georgina Fisher. We are coming down tomorrow, once we have secured all the necessary warrants. When do the boys go home for their Christmas holidays? You might have to take over as headmaster as well.'

Stan gasped. Lennon reassured him. 'Only joking, relax!'

'Whew!' Stan said, genuinely relieved. 'You got me on the funny bone there. Anyhow, it will work out. The boys go home tomorrow at midday. Then there is the staff Christmas dinner in the evening.'

'It will probably be evening before we have sorted

out the paperwork. I am afraid that we shall probably have to gatecrash the festivities. But, at least, it will give the school a chance to end its term with dignity and calm.

'Come to think of it, it will also give the staff, assembled in a congenial atmosphere, an opportunity to meet the inevitable crisis in a coherent and a united way.'

'True.'

'And, finally,' Lennon concluded, 'the brainstorming amongst the staff themselves which must follow such a surprising development will probably give us all some small insight into what in God's name has been going on at St Isidore's.'

'True, again,' Stan said simply. He added, 'God knows best.'

Relating this conversation to Molly, Lennon joked, 'I don't think I was intended to take Stan's last comment as a personal compliment.'

It was a measure of Lennon's confidence in Stan's judgement that he did not bother to remind him of the importance of keeping the police plans strictly to himself.

Chapter Twenty

It was half past six on the evening of 17 December. St Isidore's School had closed that day for the Christmas holidays. Superintendent Denis Lennon and Sergeant Molly Power were motoring down from Dublin, hoping to arrive just before the staff Christmas party which was customarily held on that evening. As usual, Molly was driving. A few miles from the school, Lennon took out his cellphone and tapped in a number.

'Stan, is all set?'

'Yes, they are in the cottage together. They are due here in an hour.'

'Right.' Lennon closed the phone. He said to Molly, 'They're in there.'

They drove up to the school, but instead of stopping near the main entrance, they continued across the façade of the castle and turned down a tree-lined alleyway which led towards the forest. They pulled up at the headmaster's cottage and got out. The headmaster's car was parked in front of the garden gate, his wife's Land Rover a few yards nearer the forest. Three windows of the cottage were lit up. Doubtless Dr and Mrs Fisher were inside ploughing up and down, busy making themselves beautiful for the Christmas party. The two officers walked briskly up the crazy pavement to the hall door. Lennon knocked, two grave and deliberate strokes. He did not repeat them, although there was an appreciable delay before anybody came to the door. The summons hung in the air, patient in its power, inexorable.

Dr Fisher came to the door. He was dressed in black evening trousers with a stripe of black velvet down the right leg. He wore an expensive dress shirt, fussily festooned with lace – a nightmare to iron, Molly thought: she had one more or less the same herself. Dancing pumps and braces temporarily completed the headmaster's inchoate costume. There would, no doubt, be a bow tie and a tuxedo to put the icing on the cake. The headmaster looked distinctly unwelcoming.

'Superintendent, I cannot say that this is a pleasure. I am, and have been always, prepared to see you in my office. I am not willing to receive you in my home, at this hour of the evening, and in the absence of the minimum courtesy of a telephone call to announce your arrival.'

'Dr Fisher, we will explain ourselves very quickly.'

'Please do.'

'I am afraid that we have to come in, and that we must insist that Mrs Fisher be present also.'

The headmaster was clearly on the point of a major eruption when a voice cut in from behind him: 'Oh, let them in, darling, and let's hear what they have to say. The sooner they're in the sooner they'll be out again.'

Fisher did not say a word. He stood back obediently from the door. As the police officers crossed the threshold, they could hear the additional police car which they had requested from Tralee arriving. The headmaster closed the door behind them. George Fisher stood at the entrance to the sitting room, the epitome of classical elegance. A full-length sheath dress in burgundy silk clasped her sculpted figure, the rich material held taut between the promontory of marble breasts and the flat triangular plain of hips and pelvis. *La Belle Dame sans Merci*, Lennon thought, remembering a poem by Keats from his school days more than forty years ago. They all went into the sitting room. Fisher closed the door. 'He is good at closing doors,' Molly thought.

'Dr and Mrs Fisher,' Lennon began without further preamble, 'I have here warrants for the arrest of each of you—'

He got no further. Fisher snorted so violently, it was as if to leave a full pint of snot on his own carpet.

'Have you taken leave of your senses, man? On what possible charge?'

George Fisher was silent. She had turned deadly white. Lennon took up again.

'I must inform you that you are not obliged to say anything, but that anything you do say will be recorded and may be used in evidence against you.'

'This is outrageous,' Fisher gasped, but less vehemently than before.

Lennon continued: 'George Fisher, I have here warrants for your arrest on a charge of having murdered Maurice Tyson, and on a charge of having murdered Neville Randler.'

George Fisher made no response. Lennon turned to her husband, to whom he read charges of having conspired with his wife to murder the same persons, and having aided and abetted her in so doing. He added that there would probably be further charges, and he repeated the formula that neither accused was obliged to make any statement, but that if they chose to do so, it would be recorded and could be used in evidence.

Fisher said, 'It is outrageous and absurd.'

Molly made a show of writing this down in a jotter, which seemed to stem the flow of eloquence and indignation. Lennon went on to explain that another police car had arrived which would take them to Tralee Garda barracks where they would be detained overnight. They would be formally charged in the morning. They could apply for bail at that time, but they would probably be remanded in custody to Midlands Prison in Portlaoise to await trial. He added that they would, of course, be allowed full access to the lawyers of their choice.

Fisher spoke again, this time in more subdued tones: 'Superintendent, this evening we are the hosts of our annual Christmas party for the school staff. You are hardly unaware of this fact. I think it particularly offensive that you should choose this night of all nights to transact your squalid business.'

Lennon did not say anything, and Molly did not bother to pretend to be writing anything down. Fisher resumed: 'It would be unthinkable that we should not attend our own party, and indeed preside. The school staff would find this deeply upsetting.'

'As I'm sure they also found the murders of Maurice Tyson and Sir Neville Randler,' Molly mused out loud.

Lennon cut in hastily, 'I should also tell you that we have search warrants for this house and for the school. There is no question of your spending the night on campus. It is our intention to search immediately.'

Eventually, Dr Fisher proposed a formula. The Gardaí who would be transporting himself and his wife to Tralee would accompany them into the castle where the guests would be enjoying a preprandial glass of sherry. They could make a short speech to their guests. They would not be handcuffed and there would be no explicit mention that they were under arrest. It would be said, in the time-honoured circumlocution of the law, that they were 'helping the police with their inquiries' into the tragic deaths of Maurice Tyson and Sir Neville Randler. Finally, Fisher would encourage the guests to enjoy the party, because St Isidore's was a splendid school and was bigger than any mere individual. He would also say that he and his wife were fully confident that they would soon clear up any little ambiguities and would be with their colleagues to ring in the New Year. They would drink a toast to that.

Lennon shrugged and said, 'Why not?'

The three Gardaí from Tralee were admitted. Lennon and Molly explained to them what had been agreed. They were on the point of leaving with their prisoners when George, who had not spoken since the first mention of charges, suddenly strode to an antique writing bureau, opened a drawer, and took out a manilla C5 envelope which could contain about ten or fifteen sheets of A4 paper folded in two. She flung this at Lennon and shouted: 'Here's what you are looking for, damn you! I hope you roast in hell! Get out of our house, now!'

Lennon said nothing. It was Fisher who reacted. 'What the hell did you do that for?'

His wife replied: 'Because they'll find it in ten minutes anyhow. It's all over, don't you realize that? We're finished!'

'You're finished, you mean. I didn't do anything.'

George Fisher vented a violent oral fart of laughter, one harsh blast. She mimicked, '"I didn't do anything." You miserable creep, you make me vomit!'

Lennon signalled to the escort and they led the prisoners out. They were allowed, under supervision, to complete their dressing for the party and pack something less stylish for life in Midlands Prison. Then they were driven to the school where the sherry party was in full swing. The Fishers staged quite an arrival. They were dressed so like royalty that a uniformed escort did not look too much out of place. But there was the inevitable double take, and a thrill of excitement rippled over the assembled convivialists.

Dr Fisher rose to the occasion. As Hamlet would have wished, he spoke the speech *trippingly on the tongue*. George rose to the occasion too, smiling unconcernedly, sipping her sherry, and announcing loudly that 'the constables' could not have anything to drink because 'the poor darlings' were on duty.

'Besides,' she added provocatively, 'you probably all think that it was Papists like yourselves who made the wine, but that it was the bloody Protestants, like us, who made the mean little glasses.'

She gave a shrill screech of laughter. People looked at each other uncomfortably. 'She's as high as a kite,' somebody murmured. Nancy McGivern, who was standing beside Stan, whispered in his ear, 'Cocaine.' The South African turned to her quickly, astonished. She nodded her head. In sad contrast to his wife, Dr Fisher, once he had made his bravura little oration, seemed to fold into himself and looked the picture of gloom. Within twenty minutes, it was George who, completely ignoring her police escort, announced their departure.

'Don't bother coming out with us. We'll show ourselves the door.'

The staff members took her at her word. They did not go out – probably to maintain what they all knew now was a slender fiction of normality. It was clear to most people that the Fishers were in deep trouble.

The staff went in to dine – for the sake of St Isidore's.

The banqueting hall, which accommodated the staff dining room all year round, was worthy of its name, though the food served up there by the school caterers was normally less than gourmet. This was school food, standard issue, with frills for the staff, mainly answering to dietary whims and fixations: politically correct rabbit food, imitation butter and sugar, fake milk, black bread made from nuts and bolts to give one's gut a good raking over on the way down, and other killjoy food items suitable for middle-aged persons determined not to fall victim to cancer, heart disease, cholesterol, blood pressure, obesity, plaque, or anything else that would prevent them living until extreme and – the boys would have thought – unreasonable old age.

The hall was an elegant room: high, oak panelled, with three full-length windows on the sunny south side. There were solid brass picture rails near the ceiling, from which were suspended gilt-framed portraits of the great and the good of an earlier age, looking incredibly noble and stuck-up. Even the ceiling was panelled, with, superimposed, strange geometric designs in bas-relief, said to be arcane Masonic symbols. Sir Neville had whispered to the boys, on one of his random visits to the school, that his ancestors had used the banqueting hall to hold seances of necromancy and sorcery, at one of which the Devil himself had made a personal appearance. A boy at heart as long as he lived, Sir Neville knew how thoroughly boys enjoyed being scared out of their wits.

This night, with Christmas decorations – including a handsome tree – a blazing fire in the monumental fireplace, Madeira already imbibed, and the prospect of an excellent meal to come, the banqueting hall engendered an atmosphere, if not exactly of jollity, at least of *Schadenfreude* centred on the bizarre fate of Dr and Mrs Fisher. People were beginning to enjoy themselves.

Inevitably, the one topic of conversation was the arrest – or was it an arrest? – of the headmaster and his wife in connection with the murders of their colleague Maurice Tyson and their neighbour and antecedent in residence, Sir Neville Randler. Nancy McGivern caught the mood of the gathering when she was heard to exclaim, 'Have I had too much to drink, or did that actually happen? Would somebody just run it by me again – in slow motion?'

After the first course, Stan de Witt stood up. He raised his voice and said: 'Please, I don't like making speeches.'

That first sentence was so palpably true – given the speaker's customary modesty, and most especially against the background of the evening's startling events – that the whole hall fell silent immediately. Stan went on: 'Thank you. The thing is, I happen to know a small bit about what we have just seen with our own eyes. I think I should share this information with you.'

There was a general murmur of interest and assent.

'As you know, I had to replace Mr Tyson at a moment's notice and take care of his boys, including those who had the awful experience of finding his body. As the police inquiry was concerned chiefly with those boys, I got to hear – well, various things to do with the investigation. Also, I had a long conversation on the telephone with Bertrand – you remember him, the French boy who was kidnapped when he went back to France. Bertrand positively identified Mrs Fisher as the person that he saw on the stairs of Tyson's tower the night of the murder. A fingerprint check confirmed that she had been at the scene of the crime and had also got out of the window in the Middle House and climbed down to the ground. Well, that is the essence of the case against Mrs Fisher. I am not quite sure how much or in what way Dr Fisher is involved.'

Several people noticed, and some were amused by, the fact that Stan referred throughout to Dr and Mrs Fisher, and to Mr Tyson, never presuming to say Maurice or George, still less Derwas, although first names were the norm amongst the staff. Celia Flood, the matron and a stickler for manners, said admiringly to those around her: 'That young man has been beautifully brought up. He even calls that hussy Mrs.'

The word *hussy* in that context was an early and accurate indication of what way the wind was blowing amongst the staff.

Stan sat down. There was a pause. Then Stephen Stritch, the vice-principal of the school and the most senior member of the staff present, stood up.

'I am not sure what I am meant to say on such an unprecedented occasion and in such an unusual situation. But – leaving aside graver issues, as we must for the moment, if justice is to be done – I think I speak for all here when I say thank you, Stan, for sharing this information with us, and indeed also for the splendid job you have been doing for those boys in the Middle House, in very difficult circumstances.'

There was a ripple of applause, sincere but restrained, in the solemn context of two tragic deaths. The main course was served, a traditional Christmas dinner with all the trimmings. People near Stan quizzed him about George Fisher's reasons for killing Maurice Tyson and/or Sir Neville Randler, and about the extent to which Derwas Fisher was implicated. Stan admitted that he was completely in the dark as to all of these matters.

'The police tell me stuff on a need-to-know basis, but they are not exactly chatty. I guess that that is more or less how it should be. We'll know soon enough.'

There were several things that Stan had not told his colleagues: about Maurice Tyson's telephone call to Sir Neville Randler mentioning the 'devastating letter', about Sir Neville's row with Dr Fisher, about accusations of child abuse against Tyson, and about his own detailed consultations with the police in Dublin. He had merely sought to bring his audience up to speed in a matter that concerned all of them, without blowing his own trumpet or indulging in pretentious speculations.

As the evening wore on, and good food and wine unfolded their blessings – at least their short-term blessings – the staff began to relax. Stan's words and those of the vice-principal had had a reassuring effect. Maurice Tyson's murderer had, in all probability, been named. People were shaken, but the devil you know is always better than the devil you don't know and now they *did* know. Besides, the simple speeches they had heard showed that St Isidore's was still strong and that they could count on themselves and on each other to behave intelligently, decently, and appropriately – even in such a difficult and bewildering situation.

Joan Sutton, the music teacher, said, 'We must persuade young Stan to stay on when his year is up.'

Nancy McGivern replied, 'That won't be easy. He has a fiancée at home somewhere.'

'Well, let him bring her along,' Joan responded with equanimity. 'They can have the Fishers' cottage. That will be vacant as of today. Nothing more certain!' This was the first oblique and not fully conscious insinuation that Stan already had the makings of a great headmaster.

Conversations and the meal were interrupted by the sudden reappearance of one of the Gardaí who had left with the Fishers, perhaps three quarters of an hour before. He seemed to be uneasy and embarrassed. He engaged some of the nearer diners in discreet, almost furtive consultations and then, evidently not finding a solution to his problem, he was obliged to cast his net wider. He looked up, excused himself profusely, and explained that Dr and Mrs Fisher, on leaving the dining room, had asked – well, actually, it was Mrs Fisher who had asked – to spend some moments in the headmaster's study, 'to sort out our medicines'. Dr Fisher himself had indeed seemed surprised at this request but had said nothing. A bit in awe of their surroundings and of their obviously distinguished prisoners, and taking his cue from the latitude already allowed them by Superintendent Lennon, the senior officer had acceded to their seemingly reasonable request. He did insist, almost shamefacedly, that, as they *were* after all prisoners, one of his acolytes would have to accompany them. Mrs Fisher graciously assented. The officer chose Garda Murphy for the task of chaperon.

Murphy was an avuncular figure close to retirement. He was selected routinely for those delicate assignments where a *bean-gharda* (a policewoman) might have been more appropriate, had one been available.

When fifteen minutes had passed, which the officer considered a generous allowance of time to sort out one's pills, he had tried the door. It was locked. He had knocked politely, then called courteously, then knocked vigorously, then called loudly, then rattled every handle, knob, bolt, or bar available to be rattled, then pounded the door and yelled at the top of his voice. He had intermingled ardent entreaties to Garda Murphy with his intercessions to a range of larger and lesser deities. All these supplications had fallen on stony deaf ears.

At last, very reluctantly, the officer had had to admit defeat. Feeling ridiculous, he went to throw himself on the mercy of the diners and winers, some of whom by this time were becoming distinctly jolly. They were not slow to exacerbate his discomfort by the sort of raillery and ribaldry that has always existed between Town and Gown – even little towns and mini-gowns.

Chapter Twenty-one

When the police car carrying the Fishers had left from their cottage for Tralee, via the castle – so that they could excuse themselves to their guests in terms of a pressing engagement – the two Dublin-based officers sat down to examine the contents of the envelope that George Fisher had flung at them.

It contained twelve quarto sheets of white unlined paper, covered in quite small but surprisingly clear black Biro handwriting. It was a letter, addressed to *Darling Sally*, and signed *All my love, Seán*. Lennon said: 'Who is "Darling Sally" and who is "All-my-love Seán"?'

Molly replied, 'I don't know who Sally is, but I bet you "Seán" is Seán Gilhooly.'

'A voice from beyond the grave?'

'Yes,' Molly answered, 'a voice from beyond the grave; a voice answering his brother's questions about why Seán had to die, and where to lay the blame. At least I am glad that the poor boy had a "darling Sally". He did not go entirely loveless into the night.'

Lennon thought to himself that he liked working with Molly so much because she was as tough as the next, and yet not afraid to say tender things that no policeman would say, and that he himself would not say in a fit. Neatly sidestepping the tender thing that she had just said – a prerogative of the Irish male – he replied with a banality.

'You read faster than me, so you read first, and pass me each page as you go.'

'Right you be,' Molly agreed. 'And let's not say anything, good or bad, until we both finish completely.'

'Good idea,' Lennon assented. 'Let's get the whole picture.'

In the event, Lennon stuck more rigorously to the agreement than Molly. Apart from a few sighs and groans, he maintained a stoical silence throughout his reading. Molly gave more vent to her feelings. From the first page, she was punctuating it with 'Oh my God', 'the perfect shit', 'the thundering bitch', and other even more vehement expressions. Once she sprang to her feet and yelled. Finishing two pages in front of Lennon, she covered her face with her hands and sat quite still.

When Lennon was done, he assembled all the sheets of paper very deliberately, taking time over it. He was shaking his head from side to side in a succession of staccato movements, as if to dispel haunting memories or evil spirits.

'Let's start with the easy part,' he said tonelessly. 'The history of this document. I mean the people whose hands it has passed through, and when they saw it.'

Molly removed her hands from her face and sat up. She blinked several times and coughed before speaking. Her voice, too, was now blank, with no hint of the emotion she had clearly felt during the reading.

'In all probability, this is a letter that Seán Gilhooly wrote to a girl called Sally, shortly before his death, that is to say, a year ago. Sally was his friend.'

Lennon took up the running. 'It somehow came into Maurice Tyson's hands. How and when?'

'We don't know how. Perhaps Sally sent it to him, but when? Very likely it was shortly before Tyson's own death. We know that he received a devastating letter just days before he was murdered. Tyson seems to have been a sober-minded man. I don't think that he would have used words like "devastating" lightly. It would probably have been reserved for something like this appalling document that we have in our hands.'

'Very well, I agree. So then the question arises, why did Sally – if it was Sally – wait the best part of a year after Seán's death to send this letter to Tyson? Or indeed, now that Sally must know that Tyson has been murdered – and that the probable reason for his murder is to shut him up, because he received that letter and, therefore, knew too much – why in heaven's name is she not raising Cain, or at the very least sending a copy of the same letter to *us*?'

'Those are difficult questions,' Molly admitted. 'I suspect that we won't have any answers to them until we find Sally, which shouldn't be too difficult. Still, I can understand why a girl would not want anyone to see this letter. It is very private, the kind of letter you would only send to somebody you trusted totally. Sally probably loved Seán very much. She wants to protect him, and also – I think this is important too – she wants to keep close to her heart the record of all that he suffered. Yes, I think I understand her.'

'And, to follow it further,' Lennon persisted, 'how did the letter get from Tyson's possession to Sir Neville Randler?'

'That is the most amazing conjuring trick of all,' Molly answered. 'We have a photograph of a green folder on Tyson's table, which then mysteriously disappears from behind police padlocks, and surfaces again in Sir Neville's dustbin. How did that happen? I just do not know – but it *did* happen.'

'And the most sinister feature of all in this terrible story is that wherever this letter or that green folder travel, George Fisher's butcher's knife follows close behind them. First is Maurice Tyson. Second is Sir Neville Randler. And I have little doubt that "Darling Sally" would be next on the list, to seek and destroy.'

Darling Sally,

This is my story – finally. How often have I promised to tell it to you? I have never found the courage to do that. There are too many things that I am ashamed of. I have made a horrible failure of my life.

You know that Eddie and I were orphaned

when we were very young. I was eight and Eddie was two. You can imagine what that must be like – indeed better than I can, because you have had the love of a family to compare it with. I have almost never known anything different from being orphaned. I could best describe that experience as like always having to feel that you are a nuisance to other people – like Harry Potter with his uncle and aunt. I have an uncle and aunt too. They are good people, but they have their own children and their own lives to live, and they cannot hide the fact that Eddie and I are a burden to them.

I am not using this business of being orphaned as an excuse for all the evil things that I have done. I know that I am fully responsible for everything. Yet I still sometimes cry for my dad and my mum, and I think that, if only they had lived, they would have helped me with advice, and encouragement, and above all with *love*, to be a much better person than I am.

My descent into hell began when I was in fifth year in boarding school. One day, on an impulse, I stole a hundred euro off the head-master's desk. Dr Fisher was his name. I believe now that he had set a trap for me and that he was just waiting for me to do it. When I was in my first three years at St Isidore's, Dr Fisher pretty well ignored me. As I began to grow up, he started to notice me, to talk to me in a friendly way, to pay me special attention. I thought that this was because I had lost both of my parents, and he was sorry for me. After all, I was alone and vulnerable, with no parents to turn to. That was all true – except that Fisher was not sorry for me at all, not one little bit. If he was nice to me, he was working to somebody else's agenda, someone who had already decided to destroy me.

Stealing the money was stupid and bad. I was seventeen. We were in fifth year, and we were going on a barbecue – one of those midnight barbecues that I told you about. They were a kind of rites of passage thing, you see. I took the money to buy beer because we fifth years were big tough guys – well, that sounds pretty silly now, but that's what we thought at the time – so we had to have beer for a barbecue, even if we hated the taste of the bloody stuff. I intended to do a whip-round among the lads and to put the money back, I really did. Besides, we didn't even need more than fifty euro. I just took a hundred because that was what was there, in one note.

Perhaps if Fisher didn't miss the money at all, maybe I would have been tempted *not* to put it back. Still, I do honestly think that I *would* have put it back because I don't steal money – I don't steal *anything*.

At the time, I was in and out of Fisher's study several times a week. He had allowed me to store a model aeroplane that I was building in the safety of his room. In a boys' school, it is hard to find a safe place for such a delicate object. I mean, it could be smashed to smithereens at any moment by stampeding buffaloes. Well, Fisher, as I said, had become very friendly over the last few months. I could see, even then, that there was something phoney about this too friendly stuff – hand on the shoulder, soft talk, shit like that. But I didn't think anything of it at the time. I just thought that it was the way a guy would *act* nice if he didn't have much experience of actually *being* nice.

That was Fisher's case right enough. He was not a nice man. I recognized all of that. The joke is that I thought that I could manipulate him, when all the time it was he who was manipulating me. So I asked him, with my most goody-goody-two-shoes smile, could I keep my model aeroplane in his study. 'Welcome, day or night,' was the reply. 'Don't even knock, just come in.'

I must say this bit up front: whatever Fisher was after, it was not sex. I guess I was pretty innocent at the time. I was into sport and outdoor stuff like that. Girls weren't really on the agenda, not yet anyhow. I used to fantasize that I would one day make a beautiful marriage, the way I'm sure my parents' marriage was beautiful, and that me and my girl would live happily ever after. Meanwhile, I was a happy-go-lucky person – not into porn, or sleazy websites, or dirty movies. I guess I was still pretty immature, but I honestly think that I was doing okay for my age and, at least, I was trying my best to get it all together.

Sally, you will probably laugh at me, but I know, and I knew then, that I was quite a nice-looking guy. Old women drool over me – and also, certain kinds of men. You know what I mean? Well, I have had one or two bad experiences that way. So, let's say – like most guys my age – I would already have been more or less street-wise about that stuff.

Well, I'm telling you, Fisher was just not the kind. I am positive sure of that. Whatever he was after by being nice to me – it was not sex. In fact, I cannot imagine what his sex life is like. I don't think he has any. What do you call that? I bet he is a eunuch.

Well, like I say, I was in and out of Fisher's study. That hundred-euro bill was thrown on his desk, or rather on a side table, all scrunched up, as if someone had forgotten it. I had seen it dozens of times and never gave it a second thought – until this emergency about the beer and the barbecue happened. So it was then that I took it – or, as I would like to think, I borrowed it. I'm not proud about this. I repeat that I should not have done it – especially since Fisher trusted me to walk in and out of his office. I felt sly doing it, and I still did it.

But 'with the wisdom of hindsight', as they say, I would swear that Fisher set a trap for me. The minute he knew that the money was gone, which would have been an hour or two later when he got back to his room, he was on to me like a Rottweiler with rabies. I was working out in the gym. He came in, brought me straight to my locker and made me search all the pockets in my clothes. He found the money. He said he had marked the bill, but I admitted it straight out. Anyway, I am a hopeless liar. Nobody would ever believe me if I tried to tell a lie.

He told me to get dressed and to report to his study immediately. I knew that I was in bad trouble. His attitude to me had changed in a flash beyond recognition. Still, I felt that if I was completely honest with him, he would understand that I had made a stupid mistake and find it in his heart to forgive me. But in his office there was no give at all. He threw the book at me. He was talking about instant exclusion, calling the police, criminal charges, and prison. I reasoned with him. I swore that I had intended to give the money back. To that, he said contemptuously that he could not believe me; that I had betrayed him, and been utterly ungrateful.

Sally, people who have not lost their parents do not realize that one of the hardest things for a kid to bear is that he or she is convinced that the parent or parents have died because of something bad that the kid has done. The bereavement counsellors – or whatever they're called – told me that, dozens of times, when my dad and my mum died. I heard what they were saying, but it didn't make it any easier to bear. When Fisher said the word *ungrateful*, it was like he pulled a trigger. I had a sickening flashback to seeing my dad and my mum in their coffins, their faces all ugly, and white, and messed up because of the car crash – and because I had been *ungrateful* and had not loved them enough.

I had been cool enough until then. Quite suddenly I began to panic. Since the death of my parents, St Isidore's had been my only real home and my friends were my only family. I was going to lose even that. I didn't mind going to prison but I couldn't bear to leave St Isidore's, and in disgrace, branded as a thief and a liar. It was as if an unhealed wound was bursting open again. In a moment I was crying. I was begging, pleading with Dr Fisher to allow me to make reparation for the awful thing I had done. I would accept any punishment, I said, do anything to atone. At that he actually smiled.

He let me sob and snivel away until he judged

that I was really abject and desperate. 'Very well,' he said then, 'the punishment will have to be very severe. Call to my private house at seven o'clock in the evening, next Monday, Wednesday, and Friday. Now, get out.'

'Oh, thank you, sir,' I blubbered, and I got out.

This was a Saturday. So I had two whole days to wait. My dominant feeling was of enormous relief that the headmaster had not made me leave St Isidore's that very evening. For the rest, I said to myself, 'I am a man' – poor child that I was – 'I can take whatever is coming to me. Whatever it is, I deserve it.' My one desire was to make it up to Dr Fisher – because he was clearly deeply upset – and even to get him to trust me and to like me again. That is precisely what I was meant to feel, wasn't it?

I did think that the two days of waiting was strange, and then the three days in the following week with a one-day interval between each. This seemed surprisingly detailed and structured for something thought up on the spur of the moment in response to my pleading. But I rationalized it as Dr Fisher's desire not to act out of anger, to let a few days elapse, and then to explain to me patiently over a whole week what I had done that was so wrong. I was eager to learn that lesson, even if he punished me severely as well. At least I would know the reason for the punishment and that it was absolutely necessary for my own good.

Poor fool that I was! Fisher's programme and timetable were, of course, a premeditated and ruthlessly cunning process of grooming, to bend me to whatever he wanted of me, however abject and degrading. The process had already begun because, despite the hopeful rationalizations, I already knew in one tiny corner of my mind that Fisher had sprung a carefully constructed trap on me – which indeed he had probably used before with other boys and found effective. But why?

I must admit honestly that there was even some element of complicity on my part, some toxic curiosity. What the hell was Fisher up to? I just had no idea. My gut instinct was that this was weirdo stuff. But what exactly? I was practically totally ignorant in the area of off-beat emotions. These were totally new thoughts and feelings for me, and I had no idea how to handle them.

The two days of waiting were intended to ratchet up both my terror and my excitement to fever pitch. What would Fisher do? Would he beat me? I belonged to a generation that had never been beaten at school. Would it really hurt? Would he make me take down my trousers, even my boxer shorts, like in all those stories about English public schools, which were so ambiguous, to say the least? If he did all that stuff, it would be pretty humiliating. Did I really deserve that? It would also be a wholly new experience – and darkly exciting. He couldn't beat me three times in a week for the same offence, could he? But the truth was that he could do exactly what he liked and I had agreed eagerly to those terms. I had agreed to anything. I promised myself – seeing that I had to promise myself something – that no matter what he did to me, I would not cry.

During those two days I hardly ate anything or slept. Several times it was on the tip of my tongue to talk about the whole mess to a friend. Something held me back. Perhaps it was the fact that I had stolen the money. I wasn't too proud of that fact anyhow, and I probably would not have told my pals about it even if everything had gone perfectly according to plan. Besides, seeing Fisher was making such a fuss of the whole thing, perhaps after all I had got it badly wrong and my friends would despise me if they knew. When you do not have parents to tell you things, or even a proper home, it is not always easy to have standards of behaviour. I felt very alone.

Perhaps above all, that tiny corner of my mind which recognized what Fisher was really after also knew that I was already compromised. The truth was that I might emerge from my three visits to Fisher's house with experiences that I would not want other people to know about.

All I did in the end was to say to Bernard Kalinski, perhaps my greatest friend, 'Bernard, I am in terrible trouble. I can't tell you what it is but, please, pray for me, please. It is very important.'

Bernard was a Pole, and, like all Poles, very religious. He spoke American better than English, so he slapped me on the back and said simply, 'You got it!'

He was that kind. Totally decent. He knew that I didn't want to talk about it. He would not dream of asking me a single question, though he must have been both curious and concerned.

Later I did Bernard a great wrong. I am sorrier about that than about anything else that happened in this sick-making affair. I truly loved Bernard. He was probably the best, the most decent person I have ever known. Sadly, I betrayed him.

I was shaking when I knocked on the door of the headmaster's cottage. He opened it himself and gestured me in without speaking. He crossed the hall and entered a room which was obviously his study at home. I followed him in and he closed the door. He stood at his desk and said one word: 'Strip.'

I said, 'Sorry?' as if I had not heard.

He stared at me expressionlessly, and said nothing.

I said, 'You mean my trousers?'

Silence.

'And my boxers?' I bargained forlornly.

He continued to stare. I started to undress slowly. I said to myself, 'Just do it now. You can feel what you like later.'

I held on to a crazy thought. 'He doesn't know that I am wearing contact lenses, so I am not entirely naked.' Crazy, yes, but it did help a lot.

He did beat me that first day, not very severely. But it was all that I could do not to cry, because the whole thing was so humiliating. And that seemed to be the whole point of the ritual, to make me lose pride in myself – I mean a good pride, like everyone should have, even the smallest child. And I was a young man of seventeen – for God's sake!

Even as Fisher walloped me I asked myself, 'What the hell is this all about?' There was no vibe coming from Fisher, and certainly no sexual chemistry in the air. He was getting no thrill out of this. He was like a hangman, just doing his job. For one hallucinatory moment I nearly gave him five euro – it was all I had – as I'd heard somewhere that you are expected to give your executioner a tip. It's such a crappy job, after all!

When it was over, I dragged my clothes on, inside out or anyway, and stumbled out of the house. I did not know where Fisher had gone, but I doubted that he needed me to say goodbye to him. At least, I told myself, I had retained this one last shred of self-respect: I had not cried in his presence.

I almost bumped into Mrs Fisher right outside the front door of the cottage, apparently coming in. She is a beautiful woman. She said to me, 'Poor Seán,' and kissed me full on the mouth. Then she said, 'We'll be expecting you on Wednesday,' and she added, 'Light at the end of the tunnel!' Then she went quickly into the house and shut the door.

I was so astonished that I just stood looking open mouthed at the closed door. Then I half ran and half staggered into the forest, to be alone and to reflect on what George had done and said to me. Our encounter had not lasted more than a few seconds, yet it had almost eclipsed in my mind anything that her husband had done to me. In comparison, he was a boring irrelevance.

I climbed into a tree and sat down with my back to the trunk, my legs comfortably stretched along a branch. This was a favourite secret place that I had discovered in second year. My ass was tingling, almost pleasantly, as a result of Fisher's handiwork, and it occurred to me that he was a bit of an ass himself. Then I decided to despise him. A phrase came to me and I said it out loud, trying to understand what I really meant. 'Why! He is only a menial, a *menial*.' And I actually laughed for the first time in two days.

She had kissed me full on the mouth. I could not remember my mother's kisses. Perhaps I had suppressed the memory of them as something too painful to remember. Various aunts and cousins had, from time to time, done the peck on the cheek routine. It meant nothing. But this woman – I knew now what the lads meant when they said that a woman was *hot*. George was *hot*. She had said, 'Poor Seán.' What did that mean exactly? Did she mean 'poor' in the banal sense that I was in trouble with her husband? Or could she have meant 'poor' in the sense that I was hungry for love and that she had guessed my secret – a secret that I did not even know myself until that precise moment in front of the cottage door? And what did 'light at the end of the tunnel' mean? I don't think I had ever heard the expression. Suddenly I thought of a sense for those words, so explicit and so shocking that I practically fell out of my tree.

Above all, I was conscious that I was now implicated in this thing up to my eyeballs. Had I lost my innocence, without even knowing what was going on? I knew now that Fisher and his wife must be working together. It was too much of a coincidence that George should be coming in the door exactly when I was coming out. And what she said was so exciting. Was it possible . . . ?

I knew that I would go back to that house again in two days' time, and in two days' time after that, and that, although I was terrified, I *wanted* to go. So it is that vampires spawn vampires of their virginal victims.

Wednesday came. This time, George opened the door. She looked – well, so *hot*, so sexy – just to use another word.

'Come in, Seán,' she breathed huskily. The sound seemed to come from somewhere between her breasts. She was inviting me in. She added, holding the door wide for me, 'My husband has had to go away for the night. Come in and keep me company.' Everything she said seemed to have a double meaning; teasing, tantalizing. I remember asking myself in a last lucid moment, 'Am I crazy, or what?' It is a question I have asked myself many times over the last four years.

She cooked a meal for us and we ate. I had no idea what we were eating. I only had eyes and ears for her. She got me drunk – my first time ever – I no longer knew what she was saying – tender things, bewitching things. Then we were standing. She was kissing me. She began to open my belt, saying she wanted to see how her husband had wounded me. She slipped her hands down my back, on to the two cheeks of my bottom, and began to push down my pants. It was like being electrocuted.

I went back to the school at five o'clock the following morning. I guess you'd have to say that, that night, she raped me. It was another first. I was a virgin.

For almost the next two years it went on and on. Very soon I had neither pride nor shame left. It was not love. It was never love. The pleasure and the pain that she gave me during those two years were both excruciating. She is a devil out of hell. It was always she that took the initiative. She would ring me on my mobile phone and say where to meet her. This would sometimes be in the bungalow which she used for her veterinary practice, which was about a mile from the school. But it would sometimes be in the house she shared with her husband.

Fisher's involvement is a complete mystery to me. He *must* have known that I was sleeping with his wife. Wasn't it he who laid the initial trap for me in his own office, and who had softened me up with a humiliating flogging, like a butcher tenderizing easy meat? Incredibly, I could sometimes hear him moving around the cottage while I was actually playing dirty tricks with his wife. The first time that happened, I nearly panicked, but George said, 'Don't worry about him. He won't disturb us.' She said nothing about his attitude, good or bad, to what was going on.

She did say a few things from time to time about her own background and how she came to marry Fisher. She had come from a working-class terrace of red-brick houses in Bradford. She had been abused sexually and physically for as long as she could remember. She had escaped into marriage with Fisher, who had put her through veterinary school. On the surface, so beautiful and intelligent, inside she was seething with anger, resentment, and hate. She sneered at her husband mercilessly, telling me, 'Poor sod, he can't get it up.' I think she was saying that they had no sex life together, and that Fisher was reduced to pimping and – what is the word? – *procuring* for her. She more or less told me that there had been others before me and that there would be others after me – all caught on the same lousy hundred-euro note.

A week after our – affair – had begun, I found my model aeroplane and parts neatly piled on a table outside the headmaster's study. That meant, of course, that I was to take it away – and also the end of the uneasy relationship between us. From that day on, I hardly exchanged a dozen words with Fisher during my last two years in the school. When I had to speak to him, I hung my head and didn't dare to look him in the eye. I was ashamed of myself – and so should he have been – even more so.

I have already used the image of the vampire's victim who, in turn, becomes a vampire. Under the influence of that demonic pair, I too became a predator. Gender was not important. What turned me on was the combination of beauty, goodness, and vulnerability. I thank God that I never became a paedophile, but I did become an abuser. I have to acknowledge that fact. Somebody has said that we always destroy the thing that we love. Why? Is it perhaps through envy? When we no longer share other people's innocence, do we want to destroy that innocence in them, to drag them down to our own level?

I have started to read the Bible. I don't really know why. I suppose that I have made such a shocking mess of my life that I just need to look elsewhere for salvation – whatever that means. Mostly I cannot make much sense of what I am reading but, now and then, I do notice things that resonate for me. For instance, when Eve had eaten the apple, it says, she gave some of it to Adam, her husband, too. What did she do that for? That is typical abusive behaviour. She had already eaten the apple. Her eyes were opened. She knew that she had landed in the shit, big time, and she was making sure that he was going to do exactly the same thing too. 'For better or for worse.' Is that what it means, huh?

Envy of the innocent is one factor in abuse. Carnal *knowledge* is another. The Bible is hot on that one also. During the holidays I wanted

to *know* sweet girls. But because of being
orphans and having no proper family, my
brother and I didn't get invited to parties. We
didn't belong to anyone's set. I couldn't get
near to any sweet girls – fortunately for them,
because I was a wholly corrupt person by then,
with only one thing on my mind.

Back at school, in the shower room, I looked
around me with *knowing* eyes. We are always
interested in naked bodies. They tell us more
than we knew, and knowing more, we cannot
help comparing. Growing up, we long for
muscles like this guy, a sun tan like that guy,
plenty of body hair, well-developed genitals –
and why not? This is perfectly natural. But it
was different for me now. *Knowledge is power.*
I lusted after a new kind of intimacy, desiring
bodies as if they could reveal to me the secrets
of souls. As a predator, I hungered to *know*
things, places, feelings, persons, in a way in
which I had absolutely no right to know them.

Contrary to common belief, there is no more
fiercely homophobic society than a boys'
boarding school. Too anxious about our own
sexuality and how it may be seen by other
guys, *macho* is the agreed watchword and, like,

the one true faith. The few boys I sounded out for an adventure recoiled instinctively. One or two might have been interested, but even they said more or less the same words: 'I just don't want to get into that *thing*.' They were damn right: my motives were as pure as Count Dracula's.

It was three or four days before the end of summer term, the night of a festive dinner to mark the close of the school year. George had been away for almost a month in the US, and I was missing her – in the crudest way. We were seniors now, entering our last year at St Isidore's. The party had gone well, with a glass of wine, topped up illicitly in some cases by more than was good for us. We were quite merry. Afterwards, four or five of us had gathered in Bernard Kalinski's room. People liked to be around Bernard. It was a foregone conclusion that he was going to be elected captain of the school in our final year. Nobody begrudged it to him. He was simply the best.

When everybody else had gone, I said to Bernard, 'Let's make love.'

He thought it was a joke, but I explained to

him what I wanted. He stared at me in disbelief. I began to coax and cajole him, arguing, grooming, pleading, lying, manipulating – and plying him with drink. It was utterly shameless and totally selfish. Again, I can quote the Bible. Somebody in there says, 'We do the very thing we hate.' That is exactly it. I hated what I was doing, and I hated myself for doing it. Finally, I began to force myself on Bernard, to grope, to kiss. There was a moment when he nearly went with it. I could see it in his eyes. Then he lurched backwards and staggered to his feet.

'Jesus, what are you doing, Seán,' he cried, 'what has come over you?'

I went for him, knowing how near he had been to caving in. He punched me in the face, and ran out the door.

I waited three quarters of an hour. He did not come back. I don't know where he slept that night. I went back to my own room and vomited.

In the last few days of term Bernard avoided me, answering in monosyllables when he was briefly cornered. He never looked me in the eyes then, or ever again. Bernard had the bluest eyes I have ever seen in a human head. It was as if a light had gone out for me for ever.

He did not come back after the summer holidays. Bernard had loved St Isidore's. He would have had, and richly deserved, a triumphantly happy final year. Instead he persuaded his parents to send him to some kip of a school in England, where nobody knew or cared who or what he was. I don't know if he told his parents about me. If he did, and if his father had come to kill me for what I had done to him, I would thank him for it. I still cry with grief and for very shame.

I am twenty-one years of age today. The last two and a half years have been sordid and vile beyond description. Fisher's woman had grown tired of me before I had even left school. I think she was only interested in depraving new people. I had a mind-blowing conversation with her when she eventually threw me out. She said so many cruel and wounding things. She told me that she hated me from the start, because people were for ever telling her how good and how wonderful I was to have forgotten my parents so completely and gone on to make such an incredible success of my life.

'Jesus,' she screamed, 'I only wish I could forget *my* parents, especially my shit of a father.'

She told me I was a smug, complacent, arrogant little prig – except she didn't say 'prig' but a word that sounds like it. She said that she had chosen me specially to 'dismantle' me, and that what she hated, above all, was my *purity*.

'I have never felt *clean*,' she hissed, 'not from the age of four on, when guys like you were *shoving*.' Sally, she said such vile things. I just cannot repeat them.

Today, I am a drug addict. I have a whole bunch of venereal diseases – well, two, to be exact, reasonably treatable ones, though I hate those visits to the STD department. They are so utterly crap. And I am HIV positive. How did that happen? It was inevitable. To get money for cocaine, there are only three ways: be incredibly rich, steal, or prostitute yourself. I am not rich. I will never steal – I know you will say that I stole from Fisher, but that was really different – and so, well, work it out.

I don't have to tell my 'customers' that I have diseases. They prefer not to know. They know full well that people like us are living in a jungle, and the jungle is a cruel place. They treat me cruelly. They are paying for it – in all senses.

Am I right to blame the Fisher woman and her poodle of a husband for all that has happened? No doubt I have done plenty of vicious things myself. Stealing from Fisher was only the first thing I did wrong. Then, when George entered on to the scene, I went ahead. I was excited and, at the same time, horrified. It was as if sex became an obsession, an addiction. She was years older than me. There was really no personal relationship at any stage. She just knew how to make me frantic, to crave and crave in the crudest and crassest way. Isn't that the saddest thing? I am sure that sex must be magic when you really love someone. They cheated me out of that too. And now it is too late.

Then that night with Bernard Kalinski: I think that that was the ugliest thing I have ever done in my whole life. It was not so much the sex – and anyhow, there was no sex at all, once Bernard stood up to me – no, the sheer ugliness was in the lies, the manipulation, the bending of someone who loved me and who, God knows, I loved too, to do what I knew he did not want to do and what I knew was absolutely wrong for him. Why did I need to drag him down? Why did I need to do the thing I hate? That scares the living shit out of me.

I admit all the evil that I have done. But it was the Fishers who could have put me on a path to growth and to life. That is what parents are for, and, God knows, I needed parents. That was precisely what made me so terribly vulnerable to Fisher and so defenceless in the arms of his wife. I had no right to ask them to be my parents, no right to expect them to take in a stray dog. But, Jesus Christ, couldn't they have just left me alone! They came on me, unprotected, rudderless, bleeding emotionally, and they devoured my flesh and my blood – my very soul. It was soul murder.

I get black depressions. I know, Sally, that you have suffered so much in that way. You will understand. My hope is that I can atone for all the evil that I have done. I am a vampire – I say it again and again – I know that I must end up with a stake in my heart. Please God, I can find the courage to face that. Then I can go home at last. I can be with my dad and my mum. I cry to be leaving Eddie alone – just another of the shit things that has happened to him in his life. But Eddie is strong. God will grant me one final wish, that Eddie will make it, and that he will be happy.

Goodbye, dearest Sally. We may not meet again.

All my love,
Seán.

Chapter Twenty-two

The telephone rang. Lennon picked it up. He listened in silence with mounting astonishment and exasperation. Then he said curtly, 'I'll come,' and put down the receiver.

Molly, who knew her chief's body language well, said, 'Aha. We are not pleased, are we?'

'Correct, we are bloody well not pleased,' Lennon growled as he made for the door. 'Imagine, Fisher gave his little speech, as arranged. Then the blithering idiots allowed him and his wife to lock themselves into the headmaster's study – and they won't come out or communicate in any way.'

'Have they tried the interphone?'

'Yes, of course. It just rings out. No answer.'

'But what can they hope to achieve? It's ridiculous.'

'I had this once before,' Lennon said, 'perhaps twenty years ago. When we eventually got that door open, the guy had hanged himself.'

'That might be a good idea,' Molly said, 'a really good idea, in the present case.'

Lennon looked shocked. 'You shouldn't say that, Molly.'

It occurred to her that he looked so shocked because he had been thinking exactly the same thing himself. But Lennon had actually been thinking that Fisher was just not the suicidal type.

They locked up the cottage as well as they could and drove back to the school.

The banquet had reached the sorbet stage and was heading for plum pudding. In spite of the gravity of the situation, or perhaps because of it, several of the staff had had too much to drink. They were in the humour to see the funny side of a grotesque scenario: Dr Fisher and his Dragon Lady holing up in the headmaster's study and refusing to come out or even to negotiate with the police. What a hoot!

Staff members were continuing to cope with the

evening's shocking news by distancing themselves energetically from Dr Fisher – like birds pecking out the eyes of a wounded companion. Fisher had been a remote figure, they reminded each other, an administrator, who had got the job done, but that was all. He saw to it that the teachers were competent – mostly – but did not seem interested, still less enthused, by any of their subjects. He had provided excellent people – namely themselves – to take games and to organize plays and concerts, but he had never come to a single match – even to the ones that the boys considered so important that they would have cheerfully laid down their lives to win them. And when a troupe from the school had won a national drama prize, he had failed to show at the award ceremony which was televised live nationwide.

In short, Dr Fisher was a strange fish indeed, and a cold fish, whom nobody had really liked.

Lennon and Molly were greeted with a volley of inane remarks about Hitler's bunker and the Princes in the Tower. Only two people on the staff knew about the second door to the headmaster's office, behind the hall stand, down the back passage. Both said that this door had been locked since before anyone could remember and that the key was lost. To break either door down would involve a lot of vandalism, serious tools, and considerable brute force. If the walls of the castle were feet thick, the doors were solid inches of heavy oak. Besides, it was not just a question of decommissioning a Yale-type lock on the surface of the wood – they actually did that with the main door shortly after Lennon's arrival, only to discover that it had obviously been reinforced with big and long iron bolts on the inside.

Lennon was puzzled by this play-acting. Fisher and his wife must know that their situation was hopeless. Within a few hours they would be in custody. That was inevitable. So what was the purpose of this escapade? And yet he had an uncomfortable feeling that – however they had managed it – they were not in that room any more. To say that they were already halfway to South America would, no doubt, be over-reacting, and indeed absurd. He had a strong intuition nevertheless that they had eluded him – at least partially – and what did that mean, 'partially'? He did not know. Lennon was a reasonable and a logical man. He did not usually have such intuitions or feelings during an investigation. But there was something eerie about this place. *Hatter's Castle*. Perhaps the boys were right. Maybe it really *was* haunted.

And what had they done to or with the luckless Garda Murphy who had accompanied them into the study? He had fallen terribly silent. The Tralee sergeant redeemed himself somewhat in Lennon's eyes by being quite concerned about his elderly colleague.

'Murphy is the most inoffensive man that God ever made,' he said dolefully. 'If they have harmed Séamus in any way, I'll be dug out of them!'

They tried dragging a ladder outside the five small windows which stretched round two-thirds of the room. The remaining one-third of the full circle had no windows because it represented the part of the tower which was joined to the rest of the castle. Perched awkwardly on the ladder, they could see virtually nothing through the windows because the lights in the headmaster's study had been extinguished. That, too, was odd.

They got a window opened, but even the slimmest of the Gardaí could not fit through that aperture. He tried it. His head, his shoulders, his chest, his abdomen – all made it, with enormous wriggling and contortions. No way could his hips and bottom slip through unnoticed. They became firmly jammed. The weight of the unfortunate man's body hung helplessly suspended ten feet up over the void inside the castle whilst his backside and lower limbs were still mostly outside. Locked in this position, he literally cried in acute muscular agony.

Molly, who had been waiting to volunteer to have a go, changed her mind. Having witnessed the sort of hands-on measures required to free her male colleague, there was no way she was going to allow any man except her husband, or possibly a gynaecologist, to take such liberties with her anatomy.

Of course, a boy could have slipped effortlessly through that window. The place was normally crawling with boys, some of whom had even slipped through that very window by dark of night – the purpose of their visitations being usually to have a sneak preview of examination papers. But, as Molly had found out growing up with her brothers, when you needed a boy, for instance to wash the car or empty the septic tank, it was as if the sub-species had vanished from the face of the earth.

Eventually, they decided to try the disused door behind the hall stand, opposite the toilet that Dr Fisher didn't believe to be a suitable statement of educational philosophy for new parents. At least, Molly pointed out, this door was probably not bolted on the inside, so that it would suffice to neutralize the Yale lock.

The whole cohort, Lennon, Molly, and the two Gardaí from Tralee, presented themselves in front of the hall stand. Stan was also there, together with a few other members of staff who had forgone their plum pudding, either out of curiosity or, as in Stan's case, because they thought that it was 'only decent' for some members of the school staff to be present. The light was quite good because there was a bulb directly over the hall stand. As they were shifting that piece of furniture, Lennon noticed with interest that the heavy dust and cobwebs below and behind it seemed to have been disturbed recently.

'I wonder . . .' he said, but did not finish the sentence.

It was assumed that the door was locked because everyone who knew of its existence said that it was. The lock was not of the Yale type but old fashioned, requiring the insertion of a large iron key and strong fingers to turn it. This would not be the kind of key that one could conveniently carry around in one's trouser pocket. It had probably not been lost but simply abandoned, as impractical in terms of frequent use. On an impulse Lennon gave the door a good shove. It opened – grudgingly, with complaints from the hinges and scraping sounds along the stone floor – but it did open. This time, when Molly stood half in and half out of the room, to try to lift the door and open it wider, it was she who noticed scrape marks on the floor which seemed to have been made fairly recently.

'I wonder . . .' she said, but did not finish the sentence.

They had trouble finding the light switches. Apart from the pool of brightness shed at the entrance by the bulb in the corridor, the rest of the headmaster's study was in darkness. Everyone was stumbling around, as in a children's game, two hands stretched out like antennae. Molly had a humbling thought: if Dr Fisher and his wife are watching this spectacle, their eyes accustomed to the darkness, how they must despise us. She almost expected one of them to shout 'Boo' into her face and scare the living lights out of all of them. It was the sergeant from Tralee who eventually found the lights by tripping on a mat, clutching the wall for support, and landing on the light switch. The result was instant illumination.

There was no Dr Fisher, and no George.

'They've done a runner,' the Tralee sergeant proclaimed.

'How?' Lennon exclaimed. 'There are only the two doors. You were watching the one, and the other was not opened this evening, with that heavy clothes rack jammed against it.'

'What about the windows?' the sergeant persisted.

'What are you talking about?' Molly protested. 'I can assure you that if your lightweight friend came away from those windows nearly minus his vital statistics, no way could either Dr Fisher or his wife get through them.'

It was Nancy who heard it first. A faint knocking sound coming from the wainscoting behind Fisher's imposing desk. She immediately said, 'I bet you, that is your Guard Murphy.'

She was right. As they approached the panelling Murphy's voice, faint and muffled, could be heard calling to them to let him out. 'I'm in a cupboard built into the wall. I can't see a bloody thing.'

Nancy gave a snort of laughter. 'Merciful hour! He's in the wine cellar – that's neat. I bet you George did that.' She explained quickly, while grappling with the antiquated latch arrangement effectively securing the door. 'It's a dinky little walk-in affair that was a wine cellar when the Randlers were in residence here. I think Dr Fisher keeps files in it now.'

'Cool and dry for the wine, I'd say,' Lennon remarked approvingly. 'Don't mind about the files.'

Soon released, and none the worse for wear, Garda Murphy rather sheepishly told his story.

'Your one,' he said, using an Irish colloquial expression for a woman to be reckoned with, 'she told me that she wanted to show me something important. She opened this door and said, "The light is not too good, so look real close." Well I was standing in the doorway, looking real close and observing the pitch darkness, when didn't she shove me in from behind and slam the door on my backside.'

'Well, where are the Fishers now?' Molly asked.

'What?' Murphy exclaimed. 'Have ye not got them arrested? Sure, isn't it the middle of the night – where would they be off to at this hour?'

Lennon shrugged his shoulders slowly. 'Vanished into thin air – any ideas?'

Guard Murphy tilted his head towards the site of his recent incarceration.

'Sure in there, the walls are so thick and the door is so heavy, you don't hardly hear anything at all. Though, mind you, one thing I do know: it must be a solid hour since they turned out the light. There is a crack in a plank of the door where you see whether it is on or off. That is how I knew that ye had arrived yourselves, more than from anything I heard.'

It was Stan who spotted yet another door, this one in the central pillar which formed the fireplace and the chimney. It had not been quite closed again. Stan strode over and swung the door wide open. It revealed the stone stairs spiralling upwards.

'There is the escape hatch,' he announced. 'They must have a lead on you of at least an hour, probably more. Does that look like a contingency plan just in case the going got rough?'

'Too early to say, but it is a worrying possibility,' Lennon answered. 'Did any of you know that this stairs existed?'

The question was directed to the members of the staff, some of whom had been with the school for several years. They all shook their heads. It was Stan, the most recent arrival at the school, who spoke up.

'The boys were telling me that Sir Neville Randler enjoys – or enjoyed, I should say – telling them about secret passages in the castle. There is one, for instance, from the infirmary practically to the hall door.'

'You're raving,' snapped Eustace Wolf, a sarcastic pedant who was jealous of Stan's success with the boys and did not like him.

'I have seen it myself. In fact, I have walked the

length of it,' Stan replied mildly, 'and I presumed that you all knew about it.'

'We never heard of it,' Nancy said loudly, delighted that somebody had upstaged Wolf, whose blatant misogyny was only one strand in the tapestry of his comprehensive obnoxiousness.

'Well, apparently, he also said,' Stan continued, 'that there was something inside this pillar, a passage or a stairs, I forget. Actually, I thought that it was just a tall story. Sir Neville enjoyed switching the boys on. I think he would have loved to have been at school in an old castle himself.'

While this conversation was going on, the police and their escort were filing rapidly into the pillar and up the spiral staircase, ten people in all – soon to be nine. Eustace Wolf, when he had gone to the second twist of the corkscrew, had to claw his way back, through, and around Nancy – which he found totally disgusting and deeply humiliating. He was claustrophobic, as well as being misogynistic.

Lennon, Molly and the Tralee sergeant led the way. The sergeant in particular was the full of the spiral cylinder. His ascent was probably the best thing that had happened in that stairway in the line of spring cleaning for more than a century. Dust, cobwebs, bat shit: he bore all before him like an upwardly mobile glacier. When the serpentine crocodile eventually slithered or stumbled out from behind a panel across the corridor from Maurice Tyson's door, Lennon said quietly to Molly: 'At least that's one mystery solved. We know now how Sir Neville ran the Garda blockade and took possession of the green folder.'

'Yes,' Molly replied, 'and he would probably be still alive if he hadn't.'

'So where do we go from here?' Stan asked.

It was a good question, and nobody seemed to have a ready answer.

Then Nancy said, 'They definitely came this way: and there is a typhoon of a draught coming from somewhere. That's unusual.' As if to head off charges of irrelevance, she added quickly, 'No, let's see.'

They were not long in finding the source of what was, in fact, a stiff breeze. A window in the south-west face of Tyson's tower was wide open in the teeth of the prevailing wind. A fire escape ladder, which normally served to connect that window to the roof of the Square Keep twenty feet below them, had been removed and was lying flat on the lower roof.

'I see them,' Nancy said.

'Where?' a half-dozen voices asked simultaneously.

Nancy pointed. 'Look at them, at the very end of the roof.'

She was right. Two figures were silhouetted against the black jagged teeth of the battlements and the cold night sky, at the gable end of the castle where it fell sheer sixty feet to the ground.

'What on earth are they up to?' Lennon enquired of no one in particular.

'Waiting for the helicopter,' Molly volunteered brightly.

'Do I look like James Bond?' the superintendent retorted.

'No, sir!' answered the Tralee sergeant, anxious to be helpful.

Fisher and his wife had obviously gone down that ladder from the window in Tyson's tower and then removed it, presumably to cool down any hot pursuit. But their respite could only be very temporary. Lennon was perplexed, 'Why?' he said again. 'What in God's name are they up to?'

'At least we have found them,' Nancy said, expressing an undefined and possibly various relief that they all felt for their own reasons. 'So how are you going to get down there?' she added, passing the buck deftly to the police.

The arrival of the search party at the window had

not gone unnoticed by the fugitives. They were immediately aware of flashlights, loud talking, and commotion clustered at the other end of the castle roof. Stan was the first to realize what effect this was having on their quarry. He gasped, then shouted, 'Oh my God! Guys, one of them is trying to push the other off the roof!'

Those whose eyesight was less acute than Stan's peered excitedly into the night, but doubted their ears as well as their eyes. Those who had seen what Stan had seen – a fight to the finish – were already dashing around, waving their arms in the air, expostulating incoherently, and not knowing what to do. There was a drop of twenty feet between the window where they were standing and the roof below. A further hazard was added in the shape of a skylight inconveniently placed on that lower roof. A jumper, if he failed to control his fall quite accurately, might easily go right through that skylight as well, cutting himself severely, and dropping God knows where further down.

'Who is winning the war?' Molly yelled, fully aware of the inappropriateness of a question that might suggest that one could have a favourite.

'I can't see at this distance,' Stan replied, already halfway out of the window.

'Don't!' Lennon warned him urgently, but Stan was already at the point of no return. Hanging by his fingernails from the windowsill, he dropped as lightly as he could to the roof below, muscles relaxed, the better to clench them as his body – not his head – would tell him. He fell on his toes, at once rippling, shimmering in the half-light, along the entire length of his body. He rolled head over heels, twice and nearly three times before coming to a halt, winded but safe and sound: a perfect fall.

Stan was followed immediately by the young Garda from Tralee – a brave man, and one hungry for notice and promotion. His jump was more in the style of Tosca, in the last act of the opera of the same name, leaping heroically to her death from the battlements and from the clutches of the lecherous Baron Scarpia. He was lucky to do no more damage to himself than a broken leg and a ruptured relationship with his sergeant, who at once recognized that this histrionic downward plunge was, paradoxically, a blatant bid for upward mobility.

Stan was already on his feet and running. As he ran the length of the roof, he could better see and even hear what was happening. Fisher was standing with his back to the battlements, arguing and pleading. George was saving her breath – except for a short burst of harsh laughter and one callous rejoinder: 'You miserable worm! We are *not* going to prison – you promised!'

Suddenly, she kicked him on the ankles. A perfect foot-trip – one of which a professional footballer might be proud but should be ashamed – a red card job, nothing more certain. At the same time she jostled him violently with her shoulder. Taken totally by surprise, Fisher toppled over backwards, shrieking. He fell straight through an interstice in the battlements, clawing frantically with both hands for the castellations on either side. George sprang forward. Grasping her husband's feet, she thrust him away and out over the battlements, for all the world like a Highlander tossing his caber. He screamed in terror all the way down. The hideous echoes of his cries filled the night air with horror long seconds after he had crashed to the ground and burst open.

Stan jolted to a halt, open mouthed, transfixed, unable to move. He tried desperately to cancel those last thirty seconds, erasing them by sheer willpower, annihilating them, compelling them not to have happened, praying, imploring with all his heart that he had not really seen what he had plainly witnessed. He was amazed and appalled by the woman's demonic strength and sheer skill. Derwas Fisher was not a small man. Yet she had knocked him over and pitched him off that roof as easily as a rag doll.

George did not spare so much as a glance over the battlements to see – well, to see how her husband was getting on. With both hands she was already energetically coaxing her sheath dress back up over her hips to free her legs for action. Stan was shocked to find that, even in this awful emergency and after the appalling scene that he had just witnessed, he was actually musing with nascent voluptuousness on the fact that George had terrific legs. 'Oh, shit!' he called out aloud in anguish.

He was running again, closing in on her. He knew that she was preparing to follow Fisher over the battlements, crashing to certain death. He realized that he was the only other person on that roof, except for the injured Garda. He must prevent George from killing herself. He was not quite sure why, but he must. Stan had never struck a woman in his life. Even in this desperate situation, he knew that he would be inhibited in the amount of violence he could bring to bear. Knowing now what this woman was capable of, and that she would stop at nothing, he was seriously afraid that in the struggle that must ensue she would not hesitate to take him with her.

It was the end game. He was certain now that this woman was cold blooded and utterly ruthless. She had murdered two men by cutting their throats – and a third, her own husband, by throwing him off this roof, minutes ago, before his horrified eyes. Besides, she was sky high, polluted with cocaine Nancy had said, and she may have taken even more of it when she had been holed up in the headmaster's study. Stan knew that if he tangled, or got entangled, with her, she would kill him too.

She had her back to him, but she had heard and understood. He ran forward as fast as he could, his arms open to clasp her in a high rugby tackle. She sidestepped at exactly the right moment. Stan's momentum carried him on towards the battlements. With perfect timing, she kicked him viciously in the small of the back, spreadeagling him between two castellations on the ramparts. Without one moment's pause, she ran up his prostrate body, digging hard heels into his thighs, his rump, his back, his shoulders, his neck – and jumped into the void with a scream, of triumph or whatever. Hardly terror: Stan was now convinced that this woman did not feel terror, or perhaps any normal emotion; not fear, not pity, and certainly not love.

By pure reflex action, Stan flung out his arms

over the battlements and caught some part of George's already plummeting anatomy. So doing, he smashed his face and his ribcage against the battlements, his shoulders against the castellations. Both arms seemed to be yanked out of their sockets. Every breath of air was slammed from his body, every muscle, tendon, and sinew screamed in protest.

It was, of course, impossible. George was much too heavy for Stan to catch in his arms and hold, especially as his centre of gravity and the hurtling trajectory of her fall were just not happening in the same space. So he was amazed to find that, seconds into the future, he was still holding her – but now without undue difficulty because she seemed to have become suddenly much less dense. He thought wildly that it was exactly as if George's carcass had continued its plunge to the earth, and to destruction, while he was left clutching her immaterial soul. 'Hey,' he said to himself, still stunned by his own traumas, 'does that mean that I am alive or dead myself?'

Whether it was some tangential effect of Stan's flailing arms or whether it was George's own failure to jump long enough to clear the battlements, she came down with a resounding thump astride a gargoyle in the shape of an ill-tempered whale, which served to spew rainwater off the roof and into the void. She had broken her pelvis in the fall and was in extreme pain. She was also physically unable to lift either leg to pursue further her project of hara-kiri. She had been literally hung out to dry on a gargoyle. Leaning over the battlements, Stan could only hold her shoulders steady, to ensure that she stayed mounted safely on her whale. They did not exchange any small talk, presumably not having anything agreeable to say to each other. Every part of Stan's own body seemed to be hurting. It would be mid-February before he had recovered fully from the damage he had inflicted on himself in those few seconds.

They came eventually. Having found a ladder somewhere, the police rather sheepishly arrived and hauled up Georgina Fisher. They didn't bother to read her the charges all over again or to warn her that anything she said would be written down and might be used in evidence against her. The little she did say was neither positive nor edifying but, as Molly pointed out with a straight face, they had omitted to caution her.

The Tralee sergeant called an ambulance for George and his Garda colleague with the broken leg. Stan pleaded to be regarded as walking wounded, whom the school nurse would be happy to care for, at least overnight. Lennon and Molly helped him up the ladder and down the now familiar staircase from Tyson's tower.

Chapter Twenty-three

The police had little trouble finding 'Darling Sally'. She was a patient in a psychiatric unit where Seán Gilhooly had been hospitalized a year before his death, suffering from acute depression. She had been fairly well at the time and they had struck up a close friendship. Seán had been diagnosed as a case of late-teen depression – no need to look further. This is an increasingly common diagnosis at a time when society holds out few or no moral values to the young. Sadly, it is followed all too frequently by suicide, especially in the case of young males.

It was not clear whether Seán was ever asked whether he had been sexually abused. What was clear was that he never said anything about George Fisher to his doctors. He spent a few weeks as an in-patient, during which he was given medication to dumb him down, and then discharged. Soon after his release, Seán stopped taking the happy pills and increased his intake of cocaine, and what he was forced to do to get the money for it.

Several months later he wrote his letter to 'Darling Sally'. She was having a bad phase at that time. She half read his letter but did not really take it in. When she was reasonably well again, Seán had already been dead for four months. She treasured the letter, feeling that it would be a betrayal to share it with anyone. When next she felt herself slipping into one of her black depressions, she put the letter into an envelope and sent it to Maurice Tyson. He was one of Seán's teachers or housemasters whom she knew he had esteemed highly and who had really tried hard to help him.

The authorities at the psychiatric unit were adamant. Sally could not give evidence. She was spiralling down into full-blown insanity. Regularly hallucinating now, she would be a hopelessly unreliable witness – even if she could be got to sit on a chair and answer a coherent series of questions.

George Fisher was charged with the murders of Maurice Tyson and Sir Neville Randler. She was also charged with the murder of her own husband. She was never charged with sexual offences against Seán Gilhooly. The Director of Public Prosecutions took the view that, in the absence of any other evidence, a trial judge would have to direct a jury that they could not safely convict her of sexual abuse on the sole basis of the 'Darling Sally' letter. That letter could conceivably be a novella, a figment of Seán's imagination, or some weird episode in a romance between two mentally ill patients, one of whom had destroyed himself in a particularly horrible way, while the other was fast lapsing into definitive insanity.

To her own surprise – because she regarded herself as a tough-minded professional – Molly was quite upset by this decision. She had been deeply moved by Seán's letter, and particularly by an expression that he had used to describe what had been done to him: *soul murder*.

'That's exactly it: soul murder. What that pair did to Seán was at least as bad as what they did to

Maurice Tyson or Neville Randler. I just cannot believe that Seán will never even be mentioned in a court of law.'

'Wait now, he will certainly be mentioned,' Lennon said gently, but Molly was not to be placated.

'Mentioned! Well, isn't that very good of them! The wonder is that George went to the trouble of killing two men when she knew all along that the lawyers would not bother their heads about Seán Gilhooly. No charges. I cannot believe it.'

Lennon persisted patiently.

'What do you want them to charge her with? He was seventeen, the age of consent. Listen, one way or the other, this thing is all about Seán and his letter. Presumably, Tyson challenged Fisher about it, and we know that Sir Neville Randler certainly did. The Fishers were frantic to find that letter. It probably never occurred to them that it could not be produced in evidence against them in the context of a trial for sex-abuse. Besides, before they did finally succeed in getting their hands on the letter, they did not know its precise contents – except that they were absolutely damning for themselves – they did not know to whom the letter had been sent originally, and they probably did not know who had sent it to Tyson. They absolutely needed to know all of these things. Ironically, it was precisely their desperate efforts to find and destroy that letter that eventually made it admissible in evidence against them in the context of murder charges – which carry mandatory life sentences. That is more than they could have got for what you rightly call "soul murder". In the end, Seán will be avenged as emphatically as the law knows how.

'And a final thing about this letter. You know the saying that a murderer always makes one fatal mistake: well, what was George's one fatal mistake?'

Molly answered unhesitatingly, 'Not to have destroyed instantly that damning letter that she had killed twice to get her hands on.'

'Absolutely,' Lennon assented. 'We are just steeped in luck. This is an original letter in Seán's own handwriting. In so far as we know, not a single other copy exists of it. Without that letter, what have we got? A few fingerprints, blood, a dubious identification by the little French boy – and no motive. A good counsel would make short work of our case.'

'So why did George keep the letter?'

Lennon lifted both hands and shrugged his shoulders. 'That's the eighth wonder of the world. I just don't know. Maybe she kept it as a trophy, or maybe as a grotesque keepsake of Seán – for whom perhaps she felt something.'

'That is disgusting!' Molly snorted.

'Or even – it is possible that when George read that heart-wrenching letter, she realized the utter evil that she and her husband had done. She kept the letter, as a judgement against them, to be found; and when it was found, she did as she had already decided to do: she executed Fisher and she had a damn good try at executing herself.'

'You are stark, raving mad,' Molly said, pronouncing every syllable distinctly.

'Maybe,' Lennon said, in the way that always so annoyed Molly.

On the other hand, the DPP – drawing a fine distinction – did believe that the 'Darling Sally' letter could be put in evidence, not as proof of sexual misbehaviour, but as proof that George Fisher had a motive to kill Maurice Tyson, who was in possession of that highly compromising document. This, together with the positive identification by Bertrand, the little French boy, of George as the person he had seen coming down the stairs of Tyson's tower on the night of the murder, and, finally, the indisputable evidence of incriminating fingerprints, all added up to a cast-iron case against the headmaster's wife – or, more correctly, his widow.

Georgina Fisher fought. She swore that, knowing that her husband and she herself were being accused of the most frightful and unbelievable abuses by a poor crazed boy, who had since committed suicide in a most horrible way, she had decided to confront Maurice Tyson and to persuade him that these terrible allegations were not true. She admitted that she had known that there was to be a barbecue that night, and turned that fact vaguely to her advantage by saying that she chose that night because her husband was away, and she knew that she and Tyson 'would not be disturbed'. She did not elaborate on what that ambiguous expression could mean, and counsel for neither side asked her to do so.

Her story continued that, arriving to Tyson's tower, she found him with his throat cut from ear to ear. She had a hard time explaining what made her look into the dormitory – especially as, according to her own evidence, she knew that there was not going to be anybody in there. But she pressed on. She said that she had checked to see if he was really dead – and this should surely account for traces of blood on her person and for her fingerprint on Tyson's spectacles.

Knowing that the presence of some highly pre-judicial document in Tyson's study, and the wholly fortuitous presence of herself at the scene of his murder, would attract major suspicion to herself and to her husband, her prime concern was to get that document – and herself – out of there as quickly as at all possible. She did both, she swore. For the rest, George freely confirmed the boys' version of the events of that evening – and specifically Bertrand's account: that it was indeed she that they had seen on the stairs, and that, seeing them, she had changed course and got out of the window at the end of the corridor. She even conceded that she and her husband had agreed to send Bertrand home because he was the only one to have identified her at the scene of the crime.

It was significant that George did claim to have found the 'Darling Sally' letter in Tyson's room that night. She said that she had retained it, instead of destroying it, because she knew that she should hand it over to the police at some stage in the future 'in the interests of total truth' – and that she had indeed done this eventually by giving it to Superintendent Lennon – voluntarily – on the evening when she was arrested. This was clever, because if she had really taken the letter on the night of Tyson's murder, there would have been no reason for her to murder Sir Neville Randler as well. George was already preparing the ground for her next murder trial, when she would be accused of killing Randler to get her hands on that letter. The Tralee Gardaí were able to confirm that, when they were called to St Isidore's in the early hours of the morning, Tyson's rooms were locked. This, according to the evidence of several witnesses, was unusual. One of the things that the boys liked about Tyson was that he seemed to trust them. So if he had locked his room on that night, this was probably because he had on his desk sensitive documentation which inquisitive youngsters should not see.

George countered the evidence of the Tralee guards with the brazen invention that when she had collected the 'Dear Sally' letter from Tyson's office – which, she insisted, was open – she must have accidentally snapped the catch on the lock on her way out, thereby unintentionally locking the door behind her.

Assuming that George had, in fact, found Tyson's door locked, Lennon wondered, did she search the dead man's pockets for his key as he lay on the dormitory floor? Or perhaps, did her nerve fail her at that point? George's nerve, the superintendent thought, was not the failing kind. But even if she had searched Tyson's pockets, she had not found that key. The Tralee Gardaí discovered it next morning in the fob pocket under the waistband of Tyson's trousers, just over his groin. Perhaps, Lennon mused, this was not a ladylike place to go foraging – even for a murderess.

So George was probably obliged to suspend operations in Tyson's tower for that night. Even as it was, the boys nearly caught her, returning prematurely from their barbecue. In a real sense, Bertrand did catch her.

The police later speculated as to whether Fisher or his wife had subsequently travelled up the chimney-piece route from the headmaster's study to Tyson's rooms in quest of the elusive letter. Lennon summed up their conclusion. 'Maybe; but Sir Neville got there before them, thereby signing his own death warrant.'

George's defence counsel repeated with emphasis that it was not his client's responsibility to solve the mystery of who murdered Maurice Tyson and Neville Randler. It was, no doubt, some deranged person.

'Let the police find that person. That is what they are paid for.'

The trial judge gave the jury all kinds of warnings about the weight of evidence required to convict in a criminal case.

'This is not a civil case where issues are decided on the balance of probabilities. It is not sufficient for you to be highly suspicious of Mrs Fisher. Unless you are satisfied beyond all reasonable doubt that Georgina Fisher murdered Maurice Tyson, you must acquit her.'

He also reminded them that Georgina Fisher was not being tried for the murder of her own husband, that of Sir Neville Randler, the sexual abuse of Seán Gilhooly, or any crime except the murder of Maurice Tyson.

'Some, or all, or any of these issues may arise in further proceedings. They are simply none of your business; you must dismiss them from your minds.'

The jury took eight hours to reach a verdict. When it came it was unanimous. The members of the jury simply did not believe the accused. The widow was duly convicted of Maurice Tyson's murder and sentenced to life imprisonment. She appealed. The jury's verdict was in due course confirmed by the Court of Criminal Appeal, and the Supreme Court decided that there was no point of law on which an appeal might lie to that court of final instance.

Bertrand, summoned from France to give evidence, was greeted like a pop star by the media and by the many people who turned out to see him with various motivations, ranging from the morbid, the macabre and the maudlin to those who just thought that he was a great kid – and so lucky to be alive. The kidnap saga had made him famous after his return to France but, even before that, Ireland seemed entitled to some share in his stardom, as he had ended up covered in the blood of an Irish murder victim and was even able to identify and name the Irish murderer.

The boy seemed to have grown at least a foot during the last year and now cut a fine figure as a hero. Before the court sat, he approached the dock – without permission from anyone – and greeted Mrs Fisher courteously. The prison officers knew who he was. Spontaneously admiring his gesture, they stood back and let him be. His evidence, given in a strong voice and in very comprehensible English, was damning for the accused. The jury had no problem believing him.

After the trial, Bertrand spent five days with his former companions at St Isidore's. He was clearly delighted to return there, and little or no work was done by his friends for those five days. Stan, the housemaster, laughed and said to Nancy McGivern, 'God love them, they have all had a rotten time, one way or another. It is great to see them enjoying themselves again.'

Bertrand had an interesting conversation with Jim Higgins the night before he left. He said that he had not seen Eddie Gilhooly around.

'He hasn't left, has he?'

'No,' Jim answered. 'He's in Argentina, on a school exchange. I think the school organized it, so that he would not have to be here when the trial was going on.' Jim paused, then went on, 'He is a much nicer chap now, Bertrand. When you think of all that has happened to him. His parents dead, his brother dead – in that awful way. And then, all these revelations about what Fisher and *she* did to his brother. The poor guy – it's just awful. That's the only word I can think of – awful!'

'What can you do?' Bertrand asked.

'Well, Martin and I have been thinking . . . that if we could run a really cool campaign, maybe we could elect Eddie school captain next year. We could do it, you know. There is enormous sympathy for him in the school, and he really has changed, into a far nicer guy.'

'And what about Jim Higgins?' Bertrand asked. 'I thought that it was written in the stars that you were going to be elected captain. It's a big thing in St Isidore's, isn't it, Jim? The very biggest.'

Jim twisted his head away, so that Bertrand could not see his eyes. He said lightly, 'Yeah, well, Eddie really needs this – to give him a bit of fun before he finally dies of old age. So, right, that's what we are going to do!'

George refused to plead either guilty or not guilty to the charge of murdering her husband. Presumably, she did not approve of the state's coming between a man and his widow, or else she did not think that Fisher was worth all the fuss of a murder trial. So, having determined that the accused was 'mute of malice', and not 'mute by visitation of God', the learned trial judge appointed counsel to defend her and proceeded with the trial.

Stan had to give evidence of what he had heard and seen on the roof of St Isidore's on the night of the Christmas dinner. Defence counsel made a half-hearted attempt to say that he had dined and, particularly, wined too well earlier in the evening. Five Gardaí and several members of the school staff swore that Stan had been stone cold sober on the occasion. Nancy McGivern put a final stop to that line of loose thinking when she declared uncompromisingly: 'That young man does not drink at all. It is against his religious principles.'

Defence counsel was heard to murmur as he resumed his seat, 'Jesus, just my luck. A Jesus freak!'

A last-ditch defence was to say that George had been insane – whether on the occasion or more generally. The psychiatric evidence was that, on the contrary, she was in full possession of her faculties and that, by implication, her actions must be attributed exclusively to drug abuse or sheer badness. She was convicted and received another life sentence.

George was charged, a third time, with the murder of Neville Randler, but a *nolle prosequi* was entered on that count. This meant that the charge could be reactivated any time in the future, but was not going ahead for the moment. In fact, she was never tried for that offence. The DPP said – privately, of course – 'She is as guilty as hell but we have no conclusive proof. Anyhow, two life sentences are enough to be going on with.'

The school authorities had thoughtfully arranged for Eddie Gilhooly to be out of the country during George's first trial. He was, as Jim Higgins had told Bertrand, on a student exchange in Argentina. Meanwhile, the 'Darling Sally' letter was providing many meals for the media. The courts had to intervene decisively to secure protection for the students

of St Isidore's School from cameras and micro-
phones, particularly those of foreign provenance.

When Eddie came back from Argentina, he was
employed almost immediately in the National
Gallery on a work experience project during his
transition year. As planned, he lived with Molly
Power and her young husband, Jan-Hein, for the six
weeks of that programme. After three weeks, when
he was well used to both the work and the domestic
aspects of his life – and very happy in both – Stan
came up and also stayed in the house, sleeping on
the sofa in the sitting room. It was a long weekend.

They gave Eddie Seán's letter to read – and waited.
At first, he went completely numb. He came to meals,
ate mechanically and without appetite, and did not
seem to hear when somebody talked to him. After
a day he began to cry, and he cried for a long time.
They took it in turns to just hold him and say nothing.
Then, in a third phase, they talked and talked in
every conceivable combination that you can have
with four people.

On the last day of Eddie's stay, which had
continued for another three weeks until his work
experience project came to an end, he said to Jan-Hein,
with whom he had got on like a house on fire, 'The
first time I ever talked to anyone about Seán, it was

to Molly – a year ago. She said that I had to forgive Seán for what he had done. I did not really know what she meant at the time. Well, now that I have had to hear all these terrible things, oh, my God, I have forgiven him with all my heart – or rather, there is nothing to forgive. Seán did the very best he knew how with the wreckage that those two monsters had made of his life. He was my hero. He will always be my hero.'

When Eddie got back to school, a letter was waiting for him. It was from Bernard Kalinski. They had scarcely known each other in school, Eddie being only a very small junior when Bernard was already a senior – and one who left before his last year. Bernard, too, had obviously read the 'Darling Sally' letter and been deeply moved by it – by the passages about himself, but also by Seán's concern for his little brother. In an echo of the words that Eddie himself had spoken to Jan-Hein, Bernard concluded his letter, 'Seán was my best friend in school. I will never forget him. I want you to know that he will always have been my best friend.'